Eraserheads:

A Hood Misfits Novel

Eraserheads:

A Hood Misfits Novel

Brick & Storm

URBAN BOOKS

www.urbanbooks.net

Urban Books, LLC
300 Farmingdale Road, NY-Route 109
Farmingdale, NY 11735

Eraserheads: A Hood Misfits Novel

ISBN 13: 978-1-60162-235-8
ISBN 10: 1-60162-235-X

First Mass Market Printing May 2019
First Trade Paperback Printing October 2018
Printed in the United States of America

10 9 8 7 6 5 4 3 2 1

Distributed by Kensington Publishing Corp.
Submit Orders to:
Customer Service
400 Hahn Road
Westminster, MD 21157-4627
Phone: 1-800-733-3000
Fax: 1-800-659-2436

Eraserheads:

A Hood Misfits Novel

by

Brick & Storm

Prelude

Auto

"Yo, Auto, some shit done went down with Lelo and Stitch."

Those were the words that started all the mayhem. If I'd known those words would come with a whirlwind of change, I would have pulled Lelo and Stitch out of that desert and just said fuck it. I would have strategically found another route to have our merchandise transported. But in the line of work I was in, if you didn't address disrespect, it was like a domino effect. Niggas would start coming out of the woodwork to test you. Would see the glitch in your system and start to take advantage of it.

My head jerked up as I sat in my office. Many days I'd sit there and have flashbacks when shit wasn't going right. Anytime something fell off course, I would always think back to those days when I was in the system. Being a juvenile offender had started me on my way to a life of crime.

Lelo and Stitch were supposed to check in hours ago, and when they hadn't, my spidey senses kicked in. I'd gotten so used to the smell of the shop that I could oftentimes taste the grime and oil in the back of my throat. Now I tasted rage.

I frowned at Seymore as he used his hands to roll his wheelchair into the room. He was covered in oil and transmission fluid. Smelled like he had been outside. I never knew exactly how to explain that smell, but Mama Joyce, one of my foster moms, always hated when we smelled like outside. As an adult, now I hated the smell too. Seymore was eighteen years old. He was a kid I'd rescued from the system. A bullet to the back had cut down his chances of ever walking again. But he could work on an engine like a pro. He was ASE certified, just like all the mechanics in my shop. The one thing I liked about him was that he never let his disablement slow him down.

"The fuck you mean, something went down?" I barked at him.

He adjusted his thick glasses. "Lelo said he been trying to call you, but you ain't answering, so he called the shop."

"Why in hell didn't he call Code?"

"Said she ain't answering, either."

I slapped my hand down on the desk, then stood, remembering I'd left my phone in my car, on the charger. It was a bad habit of mine that I had to break, especially in the business I was in.

Who am I? I laughed inwardly. I really had no idea who I was. I knew what the hood had raised me to be, but that was about it. I'd never really known my mother. I remembered faint images of her smiling face. When I was four, some woman decided she didn't like an Asian woman on her corner. Took a blade to my mother's neck. I'd been in the system ever since.

I could never really explain what it was like to grow up the way I did. From the womb right to the bowels of the hood, I'd been thrown. I was the product of rape. I wouldn't know my father if he slapped me in the face. I'd gone from foster home to foster home during my childhood. Met a lot of people along the way. Some good. Some I couldn't give a fuck about in the long view of things.

Being an Asian kid in a majority black hood, I had had to learn how to survive by any means necessary, and I had had to do it quick. There was no room for the weak in the jungle. You had to adapt. It was the survival of the fittest, and I'd seen plenty of niggas who weren't fit to survive.

All I knew about my culture I'd learned from reading. I knew I was Asian. Just didn't know which country in Asia I'd come from.

The streets of the A had turned me into the businessman I was. Me and my crew specialized in what some would call the auto business. From the car lot we owned to the industrial-sized auto shop, if you wanted something, we got it for you. We stripped cars down to their skeleton and rebuilt them. We could transform your ride into whatever you wanted, however you wanted.

Did we always get the cars or the parts legally? I'd plead the Fifth. We "borrowed" cars from all over the globe. Had them delivered to us, made the vin numbers disappear, stripped them down, distributed the parts, and rebuilt them into custom-made rides you couldn't find anywhere else. If the law had been looking to take us down, they'd call us a chop shop, but we were much more than that.

We called ourselves Eraserheads. From skimming credit cards to erasing a bad credit history and even erasing your identity, for the right price, we could do that for you. Our names resonated in the underground sector. Yet we worked only with those who we knew had our best interests at heart.

Every nigga had an agenda. One of my home-boys I'd met in one of the group homes I'd been in had taught me that long ago, and I'd kept it with me. Even as I'd selected my team, I'd kept that motto in mind. Shit had been off with Code lately. Some shit wasn't adding up. Although we were partners in this business, sometimes Code made me question if we had the same agenda.

Chapter 1

Smiley

All that nigga had had to do was die.

All he had had to do was die in that fucking car crash after leaving my mama and me. He'd beaten her ass to a bloody pulp while I lay on the floor at her feet, with his boot print on my damn face. All he had to do, since we meant nothing to him, was die.

Then we could have gotten his military benefits. I wouldn't have had to get lost in the streets just to keep a roof over our heads. Keep food on our table. Keep the bills paid up. Keep my mama supplied with the meds she needed for her sickle-cell anemia. Finish out my community college classes, which my mom had insisted I take. But no, he hadn't even handled that right. He hadn't died in the fucking car crash, like all drunk drivers should.

So I had had to snatch and take to the streets, while being smart about it, all because of that nigga. But had he died when he was supposed to? Nah. He hadn't been able to give us that peace.

While chilling in the streets and taking care of home, I had to listen to caseworker after caseworker deny my mama what she needed. Because of my thieving habits, I had been put in a scared-straight type of juvie program at fourteen, and then I had got out and started the process all over again. Yup, that crap had had me abandoning my mama for a little bit, but it had only made me stronger in the process.

I used to listen to a badass street poet in Decatur whom my mom had a lot of respect for, and he influenced me a great deal. The poet used to say to us girls, "When a woman is a survivor, if she can make it through the shards of glass that are life, then she is a queen worthy to tackle the jungles of the hood." So I remembered that. Well, I tried to at least.

Then one day, by the grace of God, I got an excellent piece of mail. One last reminder of that nigga who had skeeted me out in my mama's womb. Info on that nigga registering in New York, at the VA. See, how it worked was, since he was still married to my mama, all that type of information still needed to come her way. So that meant that they had to update her too about the possible pension coming his way.

Yeah, that nigga had messed up with that little bit of info, and now his blood was on my hands.

But it was whatever. My mama was dead because he had refused to send money to help her. She had left me a little old ranch-style, white house with a wraparound porch and a couple of grand she had hiding in her account from when she used to work for the state. All of it just for me. I had also got that nigga's pension money. Albeit a little late. Funny shit, that was.

Fuck that nigga. Glad I had watched him down too many psych meds mixed with coke and his favorite white Hennessy. Shit, what did you expect from a wife-beating, wife-raping, gloating sociopath with the mind of a marine?

Anyway, now, at age nineteen, I was about to get locked up for being stupid and trusting a bitch because she had said her baby needed some necessities, like milk and diapers. The little change I was making while working at Morton's The Steakhouse wasn't shit. Stealing was my forte. The more I stayed in the streets, the better I got it. I had learned how to skim ATMs from this white girl I used to run with. Most people did it the hard way, like busting the

ATM open and taking the cash. Actually, those people were stupid.

The white girl had taught me how to skim. Skimming was like identity theft for debit cards. We used little hidden electronics to get the information stored on a person's card and to record PIN numbers. Most people paid no attention to what was going on when their card didn't work the first time around at an ATM. They'd take the card, look at it like something was wrong with it, then put it back in the slot to try to withdraw cash again.

It had started off small, a couple hundred here and there, and then I had started to go for more. When skimming got too hot, I had started swiping credit cards. Creating new cards with fake identities had become a hobby of mine. Mix that with joyriding in cars I would steal just to get around and I was good in my little gig, until this scared-ass broad had ratted me out. Now I sat staring at a sour-faced nigga who looked like Uncle Phil from *The Fresh Prince of Bel-Air*.

Trick had ratted me out, and now I was stuck. I hated disloyal bitches, and it just proved again that the only person I could trust was myself, now that my mama was gone.

"You're too pretty to be a thug. All that pretty hair on your head. And those big copper-brown eyes lined up like you're some kind of Egyptian queen. Granted, you're sitting here looking like some Afrocentric goth too. That black lipstick on those big lips of yours clashing with your cocoa-butter skin."

Uncle Phil rubbed his double chin while eating me up with his eyes.

"Damn, you're pretty . . . but you gotta be fucking stupid to be running the streets, stealing credit cards, Ms. Gaines," he declared.

My nose crinkled up, and I felt sick to my stomach. This fool was watching me like he wanted to screw me. Matter of fact, I knew he did. It was all in his eyes. Yup, I was sitting there looking like an Afrocentric goth. It was my thing.

I sported a ripped-up black-and-white printed top that showed my bare stomach and a hint of my side tattoos, especially the ankh resting on my hipline. Ripped blue jean shorts with black leggings and black boots constituted the rest of my attire. The hair the detective liked, my black sister lock extensions tipped in purple, fell over one of my shoulders and hanged down to my breasts. Half of my hair was shaved off and revealed the hooped ear cuff in my ear. In my nose was a small gold hoop. I tapped my middle finger, the one that was missing the midi knuckle ring I usually wore. It was back in my locker at work. Assholes had snatched me up before I could change into my work clothes.

While Uncle Phil babbled on about how pretty I was, how well my curves went with my thin frame, and how he liked that I had tits big enough to play with but small enough that they weren't smothering, I yawned. Dude was trying to get me to respond. I had nothing to say. Nada. I sat with my well-known blank stare and counted off the time. Five-o had me in here on suspicion. That had become apparent when the Michelin Man, the man sitting next to Uncle Phil, revealed that my supervisor thought he had seen me taking cards with Keisha on camera.

Shit was funny, because I never was that open with it. Why? Because I had a photographic memory, plus an app I had created on my cell. I took all the personal information I needed, then used it later to track them down on the Net and go from there. Sometimes I'd also overcharge a card by ringing up a greater amount, as if the customer wanted cash back. That way I could pocket a little change. Well, this time, I had been trying to get Keisha to charm and distract the customers as I worked their card and hit them with tiny surcharges. This broad instead had got scared and had freaked out in the restaurant.

I had had to stop what I was trying to do, clear out the app I had on my cell that was the hidden card-jacking program, and do things as normal. So what the cops had got on the cameras was really me acting normal and charging the customers as I usually did. I realized that Keisha hadn't played me all the way to the left. She couldn't have, anyway, as I had never told her how I took from the customers. Keisha had just said that I was helping her take cards, which was a damn shame since I had been helping that bitch out.

"So tell me, Nia, why would you mess up a good thing at Morton's and steal from your employer and their customers? From your records, it looks like you've been doing right. You were raised well, and you're going back to school too, little thief. Shit, what's up your sleeve, then, little Miss Brown Sugar?" Uncle Phil said.

My eyes got wide. I looked away and bowed my head in fake shame. "I didn't steal anything. Keisha is just tripping from all those hormones and stuff because she's pregnant again. I promise. What you see is me doing my job. I'm not stealing from those people."

Like hell I wasn't. The customers I would steal from were mainly the rich assholes with the nasty attitudes and blinged-out wrists. So

I was lying, and since Uncle Phil was all on my pussy, I figured I'd play the game. Besides, I was mentally freaking the heck out. I didn't want to get caught. I didn't want to be locked up again, and I really wanted to go home. But if I showed fear, these cops would chew me up. I hated cops, anyway, due to their crooked-ass ways.

Anytime my mama had called those niggas for help, it was as if she had called for nothing. My daddy's last name being what it was, the cops were in his pocket. So I was playing hard just to figure out how to get out of this mess. Tears rimmed my eyes. I glanced up at him, then down again. I crossed my arms, then shook my head, as if I was angry. I was a good actress. Could get an Oscar for most of the shit I'd acted my way out of.

"I just lost my mama, okay? I don't have time to think about taking shit. I mean that. I just want to go home and try to get my mama's shit together so I can bury her peacefully," I said, choking up. I bit my lip.

That was another lie. In keeping with my mom's request, I had had her cremated and had snuck her ashes into the Atlanta Botanical Garden and had poured them out among the yellow lilies, her favorite. I checked out the detectives, but my stares were greeted with silence. I wasn't sure if the punks believed me, so I turned in my chair, and that was when I noticed a new face. Some blond guy in uniform. He whispered something to the Michelin Man.

A frown formed on the Michelin Man's face, and he addressed me. "Ms. Gaines. It looks like we can't hold you any longer. This is your lucky day, but we will be looking you up again."

Delight flashed in my eyes, but my face didn't show it. My mama had called me Smiley. She'd given me that name when I was a baby because I was always smiling. But I had stopped smiling long ago, when my pops had started beating her. Those memories haunted me no matter how far I ran from my past.

I asked the detectives why they were letting me go. They igged me, but then the blond told me it was because they had nothing on me, except a camera shot of me that wasn't clear. And, of course, the detectives then opened their mouths to let me know that they would be watching me and hauling my ass back in once the investigation was done.

I really didn't care about all that. I just needed to get out of this place. I didn't need these fools breathing all down my neck, all because Keisha had got scared and hadn't been able to follow through. I couldn't blame her for that, but there was something about her that was rubbing me the wrong way about the whole situation. But I didn't have time to think about it.

Once the paperwork was processed, I was taken from one holding cell to another one. About two hours later, they finally let me out. I went back to my job, cleaned out my locker except for my uniform, and headed home. I didn't want to talk to my bosses. I knew they already viewed me as sketchy due to all of this, but I kinda hoped that it all would blow over somehow. Maybe my mama would look out for me, because I was doing all of this just to survive until I figured out what I wanted from this life.

Back in my neighborhood, I clutched my bag and rushed past houses and neighbors, who always looked out for us in this dangerous but safe zone. I knew it sounded crazy, but even though this neighborhood was kinda dangerous, we weren't the trap. My area was actually cool. Every Saturday there was an event called Spoken Word in the Park, with damn good barbecue, soul food, and all kinds of vendors.

That was where I'd listen to my favorite female MC and poetry chick, who was on another level. Too bad she had disappeared. At the local high school, where I used to go, we'd see the step squads battle the cheerleaders, as well as banging football and basketball games. Everything was cool except for the occasional shoot-outs, which involved niggas trying to create some turf war. I'd occasional spot these chicks, known as queens, who protected us.

Glancing at an empty, well-kept house, I smiled at the memory of the old lady who used to live there. I used to go to her church. She'd hand out bomb cookies and frozen slushies to us kids in the summertime. Was crazy how she was found dead in her home. Shaking off that thought, I kept going until I rounded the corner and ended up at my mom's home . . . well, my house now.

After stepping inside, I glanced around at the familiar items all around me. Pictures of my mom and me during our happy times adorned the walls. Me at graduation. Me as a little kid. All the pictures of my father were gone, which was how we had both liked it, and now I was left with the reality that my mama was gone. Sadness filled me, and I went to my bedroom. The cops were on my ass. I knew my neighborhood inside out, and I always knew when people were watching me. I had some cleaning to do just in case.

So I left my bedroom and began rushing around my house. Went to my attic and basement to hide all evidence of my illegal activities.

I cleaned thoroughly. Wiped my hard drives and then moved them. Broke down the machines I had around and placed them in spots where they blended in with the furniture in the rooms. If the cops decided to search my house, they wouldn't find a damn thing. I'd been doing this long enough to know how to hide microchips in picture frames. I knew how to make my tiny ATM cameras look they were just a part of my home security system. If the cops searched upstairs, they'd just think I'd made myself a security room.

I then changed out of my clothes, showered, and went into the kitchen. The sound of my burner cell going off drew my attention. Keisha's ugly mug, with her bubble gum–pink lipstick, appeared on my screen.

Annoyed, I snatched up the phone and sucked my teeth. "What?"

"Ah, ew!" she said in her nasal voice. "Oh my gosh, Nia. You a'ight? I'm so sorry I was scared, girl."

Keisha had to be a stupid bitch. Why she would call me and try to talk about this shit over the phone was beyond me.

Bitch was killing my vibe and lying through her teeth. "Scared of what? We weren't doing anything."

"Nia, what you talking about, girl? Come on. We were going to grip those people, and I was going to be able to feed my kids."

Again, that feeling that this chick was off her rocker was working on my nerves. "Keisha, what do you want?" The sound of Keisha's babies crying in the background had me feeling soft for a moment, but the fact that she had played me pissed me off. "You know what? I should stomp your ugly, goat-looking ass for lying on me. Next time you contact me or come in my face, know you will get handled."

It was almost as if Keisha hadn't been sad just moments before, and I knew she hadn't. I'd feigned hurt and regret enough to know when another bitch was faking it.

"Bitch, you ain't shit any damn way, and I'm tired of your ass talking to my baby daddy!" Keisha shouted back at me.

I hung up on her face.

Fuck her, for real. She was another stupid bitch having sex with nothing-ass niggas and producing bastard babies who would grow up to be menaces to society. No one wanted that nigga. No one! I couldn't believe that after whining to me about that nigga not paying her child support or handing her even a dollar, she'd play me like that.

Everything I had done for her was really for her kids, because I felt really sad about them not eating and not having diapers, so forget her. She could choke on that nigga's dick as far as I was concerned. Ramon was her dude, and he kept flirting with me. He beat her ass, and I had tried to help Keisha. I hated niggas who thought using their fists on a woman would get them the glory, respect, and power they sought. That was why I had got caught up and had allowed myself to feel sorry for this broad.

Annoyance had me talking to myself as I cooked. I mixed together a cup of ground beef, chopped-up onions, and green peppers in a pot and cooked it on my stove until the beef had browned. I then drained off the fat and added onion soup mix. Then I opened a can of crushed tomatoes, dumped the tomatoes in the pot, and stirred in some ketchup, brown sugar, soy sauce, and hot sauce. I mixed it all up for ghetto sloppy joe's. I hadn't gotten a chance to cop any real groceries, and this was all I had found in my kitchen. My mom would try to eat healthy due to her sickle-cell anemia, so this stuff was left over from before she went into the hospital.

I grabbed some bread and a plate, I slapped everything together, and plopped down at my table. Chilling in my small T-shirt, bikini-cut undies, and socks, I thought back to all the bullshit Keisha would say about Ramon. She'd always yapped about his good dick, his tongue, and about how she missed him and how pissed she was that he kept flirting with me. My locks fell over my shoulder, my mouth was full of food, and my head hurt from her stupid bullshit. I didn't want Ramon's evil ass. Keisha should have been checking Trina. She was the one who wanted Keisha's man's dick, not me.

Dude was ugly as shit in the soul. So his dick was nothing I was thinking about. Fucking was nothing I was thinking about. Never had had time for it, anyway, or had wanted it, because my mind was on protecting my mama.

Every guy who tried to get at me, I ignored. I didn't want to get pregnant. Didn't want no STD and didn't want to be Keisha, since all she talked about was dick. I had my mind made up to have a different life. Guessed that was why I was a virgin still. I didn't care. But I knew if I got hot in the ass with the way chicks always came up missing in the trap, I knew I could be a target. I mean, I could become a target, anyway, but at least sticking close to home and not running the streets kept me safer. There were some guys I was into, but when my mama got sick, nothing else had mattered to me.

As I sat in the kitchen and ate my sloppy joe, the silence hit me. I was all by myself now. No one to take care of anymore besides myself, and it seemed strange. It scared me. Stuffing my face, I looked across the kitchen table at the empty chair that had been my mom's, and my fork dropped, and the tears followed. I missed her. I just wanted some peace. I could tell by the way Keisha had talked to me on the phone that the bitch was trying to set me up. So I wouldn't be talking to that raggedy ho again.

When I was finished eating, I tossed the left-over food in the trash. Cleaned the kitchen, then headed to bed. Wasn't no need for me to sit and have a pity party.

I woke up the next day, knowing something was off. On my way to work, I used one of my dummy cards to get some money to stash, just in case I needed to hide and lay low. A dummy card was one that I'd made with someone else's card number and information. Back in the day when I was stealing, you had thirty days to get three hundred dollars a day from a dummy card. It used to take thirty days for the billing cycle to come around or thirty days for the statements to be mailed. Before all the high-tech security shit took over, shit had been simple. Now, for those of us in the business I was in, you had only fifteen days, max. Banks and credit card companies were more alert and paid attention to suspicious activity.

In hindsight, I could see how fucking stupid I was to try to use that damn card. For some reason, I didn't think the cops would really take the time to bother me when there were other, more serious crimes afoot.

People rushed past with no cares in the world. I stared at every passerby, because I kept feeling like I was being watched, and I hated that shit. Sliding my hands in my pockets and keeping my head down, I kept it pushing.

Cars zoomed past me, but it was the nice blacked-out Audi R8 that drew my attention. I couldn't really see inside it too well, but then I did make out the top half of a dude, who locked eyes on me. He revved his engine, then darted his eyes before driving off. If that dude had parked that shit and had left it near me, I most definitely would have stolen it, checked out the engine, and enjoyed the pleasant weather. But I had work to do, even though the hairs on the back of my neck were standing up.

As I turned to head off, I stopped in my tracks when flashing lights quickly surrounded me.

The police had me surrounded, guns cocked and aimed. People gave the police a wide berth. If they weren't running and screaming, they were standing around, staring. I held my hands up and stopped. I didn't want to end up shot.

"Get on the ground! Get on the ground," a cop shouted.

I quickly dropped to my knees, then lay on my stomach. I swore, it felt as if those niggas were trying to paralyze me. Knees in my back and on my spine. My hands and wrists twisted awkwardly so they could get the cuffs on.

I guessed the investigation was over, because now my ass was being hauled back to jail. I sat in a holding cell at Clayton County Jail for a good three or four hours before I was pulled out and placed in an interrogation room.

"Look who we have back here with us, man. This lying bitch," Mr. Blond taunted me sarcastically. I remembered him whispering to Mr. Michelin the last time I was here.

Guessed I wasn't too sweet or too cute to be a thug anymore, because these fellas were all the way turned up, and Uncle Phil was nowhere to be found. They tried to get me to answer questions, but I refused. I had the right to remain silent, so that was what I did, until they got frustrated.

"Get her ass up outta here, and let's see how she likes sitting behind bars. These goddamned kids are getting too smart for their own good, and we're not about to have another punk act the hell up and tear up the interrogation room. Two is enough. Stop playing with her, Derrick," Mr. Michelin barked.

So Mr. Blond is named Derrick, I thought.

"I will, but we should let her see at least a piece of the evidence. Let her see what got her in here, since she wants to be all smug and silent," Derrick suggested.

Derrick took out his cell and angled it in front of me. He slid his hand across the touch screen, and I watched as a video started playing.

I heard Keisha's voice. "Look in her locker. I promise, she put me up to it all. I ain't want to do it. Was going to wait on my baby, Ramon, to pay his child support check, but she told me it would help me with my babies. She planned it all!"

I felt the need to speak up. I could admit I was panicking. The shit I had been doing could get me some serious federal jail time.

"She's lying, and I don't know why, but she's lying," I pleaded, cupping my face.

Derrick stopped the recording and smiled. "We searched in your locker, Ms. Gaines, and guess what we found in your uniform pocket."

Anger bubbled up inside me at the bullshit I heard. My eyes narrowed while I ran my tongue over my teeth, then sucked them. "My ass to kiss, because I ain't did anything!"

"Excuse me?" Derrick said in my ear, causing me to sigh and pray to the heavens. Derrick, with his sour breath, was all in my face, trying to make my life worse than it already was.

Pictures flashed in front of me, and then various IDs, credit cards, and money in a plastic grocery bag. My mouth dropped open. I sat back, tight lipped, because in front of me was also a video of me handing Keisha that very same bag days before all the shit had hit the fan. That bitch Keisha had really sold me out. All the IDs and credit cards I'd gotten for her lay in front of me now.

Suffice it to say, the bitch had set me up real good. She had set me up so well that days later, I was still being held at Clayton County Jail. After that, they found more shit and so-called proof that I was a thief. A few days turned into several weeks and counting. I'd been arraigned and brought up on charges, like identity fraud. That alone could have me sitting in prison for ten years.

Mix that charge with all the others and the DA was trying to plead me out for twenty years.

Twenty years for all that bullshit? Wow! I knew Keisha had sold me out to save her own ass. I got it. But if I ever saw the light of day again, I was going to kill that bitch. Maybe she'd done this because she was jealous or some shit. Whatever it was, I knew I shouldn't have trusted that broad. I felt like an ass for feeling sympathy for her fucking snotty-nosed, crying babies. Damn, man!

Chapter 2

Code

I moved with a purpose. Anxiety was riding me like a two-dollar whore. Sweat beaded at my temples. Normally, I'd stop and chat it up with the guys around the shop, but I was in no mood to. The auto shop was loud. The smell of oil, tar, and grease assaulted my senses. My heart thumped in my chest as I speed walked in the direction of the back office. Male and female voices were chattering as I went, but I kept going. I needed to be in the security room.

"What the fuck took you so long?" said a voice behind me as I kept walking.

I glanced over my shoulder at Auto, the manager of the shop. He was also my partner in crime. Auto's black, shoulder-length hair was drenched in sweat, as the shop felt like a sauna. His Asian features were set in an impatient scowl. Sweat rained down his chest, which was covered with black specks, no doubt because of the oil and grease from cars. Abs constricting with each breath he took, he looked anxious, like he had something of importance to tell me.

"Cut me some slack, a'ight? The old man had me tied up with family shit," I countered. The "old man" was Papa, my grandfather.

He looked like he wanted to counter what I'd said, but he knew that the new package coming from Vegas was needed and that we had no time to be arguing about other shit. We'd run into a lot of interference lately because of an unforeseen enemy. He sighed loudly, then shook his head as he fell into step beside me.

"Yeah, well, this shit here is more important than that old man," he snapped as we walked.

"You know when he calls, I have to answer."

Auto shook his head. For as long as we'd been partners, we'd had words when it came to where my loyalty lay.

He said, "One day you're going to have to choose between us and him. We got a lot of money involved in this shit, and you letting that old motherfucker get to you again."

I shook my head and stormed on behind him toward his office. No matter how many times I had explained the dynamics of my family to him, he had never got it. Auto didn't know where his family history began or ended, so a long time ago,

I had stopped expecting him to get why I had to show loyalty to the old man, my grandfather.

"Look, I'm sorry, okay? Just tell me what the fuck is up." I didn't know if he believed my apology. All he did was shake his head.

"Those new parts we're supposed to be getting . . . seems like our supplier also made a deal with a set of dudes who run a similar operation out in Minot, North Dakota," he then informed me.

Nervousness settled in my spine. We couldn't afford to lose another shipment of parts. "So he played us?" I asked.

"He's been playing us. That shipment we lost last month, he told them about it. That was how we lost it. It cost us only three hundred thousand then, minus what we paid him. If we lose this, we're fucked."

Both of us were silent as we walked into his office. He closed the door behind us. We both made sure the door was locked before he laid a hand on the digital panel beside the wall. I dropped the bag in my hand on the floor, then waited impatiently as the file cabinet slid over like it had an invisible motor. My breathing intensified when the wall glided over and revealed a hidden room. We stepped into the room, and six fifty-inch flat-screen TVs greeted us. Then the movable wall slid closed behind us.

"Get Lelo on the line," Auto ordered me.

While he was my partner in the very lucrative business we ran, sometimes he lost track of this fact and treated me as if I was the help. When he was angry, he always threw his weight around. Luckily, I knew him and knew he meant no harm. He also knew I loved him as if he was my blood. Our different races didn't matter. I was older than he was by three years, too, so sometimes my bossiness kicked in as well. But Auto was a businessman, and when something didn't go right, we all saw a side of him he rarely showed. Fear.

While he may not have known where he came from in a sense, he'd made his own way. Made his own family. Our connection had started after I purchased a car from him. He'd already had this business up and running by the time I'd come around. But I'd never been one to turn down money, and since I'd never been like most of the women in my family—they lived off family money—I'd asked him for a job. It was only when he fell in the hole monetarily that I was able to buy into the business. Even so, the Eraserheads belonged to him, and he made sure we all knew it.

It took a little less than a minute for me to get Lelo on the main screen. Lelo's butter-pecan face could be seen as he shielded his eyes from the sun. The Las Vegas sun had darkened his already brown skin.

"Talk to me," Auto spat in a no-nonsense tone. His breathing intense, Auto stood with his arms crossed over his chest, legs wide. With each breath he took, I could see the expansion of his chest, the rise and fall of his shoulders.

Lelo was looking around like he was paranoid. Fear was written across his face, and that alarmed me.

"They got the shipment," he said, clearly stressed out.

"What?" I yelled.

Auto came up behind me. "How? What the fuck happened?"

"We got robbed," Lelo roared. "These big, blond white niggas robbed us. We took a different fucking route, and they still got us. They took the fucking truck. Every fucking thing except the tracker and the device in my glasses."

My blood was boiling. Something akin to indignation was overtaking my senses. The tears burning my eyes told of the plethora of emotions I was feeling. Still, we needed to make sure he and Stitch were okay. Auto kicked a chair around the room, then stalked across the floor with his fists clenched.

"Where is Stitch?" I asked Lelo.

The camera started to shake as he moved. Lelo turned his head and showed me Stitch, who was sitting on a boulder, holding a bloody T-shirt to his left eye.

"He took a hit to the eye from one of their guns," was all Lelo said.

Silence settled loudly in the room before I asked Auto, "What are we going to do?"

"I'm thinking."

"We have to do something. This is the third time," I noted.

As much as I knew he hated to agree with me, he knew I was right. It was rare that Auto had to flex his muscles, but he knew we had to do something. If we didn't, others would think it was okay to come for ours, and that would never be the case.

You embarrass yourself, you embarrass this familia, I could hear my grandfather saying in my head.

His Cuban accent was as thick as his face, and he was stoic. He'd made it clear that when I branched out on my own, I'd better keep our family's name as revered as it was before I branched out. He was livid that I'd chosen to do my own thing instead of family business, but I was his favorite. That meant I got away with shit no one else in our family could. There was no way we could let this go unanswered. If the old man got word that my crew was being robbed and basically bullied, he'd have a problem with me not handling business.

Auto told Lelo, "Find a safe haven."

Lelo asked, "You don't want us to dip?"

"Nah," Auto said, then turned to me. "Call Reagan and tell her to get the Cessna ready."

Reagan was another mechanic, friend, and crew member. I nodded, and then I headed back out to the main floor.

Bullets rained down all around us. The yells and screams of those who had become victims of war serenaded me.

"Get the truck!" Auto yelled at me. "Get to the fucking truck!" he roared.

My heart was beating so hard against my chest, it hurt. A bullet had grazed my arm. The thick T-shirt I had on had been dyed red. I didn't know if it was all my blood or not. I was sweating. The Las Vegas heat wasn't being nice to me. I didn't know where Lelo and Stitch were. Two big rigs had been abandoned on the side of the road.

"Code, y'all gotta get the fuck outta there," I heard in my earpiece.

Seymore had been tracking us. Through the crew we had in Vegas, he had been able to pin-point the exact time when five-o would arrive.

I shouted, "We can't. We ain't got the truck yet."

"Don't matter. You got twenty minutes, and then them folks gone be on your ass. Get the fuck outta there!" his voice thundered in my ear.

I slowly peeked around the bumper of the car I was hiding behind. A bullet whizzed by and almost sent me to my Maker. I could hear Auto yelling for Lelo to get down. Auto had never been one to like guns. He'd never been a fan of murder-death-kill-type shit. But sometimes, sometimes one had to get dirty when one's hand was forced. That was where my skill set came in. I didn't mind dancing with the devil. Didn't care to let my hammer loose and watch it praise the gods of death.

The grunts of my brothers could be heard in the distance. I knew we were surrounded. No way were we getting out of there. We had flown all the way from ATL in a Cessna 172 Skyhawk, following a half-cocked plan to retrieve Lelo and Stitch. Now it was possible that we were all on our way to hell.

The smell of gasoline from wrecked cars burned my nose. My hand was steady as I held on to the Beretta Px4 Storm. Even though I was one of the best shooters on the team, I still knew we were in a fucked-up situation. The heat had my skin tight and was pulling all my electrolytes out through my sweat. Dusk was on the horizon, and I knew if we got caught out there at night, we were in for it.

"Auto, we can't get out, bro," Stitch yelled over the melee.

A shrill laughter echoed. "Fucking right. None of you getting out of here alive," a male voice taunted. "None of you."

"Auto, we tried to do right by you. Tried to come to you like men and discuss a way around this, but you had to do this shit the hard way," another male voice shouted.

I knew it was the voice of the boss running the shakedown operation, Mouse. My research for Auto, which I'd done while we were waiting for Reagan to gas up the Cessna, had told me he was a Scandinavian low-level crime boss who had worked his way up to create his own crime syndicate. I had no idea how we'd gotten on his radar, until Auto confirmed that our connect had been selling us out. Despite all the years we'd been doing business with Chandler, he had sold us out to the highest bidder.

My ears perked up when I heard Auto's voice. "No, no. What you did was try to infringe on my business. You tried to muscle me out of something I built from the ground up."

"Anything that passes through our territory, we get a cut of."

"This isn't your territory," Auto yelled at our enemies. "We've been running this route for years. This is Chandler's highway."

"This is new management, and unless you give us what we want, you'll run into this problem every single time," our rival assured us.

Static rattled in my ear. "You have only sixteen minutes, Code. Tell Auto to get out of there."

I knew I had only four bullets left. No way would we get out of here without some kind of help. As if the gods had heard my pleas for help, I heard Panjabi MC blasting in the distance.

"Pascal," Lelo and Stitch yelled.

I sighed in relief, made a cross over my chest, and blew a kiss to the skies. That *Knight Rider* theme, laid over that Panjabi beat, with Jay-Z spitting, was music to my ears. Pascal was always our ace in the hole. Anytime we came out to Vegas, Auto always hit him up to let him know we were there, just in case we ran into trouble. He and his crew specialized in explosives weaponry. If anybody saw Pascal and his crew coming, they prayed Pascal was on their side and was not the enemy. It was only after getting to know him that we found his fascination for Trans Ams comical, especially after we discovered he liked the cars only because of KITT from the old TV show *Knight Rider*. That was why he had had Auto transform all his cars so that they were similar to the old car.

"Hell fucking yeah," Auto belted out as I heard bullets fly through the air again.

As those ten modified 1982 Pontiac Trans Ams bent the steep curve, I used it to my advantage. I stood quickly, fired two of my last four bullets into the skull of one of Mouse's men, a dude who looked as if he ate steroids for breakfast, lunch, and dinner. Ducking and dodging, I took a running leap over the overturned car I'd been hiding behind. The earpiece fell from my ear, and I cursed. Grabbed ahold of the open driver's-side door of the big rig and tried to get in. Old man Law, the neighborhood creep who'd taught me how to handle what I'd called an eighteen-wheeler when I was a kid, would have been proud. For a few nude pictures and a couple of fresh feels every now and again, he'd taught me all I needed to know.

I jumped in with a wild, panicked look in my eyes, hoping the keys were still in the ignition.

When they weren't, I went into a profanity-laced fit.

"The keys, Auto! They keys are gone," I shouted.

I got no response, though, at least not from Auto. I looked up to find Mouse, a Mads Mikkelsen look-alike, breathing down my neck.

He swung his fist. Missed breaking my jaw by an inch. I jumped across to the passenger side of the truck only to have the door snatched open behind me. I took a long tumble down to the hard ground. I swore I felt all my bones break. That *Knight Rider* beat was still in my ear as my body rolled. Then big black boots tore into my sides. One caught me in my privates and made me curse the day I was born. I saw no way I could go head to head with the blond-haired, blue-eyed superhuman. His strength had to come from some kind of god.

My whole body shook from the kick to my womanhood. I got my bearings, though. Found a way to my feet and put the training my grandfather had instilled in me to use. Even while I was fighting, the old man stayed in my head. I didn't know what was taking Pascal so long, but I needed what he specialized in to get under way, and soon. I did a roundhouse kick and backed the man away from me far enough to put some distance between us. It only angered him, if anything. He rushed in, threw a punch, which I dodged, and then he caught me with a kick to the stomach.

In his hand was a knife, which I didn't see until it almost sliced across my chest.

"Son of a bitch," I spat.

"Your boss should have left well enough alone," he growled at me.

"And you shouldn't have fucked with me to begin with," Auto growled.

I looked up and saw Auto throw a swing, which rocked the man. The man's lips turned up into a menacing smile. One that would have put the fear of God in most niggas. It only strengthened Auto's resolve. He pulled his shirt over his head and quickly wrapped it around his hand. I stood there in pain and watched as Auto dodged that knife-wielding Viking. The Viking went right. Auto ducked left. Caught the Viking with an uppercut that bloodied his mouth. Auto didn't give him time to recover; he rushed in with a flurry of punches that had blood dripping down the man's nose like water from a faucet. The Viking fell down to one knee. Auto ran in and gave him a foot to the face that sent him sprawling onto his back.

I heard Pascal's voice. "Happy Independence Day," he yelled.

Something oval shaped and green came sailing over the big rig and rolled right between us. Our Scandinavian opponent looked confused. Auto grabbed my hand, and we took a running dive behind a big boulder. Only seconds later the ground shook, rattled, and rolled underneath me. The explosions sounded like a symphony as they occurred one after the other.

"Auto. Code. My friends, take your team and go," I heard Amina say after the dust had settled.

I had no idea where she'd come from, but I was happy to see her. Amina was Pascal's sister. She was just as dangerous as he was when it came to explosives. I swore it was like looking into God's face when I saw her beautiful earth-toned eyes looking down at me. She was wearing a full hijab, but in her hand was a gun that would put the biggest and strongest of niggas in the dirt. I couldn't see her face, but the twinkle in her eyes told me she was smiling.

"Thank Pascal for me and tell him his payment will be there before morning," Auto told her as his breaths came out rapidly.

She nodded. "We thank you, as always."

I ran for the truck and then remembered we didn't have the keys. I cussed again. "Shit!"

"Looking for these?" a voice said behind me.

I turned to find Jaahlive, Pascal's brother, standing there, holding a set of keys in his hand. No matter where Pascal went, his siblings were never too far behind him so I wasn't surprised to see Jaahlive. He looked as if he should be in someone's modeling agency. Eyes as golden as honey. Long lashes and dark brown hair, which hung to the middle of his back. His body showed that he worshipped it as he did his religious deity. He was tall, long, and lean. Looked like he could run track or dribble a ball up and down the court. Looking at him, you couldn't tell his race, but when you spoke to him, you knew that he was proud of his Hindu heritage.

At any other time, we all would have taken the time to catch up on what we had been doing since the last time we spoke, but now wasn't the time. I took the keys as I gave him thanks. Promised to check in with him and the fam soon. I rushed into the truck, closed the door, and made that big highway bully roar to life. Auto jumped in on the passenger side. Blood decorated his face, and cuts and scratches adorned his arms and torso.

While Mouse and the rest of his men ran for cover, Lelo and Stitch hopped into the back of the truck, and then we got the hell out of Dodge.

Chapter 3

Boots

My responsibility and my family were also on my mind. The man I was named after and the family we had been searching for, for a very long time, stayed with me. Now that we had found them in Atlanta, everything was set in motion. That would be something to discuss later. Right now I switched my mind to my money and my product. My mind was now on Nevada.

As I was rolling through the A, headed to see a man who made my nuts hurt because of my hatred of him, I leaned back and listened as Scarface thumped on the speakers of my Audi R8. I'd just seen a cutie with a phat booty and nice tits get shaken down by five-o. Now, what they wanted with a chick sporting ghetto-goth attire, I had no idea. But being the gentleman that I was, and a brotha who had no love for cops, I had to ghost my whip and try to signal to the shawty about the crew that was following her. I mean, it was only the right thing to do, black man to black woman.

In the South, especially the dirty South, if we couldn't look after each other, then there wasn't no point in living. Sadly, the latter was going on with all my people, and if my pops were here, the whole thing would have him pissed off. But that was neither here nor there. That was the past, shit back in the city of my birth, which matched my initials: BK

But back to little Miss Rihanna. Other than the long locks she had, the slightly darker skin tone, and the way her ass and breasts were just a few notches fuller, little mama was RiRi. She had my attention, especially with the seriousness in her eyes. But, again, that was neither here nor there. I didn't want her. Just enjoyed the view, and something in my gut said—my gut was a gift that I had learned to listen to—she might have an interesting story. However, I wasn't about to find it out. I had business to attend to, and she had too many cops on that ass.

I revved my engine. Watched her eyes light up, then narrow. I nodded, then headed on my way. Money was on my mind, as well as a hidden agenda. I was a knight with a thug mentality. A killer with an honorable disposition.

People on the streets to whom I made my presence known called me BK. People back in Houston called me Boots, and my old man called me Junior or Radio Raheem, while the government called me Raheem Kweli. But that was a lot of information for one sitting, and what the government called me was my business and no one else's.

After I stepped out of my ride, the comforting and familiar sound of my shitkickers, also known as cowboy boots, scraping the pavement put a smile on my country face. I reached back for my blacked-out, wide-brimmed cowboy hat, which shielded my eyes and kept my face slightly hidden. Was I being cautious about my identity? Not in the least bit. The man I was doing business with had a long history with my family.

As for my identity, in terms of most of my physical attributes, I took after my deceased Eritrean mother. But I took after my pops when it came to my mentality, swag, height, girth, dimpled smile, and amber eyes. My soon to be business client would not be able to recognize my true lineage at all, which was perfect for me given how I ran my business.

Again, I was an enigma.

So, I ran a hand over my long, thick chin beard and wavy fade. Rolled up the sleeves of my black

button-down shirt, which was open just enough
to reveal my white beater but not the bulletproof
vest under it. I allowed my bourbon-red flesh
to soak up the rays while I smoothed down the
vest, which hid a sample of my product. Sliding
my cell into the pocket of my dark gray jeans, I
headed into Morton's The Steakhouse. Once
inside, I enjoyed the smells of the food, which
caused my stomach to break down in the Holy
Ghost.

Not that I was a Christian man. In my practice,
I was a god. However, I gave my respects to
my version of the Most High and to my Yoruba
deities. Right there I kissed the Ankh around my
neck while chuckling to myself. Pops would enjoy
seeing this meeting go down, and so would I.

At twenty-two—thanks to the education I had
got from my pops—I was considered an old
soul. I handled myself very differently than a
lot of dudes my age. Yes, I could act my age if I
wanted to, but in business, I had to be ancient as
a means to keep people out of my business. This
was why I had many contacts, and why I could
be professional in this seedy world. Besides
the fact that I made banging product—a special
grade of military-issued bullets and other weapons I chose to re-create just for fun—I was a
shrewd businessman.

Today my client wanted to talk to me about my shipment coming his way: Grade A bullets that could go through any kind of vest and implode in the body. This type of bullet I was selling him was my low-grade version, called Blazers. The real deal, my Reapers, would put that bullet to shame. I always made sure *I* got the next upgrade and no one else.

As I stood in the restaurant's lobby, I was greeted by the house attendant. "Mr. Sunjeta, welcome to Morton's The Steakhouse. Your private room is this way. Follow me."

I followed the attendant, and a minute later we arrived at a decent-sized room with various square wooden tables covered with green table-cloths. The walls were a dark green, with chocolate-brown trimming. The lighting in the room was a little dim. While the incessant chatter behind me told me the place was full, my private room afforded me seclusion to do business. The smell of succulent steak wafted through the air. Sitting at a table at the very back of the room was my client, with two of his people.

Now, don't think I came alone. I gave a nod to my own people, Oya and Shango. They wore matching colors, royal purple and black. Shango was in all black, with a purple tie; and Oya wore black leggings with thigh-high boots, a small feminine black suit jacket that flared out, and a purple shirt under the jacket. Each one sported my insignia, BK, somewhere on their person, a location that only I knew.

Pride had me acting arrogantly. However, my face held no emotion as my team nodded at me, letting me know everything was good. I approached my client. Held out my hand to greet him. My client stood, acting equally smooth and suave, and took my outstretched hand in his firm grasp. This well-known intimidator was a man who made NYC quake with just his last name, and he was making Atlanta slowly become murder capital number one. All while operating from his home base of Cuba.

My Houston accent ebbed and flowed like smooth molasses as I gave this man a show of respect in Spanish. "Senor, I am pleased to have this time with you to discuss our doing business with each other."

"*Gracias*. Senor . . . ?" my client said with a raised eyebrow upon his face.

"For now, in here just call me Mr. Sunjeta. Please have a seat." I waited for him to sit in sync with me after I removed my hat and handed it to Shango.

"You speak as if you were born in Cuba. I am impressed," my client said, praising me.

Oya stepped forward at that moment with a wooden box, a gift to show respect. She held it out and observed my client. Motioning for one of his men to take the box from her, my client gave an appraising nod. Inside the box were imported cigars from South Africa and a bottle of the best Cuban rum one could buy.

"In my view, Texas can feel like Cuba, so thank you. Now, shall we have wine?" I asked, then waited for my client's permission. I was a man who liked to give a show, just to make others assume the worst or best of me.

He nodded.

I motioned to Oya, and then I got down to business. "You were interested in a stake of my company, precisely the distribution of my Blazers."

Oya poured exotic wine into both of our glasses while I spoke, and then she stepped back into the fold.

My client drank from his glass and savored his sip, then gave me a smile. "Sí, I am. I see you're a man of the world, however young you are. You've been schooled well—and several of my associates within and outside the United States have vouched for your reputation—which is why I'm choosing to do business with you."

"Yes, sir, and it's the same with me. I knew, once we discussed the manner of our association, that working with you would be quite an experience." I reached in my vest, retrieved a small box, opened it, and pulled out one of my bullets with my initials engraved on it. "As a gift of good faith, I leave this small sample in your hands for a demonstration of my value."

After placing the bullet between us on the tablecloth, I leaned back and watched my client study it with deep interest.

"So this is the little beauty?" he asked.

"Yes, sir. there it is. You ready for a show?" I said, my pride showing.

"In here?" my client asked with suspicion.

"No better place. Besides, no one will hear a thing." I reached under the table, undid a strap, and pulled out a silencer.

Both of my client's men bristled, then moved to try to take me out, but their boss stopped that crap at the pass. He raised one hand, and they paused in their tracks. "This young man is no fool. Let him work, *me entienden*?"

"Thank you." I nodded to my people, and they walked to the other side of the room. There they pulled out a life-size dummy, behind which was a solid block of cement with steel running through it.

After standing up, I put my Glock together and added the bullets. "As you see, gentlemen, the dummy is wearing the standard gear worn by the military. When using a conventional gun and conventional bullets, like those found on the street, as you see . . ."

At that moment Oya whipped out her Glock and sent several bullets into the dummy before concealing her weapon. The dummy remained stationary.

I purposely left my gun and silencer on the table to show I was no threat, at the moment, stepped away from the table, and continued my presentation. "So with conventional bullets, this is a typical result." I pointed at the dummy. "Of course, the higher the grade, the more damage you get, but death is what we are seeking here. Now let's introduce my Blazers, and then you tell me what you think."

I snatched up my silencer, screwed it onto the gun, and then pumped two bullets into the dummy and watched it shake with the force. It rocked forward, then slammed back.

Quiet filled the room before I heard one of my client's men mutter, "Dios!"

Satisfaction filled me. I knew they were hooked now. I turned, took my silencer off the gun, then laid both back down on the table.

"I knew when I heard all good things about you that you, young man, had something I needed. Does this bullet work only with silencers?" my client remarked, getting down to business.

I explained my product. Explained to him how it was made and informed him that it could fit any style of gun he wanted to use. I showed him what I meant, and a smile lit up his face, but it was sinister.

"I knew that once you saw my presentation, you'd want a shipment. Because of our previous conversation, I already have a load ready and on its way to you now." As I was speaking, Shango tapped me on my shoulder, so I paused and tilted my head to hear him whisper that we had a problem. "Excuse me, senor," I said, then stood and left the room with Shango.

After moving away from the door, I stared into Shango's cold gaze. "Who fucked up?"

Shango shook his head and pulled out his cell and handed it to me. "The Scandinavians."

My eyes narrowing and, I knew, darkening from my anger, I snatched the cell away from him. "Shredder. What the hell is going on, homie?"

"S-s-sorry . . . boss. I t-t-tried to get our g-goods, but . . ." Shredder began, falling into his typical stuttering pattern.

I hated when he got so pissed off that he stuttered, because that meant that I'd have to wait ten years to find out one minute of intel. But because Shredder was stuttering so hard, I also knew shit had gone wrong in the worst way and there was no way to fix it.

"Shredder, where's Alize? Get her ass on the cell so she can tell me what went down. You go chill and see if you can fix this bullshit, a'ight?" I ordered, my accent becoming thicker in my frustration.

"Y-y-y . . ." Shredder paused, then swallowed. "Yup."

A silky, smooth Girl 6 type of voice hit my ear, and I knew Alize was on the line. She sighed, showing she was pissed off too, and it only made my blood pressure rise. "Break it down, Ally."

Alize broke it down for me. "We were robbed. The Scandinavians lost the product, and we got whipped out by some crew we've never heard of before. Took our ride, with everything in it."

Irritation had me scratching my jaw and looking at the ceiling with eyes that were slits. "Tell me that again . . ."

I could hear Alize swallow slowly. She knew me. She understood that I was about to go all the way off, so she tried to soften her tone and hit me in my nuts with her voice. "The Scandinavians lost our product, but we are tracking it. Shredder is following the chips in the bullet cases and trying to follow it. We have your back, I promise."

I always put untraceable trackers on all my shit when it was in transit as a means of knowing that the product safely got to where it was going. Once the product changed hands, it was hit with the deactivation code. The point being? I was an anal person with what was mine. If something went wrong, I needed to know why, even if there was not always a clear path to understanding the reasons. Because my stuff was en route, my transporters hadn't done the deactivation yet, and now we had to scramble to find my shit.

"You have our back? I told you we shouldn't have fucked with those . . .You know what? I'm going to calm down and let you all handle it. That's the point of this team. I want my shit back, and I want it back now. Now I have to smooth this over and figure this shit out! Fuck me!" I shouted and punched the wall behind me. I guessed I wasn't able to be calm, after all.

Shango stepped to me and rested his hand on my shoulder, causing me to jerk his way. "We have some stashed in our warehouse here," he said.

He was right. We did. I exhaled and spoke in the phone. "Find my stuff, Ally. Call the team here," I ordered, then started to break down the amount I needed. Once I was done, I hung up the cell phone, then handed it to Shango.

"Don't stress it, bro. He's interested, trust. We got him, and the rest will follow," Shango said encouragingly.

"It better," was all I said before I walked back into the meeting.

My client was sitting back with a smirk on his face, sipping his wine and watching Oya hard. I almost felt like being a smartass and asking him what the fuck he was looking at that was so interesting. I didn't play when it came to Oya. She was like blood, but I knew she could take care of herself, so there was no issue.

"Your guard, she is Afro-Latina. I can see it in her," my client said, then glanced my way. "Is everything good, young man?"

Oya was Brazilian, black, and Portuguese, so he wasn't wrong.

Taking a seat, I cleared my throat. "Unfortunately, there has been a delay in the shipment. But I give you my word that you will get what was contracted."

"Then you will not get the rest of my money until I get my merchandise, *me entiendes*?" he said with a slight irritation to his voice.

Though I was ticked off, I kept everything professional. "Yes sir. That I understand," I said, smoothing my voice out. "Which is why, to make up for the delay, I am sending you five hundred cases right now, while you wait until your full shipment comes in."

My client snapped his fingers, then pushed back from the table, stood, and pushed back his jacket. "Once you send notice that those cases have arrived and are ready for me to pick up, I will send you your money, *sí*? I hate to miss this opportunity with you, young man. I see a future where we can do business together long term."

After standing, I gave my client a nod in agreement. "Yes sir. I hope that will be the case."

I held my hand out, and Oya laid one of my business cards in my palm. I gave it to my client's bodyguard who stood to his left. "That is my drop-off and pickup zone. You will be contacted about when to meet there and complete half of the transaction."

"*Bien*, because I'd hate to come to a disagreement. Too many have spoken well of you," my client replied. I sensed a threat in his words.

He seemed to think that by threatening me in a quiet voice, I'd be scared, but he had the wrong one. Death, I embraced, because we all had to go at some point in time. But the thing was, I refused to go by his hand. So I was not intimidated in the least bit. I was also a killer. Had the ammo and the patience to send one of my many special bullets into his temple. One day he would learn that.

With a composed smile, I walked alongside the old man as he headed to the restaurant's lobby. I chuckled. "They say a man's reputation can be his curse or blessing. I embrace both. Don't ride the bull unless you can take it by the horns."

My client turned my way. I felt him size me up; then he extended his hand. "Sí, I think we'll do well together. Until later."

That was the end of my meeting with my client. I watched him leave the restaurant in style, his black limo drawing the attention of many ATLiens. But for me, it was just another way for him to show that he controlled his environment. A man with his type of power was dangerous, and he'd already shown how crazy he could be.

After leaving Morton's, I got in my Audi and watched my team go their own separate ways. Then I whipped out of the parking lot to travel to my side of ATL. I was a hider. Where I did business and where I laid my head were two entirely different places. For a man like my client, I had to look like I had money. But in order to go back to the place where I laid my head down, I had to look like another resident of the hood. So I made it to my private garage in Marietta, swapped cars, changed clothes, then walked a mile through some woods to wait to be picked up by Shango and Oya.

Dressed in everyday clothes, they pulled up in a simple Honda Civic, and I climbed into the backseat.

"I got a text from Shredder. But I was too pissed to read it. Is everything being handled?" I said.

"Yes. Looks like our product is coming our way as planned," Oya said.

"Just not by our hands," Shango added.

A frown overshadowed my face as I pressed the CALL icon on my phone. "He's down with our product," I said as soon as the person on the other end picked up.

"Good. Ain't no thang. Keep me updated and find out where our product went, a'ight?" came the reply.

My gaze focused on the trees as the Honda approached our familiar hood. "Yes, sir, you know I got it. I plan to leave a nice bullet between the eyes of the one who took our shit."

"I know you do, son. The animal that is careful lives long in the forest. *Ashe*?" said the voice on the phone.

I smiled. "*Ashe*," I replied before hanging up the phone.

I rode in the backseat in silence. Oya and Shango conversed in the front. My mind was all over the place. I needed to know who had stolen my shit and why. By the time we got off the expressway and made a right onto Upper Riverdale Road, I was more than a little annoyed. I gazed at the cemetery across from Little Giant Farmer's Market as we passed it. Somewhere in that big place was a set of bullets and a rose lying on a marker for a man and his wife who were once the community's only protection.

Tapping Shango on the shoulder so that he would speed up, I said, "Let's ride out this hell and get to our hood."

"Already on it, bro," Shango said as we rode out.

My name was Boots, and I had an agenda that was all mine, but for now, my focus was on one thing: getting my shit.

Chapter 4

Auto

"You have got to be fucking kidding me," I yelled as I punched the walls of the tractor trailer.

Code was freaking out. We all had damn near killed ourselves only to get the big rig to our hideaway garage and find out the Vikings had still gotten the last laugh. The only thing in the back of that truck was the replicas of the cars we were after. Shells of cars. Dummies.

"All of this! All of this, and for what?" I hollered. "For fucking what? They fucking baited us, and we fell for it. Meanwhile, they have our shit, and we have fucking nothing. Nothing!"

Code stood there, just eyeballing the back of the truck like she couldn't believe what she was looking at. Out of the blue, she yelled, "Fuck!" so loud that it echoed around the whole warehouse. "Fucking fuck, Auto. What are we going to do? We're screwed!" she cried.

All I could think about was the money and the merchandise we'd lost. I sat down on the back of the truck. I didn't have any more strength to stand. My ribs ached. Thighs and calves were hurting like I'd overdone it in the gym on leg day. My jaw felt as if it had been knocked out of its sockets, and my shoulders were tight with tension.

Lelo and Stitch argued behind me. Lelo was pissed at Stitch for pointing out the wrong truck. Stitch was pissed at Lelo for depending on him to remember when he had a head injury. I was pissed at both of them. That was what they did, though. They were a couple who argued over everything when one didn't get something just right. Most people wouldn't look at them and think they were a couple. They were both males with what the world considered a thug disposition. Lelo was Puerto Rican, and Stitch was black.

None of that mattered to me. In our makeshift family/crew, their sexuality meant nothing to us. Still, their arguing was sure to set me off soon. I needed silence so I could think. When I couldn't think, too many voices annoyed me.

"Auto, what the fuck are we going to do?" Code asked me again. "With this shipment and the other two, we're a million in the hole. Two

Porsches, a Lamborghini, and a Bugatti that isn't even out yet. We're fucked! We paid all that fucking money to get it through the weigh station illegally, and they still got us."

I stood up and started pacing the floor again. In the business we were in, you sometimes had to pay weigh-station agents to look the other way. Cars were supposed to be shipped in open fleets. Before getting into the business, I had had to learn all I could about the car-shipping industry. There was no way we could expand if we stole only cars within driving distance, so I had taken to the Internet and had studied.

Old man Law had been driving big rigs for years. When the Internet hadn't yielded enough information, he had been the next best option. He'd shown me how the paperwork was handled. Taken me on a few routes when he drove. Introduced me to a few weigh-station agents whom he trusted. I had soaked in all he told me.

As our reputation proceeded us, people from as far away as Canada had started to request our services. One of my best clients was a Latino drug lord named Armando. Through him I had met a Russian cartel leader, Nicola. It was because of my link to them that I had been able to find a connection to a man who ran a car-shipping company. For a little extra money lining his pockets, Chandler would exchange a few numbers on his paperwork and switch out a few cars on his fleet shipment. We'd pay him enough to compensate agents at a few weigh stations, and everything would go smoothly.

That had been our routine for the past few years. All had worked well. Until now.

Code went on. "We needed the money this lick was going to bring in. We borrowed what we lost last time from my grandfather, with the promise to pay him back with the take from this. God damn it all. I don't feel like dealing with that old man."

"I don't, either. I didn't want to borrow, anyway."

Code sighed. "I'll go to the bank tomorrow. I'll make a wire transfer—"

I stopped her before she could finish. I knew what she was about to say. I'd already had to sell half my business to her when she bailed me out of a jam before. Now I had to worry about how I was going to pay her grandfather, that old man, back. There would be no way I would take more money from her.

"That fixes only half the problem," I said. "With what we have to pay Pascal and what we have to take out for the old man, we're still in the hole. And I'm not about to let you do that. I'm not trying to be in more debt. I already owe money. This is *my* problem. I should have handled Chandler the first time it happened."

I yelled for Lelo and Stitch to stop fucking arguing. They stopped, but Stitch kept kicking one of the tires on a dummy car. The area around us smelled stale. The warehouse we were in hadn't been used in months. The only time we used it was when we ran out of space or when we needed to hide certain merchandise until the heat died down. Transmissions, engines, old cars, fire engines, and police cars you hadn't seen since *The Andy Griffith Show* were scattered about. The big windows were covered in dust and spiderwebs, which swayed in the breeze blowing through.

"I know, but what do we have left to do? We can't risk another shipment through or from our connect in Cali until we scope out those damn Vikings more. Can't believe old man Chandler sold us out. I need permission to handle him," Code replied, basically pleading.

It wasn't often that I let her loose on the world, because she had a hidden anger issue that would cause us lots of heat if she fucked around and did the wrong thing. But this had to be handled.

"Let this heat die down first, and then we catch him when he isn't looking," I said. Code looked at me as I spoke to her. "I want you to make sure that even his great-great-great-grandchildren feel the aftereffects of what you do to him. You understand? You make that motherfucker regret the day he ever crossed us."

I looked at my partner in crime, watched as Code paced the area in front of me. Sometimes I forgot the fact that the ruthless person in front of me was a woman. As feminine as she was, she was as deadly as a black widow. For as long as we'd been friends, she'd been like the sister I never had, but I'd seen her in action when she was angry. Shit wasn't a pretty sight.

She snatched off her bloodied T-shirt, pulling it over her head. I noticed she was walking like she was sore. He breasts bounced and jiggled in her bra. She cursed in Spanish, putting her Afro-Cuban ancestry on display.

"Yo, Auto," Lelo called out to me just then.

I ignored him as I listened to Code. "I need a few days to get to him," she told me. "Need time to set up my kit."

I nodded. "Whatever you need. Take whomever you need. Before you're done with him, though, make him tell you all he knows about those motherfucking Vikings."

A deep crease formed between her brows, a sign she was lost in thought. "Doesn't make sense to me, though."

I asked, "What?"

"Why they were trying so hard to get this truck away from us. They knew there wasn't shit here but shells."

I waved a dismissive hand. "Probably trying to distract us long enough to get the real shit out of range."

She shook her head. "I don't know. They were really trying to kill us."

Stitch called out to me this time. "Hey, Auto!"

Once he and Lelo saw I was ignoring them, Stitch tried getting Code's attention. "Code, you and Auto need to—"

Annoyance finally got the best of me. "Motherfucker, don't you see us handling business!" I snapped as I turned to scowl at them.

In Stitch's hand was a crate. His voice was calm and had a tinge of frustration when he said, "Just saying, boss man, that y'all might wanna take a look at this."

Before I could ask him what he was talking about, he had brought the crate to the edge of the truck, had hopped down, and had set the crate on the floor. Lelo trailed behind him. Both Code and I walked closer as Stitch knelt down and opened the crate. Lelo knelt down beside him once the crate was open.

"Look at this shit," Stitch said as he pulled out a small, clear rectangular box with bullets inside it.

"These ain't no regular bullets, bro," Lelo chimed in as he looked from the bullets up at me. "Look at 'em."

Stitch passed a box of bullets to me, then handed one to Code. I examined the box. Turned it upside down and saw the initials BK engraved on the bottom of the bullets. I tried to figure out a way to open the box, then noticed there was a small hole where some key was probably supposed to go.

"Can't open this shit," I said.

Lelo stood, rushed to the back of the truck, got on his knees, and felt around under one of the dummy cars. He found what he was looking for, then rushed back over.

"Here," he said, passing me a small dimple key. "Found this in the crate but thought it was just some random shit. Looks like it fits the box, though."

"Oh, this is some high-tech shit," Code said, speculating. "A dimple key like this means whoever made these bullets is some other level government-type shit. Dimple keys have cone-shaped dimples that match up with two sets of pins in the lock."

"Speak English, Code," Stitch remarked.

"What she means is, whoever made these bullets knew what they were doing. Being that the boxes are locked down tighter than Fort Knox means they didn't want them to fall into the wrong hands," I said.

I fumbled around with the lock and key on my box of bullets. Made sure I lined up the key just right, then slid it into the lock. Like magic, the box popped open. Code reached inside my box, pulled out a bullet, and studied it. Golden on the bottom, copper toned in the middle, and the color of a brand-new penny at the top, the bullet was designed like one I'd never seen before. It looked like the top had been drilled into and then the opening had been filed into eight picket fence–like prongs.

"Found some guns back there too," Stitch said.

I found it odd that Code hadn't said anything about these bullets yet.

I asked her, "What do you think?"

"Let me get one of those guns," she told me.

Stitch rushed to the back of the truck, grabbed a case of guns from where the engine of one of the dummy cars should have been, hauled the case over to us, and opened it. Then he handed a black Glock 9 to Code. She needed a target, so I ordered Lelo to set up a few of the cinder blocks that were lying around. Took Code all of a few seconds to load a clip into the gun. She stood with a perfect shooting stance: weight shifted forward, her feet shoulder width apart, one foot slightly forward of the other, and the gun pointing at the target. She'd more than likely developed this stance from all the training her grandfather had demanded she undergo when she was growing up.

When she let the hammer loose, the sound of the gun firing echoed loudly. Bullets tore through the cinder block so violently that it crumbled into pieces, sending ash clouds into the air. She turned quickly, aimed the gun at a tire on the big rig, and fired. The rubber tore apart like it had been shredded, causing the truck to shift like it had hydraulics.

"Holy shit," Lelo and Stitch said at the same time.

I rushed in to inspect the bullet casings. Code smiled like she knew something we didn't.

"Load this up," she ordered.

"What you smiling at? And what the fuck you mean, load this up?" I asked her. "We don't deal in weapons."

"Trust me when I tell you, we just hit the jackpot."

"I ain't trusting shit until you tell me what the hell you're talking about," I replied.

Code rolled her eyes hard. She knew I didn't play that shit. I never went in blindly on anything, and this wouldn't be any different. I needed to know the risk factors for everything, and since we didn't deal in weapons, illegal drugs, or anything that caused genocide in the hood, she needed to run this shit down for me, and she needed to do it in a way that didn't make me want to blow her head off afterward. I wasn't about putting my family in jeopardy, and they all knew that.

"I have to meet with my grandfather, the old man," she informed me.

I took a seat on the back of the truck and watched her intently. "About?"

"I have a feeling he'll be pissed about a shipment he may be missing."

I quirked both brows, curiosity riding me. "These bullets belong to the old man?"

"If my suspicions are correct, yes, yes, they do."

She was smiling. My lips had turned down into a frown. I didn't like dealing with that old dickhead she called her grandfather. I'd never met the man, but I knew psychological abuse when I saw it. Had dealt with it all my life from the system. He had a hold so tight on Code mentally that she often questioned her own sanity.

"And you're going to do what with that knowledge? Try to sell the bullets back to him? He'll kill you, and you know he will."

With as close as we were, there was no secret between us that the old man she called her grandfather was nobody you wanted to cross. Even though she was his favorite granddaughter—according to her, though I begged to differ—he wouldn't hesitate to punish her for going against the grain, against his word. I'd seen how he punished her before. She had the scars on her back to show for it.

"I'm not that stupid, Auto. But I figure if I can find out who created these suckers, it will be to our advantage, as they will be in dire need to get them back. Nobody in their right mind wants to cross the old bastard. And since I know for a fact he's already paid a hefty price for something coming out of Vegas, from the gun show, whoever lost his shipment is going to be looking to get it back by any means necessary."

"And yeah, that means they'll be willing to kill for it too. So no." I glanced over my shoulder. "Lelo and Stitch, pack up the Cessna and tell Reagan to gas up. We're getting out of here." I stood, then made my way across the room to make some phone calls back to the A.

"Auto, please, you have to let me do this. We need this money," Code pleaded.

"We don't need it bad enough for you to try to go head to head with that old man." I spat on the concrete, like the whole idea left a bad taste in my mouth.

"Auto, all I have to do is find the person or persons who lost this merchandise. The rest is easy going."

I shook my head. I was seriously thinking about dumping this shit off in a landfill somewhere and calling it a day. But Code wouldn't let up. I listened to her stress the fact that we needed to go with her plan because we were in the hole.

Lelo and Stitch were quiet, but I could tell they were listening. I knew if word got back to the rest of the crew about how much this latest fiasco had set us back, there would be questions. Questions I didn't want to answer. I didn't know exactly how we were going to recoup what we had lost.

Against my better judgment, I agreed to what Code was scheming.

"You get one shot," I told her. "One. If it even looks like you're about to bring heat to this team, you back the fuck out. We don't need the Feds breathing down our necks. We don't need heat from any hoodlum at our door. Got it?"

Code nodded and kept telling me her plan as we got ready to fly back out. I had people to pay and mouths to feed. If we didn't recoup our losses, I'd be breaking my word to all those I'd told that they'd never go hungry or become homeless again. Needless to say, I saw Code's vision, a vision that would come back to haunt me when it was all said and done.

It had been seventy-two hours since we'd landed back in ATL. I sat in the office at the auto shop. We were still no closer to getting our merchandise back or recouping our losses. I'd cleaned up. Talked to our team and assured them we had everything under control. I wasn't too sure of that, but my job was to be sure they stayed on task and let me worry about the heavy-duty stuff.

Code was in her signature tan pencil skirt, white blouse, and matching blazer, which she'd paired with six-inch tan, red-bottom shoes. A vast difference from the greasy jumpsuit she'd had on before. Her hair was no longer in six cornrows but had gone wild, with small spiral curls framing her oval-shaped baby face.

My black button-down, dark denim jeans, and black loafers showed the team that I was back to business. Yeah, I was young, but I had put in enough work to make me feel and seem older than my age. Truth be told, I was still young enough to be in college, but I had lived a life that had made me too street wise for corporate America.

I was deep in thought when there was a buzz in the shop. I looked through the two-way mirror. Twenty people in the shop. Loads more in the street, handling business for us. I was still nervous as fuck about what Code was trying to pull off, but I was in a bind. Wanted to call in the cavalry but hadn't heard from my boy Trigga in weeks. I knew what the deal was with that, so I wouldn't call him unless I had no other choice.

"What are we going to do about those damn Vikings?" Code asked me from her seat on the other side of my desk. "After I handle Chandler, we still have to get after them."

"You let me worry about that. I'm still thinking. One thing at a time," I told her. "Now, what about this new potential you were telling me about?"

She knew my transitioning to the topic of the new potential was my way of telling her to drop the subject. She and I had been friends long enough for her to know when something was a done deal. She got up and walked to the file cabinet to pull out a file.

"Got a hit today in the system. Street name
Smiley. Got caught up when one of her friends
was trying to pull a credit card switch at Morton's
The Steakhouse, where they worked. The friend
got spooked by the time she was facing and sold
Smiley out," she informed me.

She slid the file across the desk to me and
sat back down in the chair she had occupied.
Watched quietly as I opened it and looked down
at the face of a girl who clearly had no soul
behind her eyes. Her hair was shaved off on
one side of her head, and long black locks with
purple tips adorned the other side. Piercings
and hoop earrings lined both of her earlobes.

I looked through the papers in the file, then
back up at Code. "What's her specialty?"

"She's got a record. Credit card skimming.
ATM fraud. Card switching. But her claim to
fame? She hijacked a police car at fourteen and
took it on a joyride. On her sixteenth birthday,
she stole ten cars in less than twenty-four hours.
Max time she kept each one was two hours. She
was an hour outside New York when she was
caught."

"So she stole a string of cars to go on a road
trip? What the hell was in New York?"

"Juvie file says she was going to kill her father
for beating her mother damn near to death."

"She told the cops that?"

Code nodded. "Says it right there in the police report."

"Well, did she kill him?"

She shook her head. "Nope, but he did die about a year later of a drug overdose."

"She has family?"

"Just her and her mother. Mother's dead now, though. Died a few weeks ago."

"So why is she stealing? Out of greed or necessity?"

"According to Officer Bryant . . . from what he told me of her history, it looks like she's doing it out of necessity. Her mother was sick—cancer, I think—and she was paying her mom's doctor bills and for her meds, treatments, and such."

Officer Bryant was Code's cousin on the Atlanta Police Department. She had him in her pocket. Which worked in our favor.

I sat forward, clicking a pen in my hand, as she watched me. "You want me to bring her on, then?"

She shrugged. "Want to feel her out. See what she's about. She's facing twenty years. If I feel the vibe is cool, I can offer her a way out by joining us. We could use her. She's multifaceted. And you know we need someone who's good with credit cards, since Kitty died in that shootout in East Lake Meadows."

"A'ight. I'll call Officer Bryant and take the lead on this. Have him bring her out of the cell so I can speak to her. I need to feel her out myself. If I decide she's cool, I'll introduce her to the team. If not, she'll never see me again."

"What angle are you working?" Code asked as she stood and grabbed her clutch.

"Lawyer. Going to see whether she'll bite if I dangle the bait."

"What are we offering?"

"She works for us, we'll find a way to make her charges disappear, and the chick who sold her out will be on the hook for it all."

Code nodded, then walked around the desk. I could tell she was still in pain by the way she had to slow down her walk. She hugged me, then kissed my cheek. In her heels she was almost as tall as me.

"Can I meet you back here in the morning? I have to get to the old man while he's eating dinner, or he'll be a dick otherwise," she said as she headed toward the door.

"Sure," I answered. A sinking feeling settled in the pit of my stomach. Made me uncomfortable. I looked at the young woman who'd been the only true family I'd known as she walked with the regal disposition of a goddess and the stride of a boss. Even through her pain, she held her head high. "Hey, Code," I yelled behind her.

She turned on her heels. "Yeah, bro?"

"Be careful, even with the old man."

She smiled. "Don't worry, Auto. I got this."

I sat there, wishing I was as confident as she was.

An hour later I sat in a drab room with a light in the middle of the ceiling, a table, two chairs, and four walls. My hair was in a ponytail. Black-framed glasses adorned my eyes, and a black tailored Brooks Brothers suit was my attire. I was still sore in places I didn't know I had. Goddamned Vikings had hit like anvils were attached to their hands.

I waited, quite impatiently, as they brought the young woman in. She looked worse for wear. Like she hadn't slept or had a decent meal in weeks. There was a bruise underneath her eye. All those piercings I'd seen on the photo in her file were gone. Her eyes were red, and she had a frown on her face that told me she wasn't in a good mood. Even through all of that, her beauty couldn't be denied.

"Hey, I don't know this man," she yelled at the officer as he walked to the door.

The officer ignored her. Turned his head and walked out like she didn't even exist.

Her hands were cuffed in front of her as she studied me.

"Have a seat, Nia," I told her.

She shook her head. "Nah. I'm cool standing up. Who are you?"

"That all depends on you."

She gave an exasperated sigh. "Look, I'm not for bullshit and games, man. What the hell do you want with me? Because I don't have a lawyer, and I for damn sure don't know no Asians like that. So if you in here just to fuck with me or you a public defender, you can kiss the blackest part of my ass."

I licked my lips and leaned to the side in my chair, not impressed by her show of defensiveness.

"You just blew out all that hot air," I said. "You're talking a lot but not saying anything. It's cool if you don't trust people. I get it. I understand it, but I'm not out to get you. I'm here to help. You're facing twenty years because you trusted the wrong person. Now, if you're willing to help me, I can help you. You'll be out of here in a few hours. Curb that anger. Take a seat. Listen to what I have to say. If you don't like it, I'll walk out of here, and you'll never see me again."

She was hesitant, but she plopped down on the folding metal chair. "Talk," she snapped.

"I'd like to talk to you about employing your services."

She frowned. "I work in a steak house. I serve food."

"And I'm in need of another server."

"What?"

"I need a server. I'm one member short on my staff, and I'm looking for a replacement. Would you be interested?"

"I thought you were a lawyer?"

"Of course, I'd have to skim a bit of your earnings off the top until you pay me back for bailing you out," I observed. "You're familiar with how skimming works, right?"

Nia said nothing. Sat back in her chair and watched me with a deadly glare.

I had her attention, so I continued. "You're facing twenty years, which means your coconspirator has sold you up shit creek without a paddle. It'll be your word against hers, and I can assure you she has already made a plea deal."

"So what? They can't prove I did shit."

"If that was the case, you wouldn't still be sitting in here. Now, my offer is clear. You work for me, and I'll make all this disappear."

If she agreed to my deal, Officer Bryant would start the process of making sure any evidence against her disappeared. She looked like she wanted to jump across the table and fight me. I could see her wheels turning behind her eyes, though. No sane criminal wanted to be locked up. Whether you were a petty thief or not, in lockdown they placed you with the murderers, rapists, child molesters, and violent criminals alike. To the system, all criminals were the same. I could tell by the bruise and her anger that she'd already been in a fight or two.

"Let's say I considered your offer. What would I be doing in your employment?" she asked me. "I'm not about indentured servitude, either. So if you bail me out, I can give you your money back."

I smirked, then tilted my head. "Tell me something. How would a waitress at a steak house be able to pay me back fifty thousand dollars?"

She gave me a smirk, then squared her shoulders as she looked at me. "I can skim a little here, skim a little there. You know, from my life savings and my mama's insurance money. Daddy had a pension. I can make it do what I want it to."

I grunted, then chuckled. We both knew she was full of shit. If she had that much legal money lying around, she could have bailed herself out and got an attorney. The fact that she had used the same code word I had let me know that she was exactly what the charges painted her to be. I had done enough talking inside these county walls, though.

I stood, picked up my briefcase, and asked her, "So is that a yes or a no, Ms. Nia? You in, or are you on your way to prison for the next twenty years?"

Chapter 5

Smiley

When I'd woken up in my cell and gone out into the general population this morning, I'd had no idea I'd have to fight. Some cunt had told me I was looking at her too hard. Truth be told, I hadn't been thinking about that bitch. I'd been too busy trying to figure out what was crawling through the shit they called oatmeal. How she figured I'd been staring at her had been as lost on me as it had been on her when I beat her ass.

Through it all, I hadn't thought that I'd soon be sitting in front of some dude, talking about getting me out of here. Yet there I was, looking into the face of a guy who was holding out a carrot like bait. Now, a huge part of me didn't want to trust the pretty-looking dude.

I really wasn't trying to put my faith in some Asian who, if I closed my eyes, sounded like a brotha from my hood. I didn't know him at

all. But as I checked him out, I gave a slight
laugh, because he looked too young to be a
lawyer. Already I was peeping game, because I
was tripping on how he was able to set this up
without being suspect.

Yet here I was, thinking about what he was
offering me. Weighing the pros and cons of all
this shit, coming to terms with the reality that he
had just offered me my freedom. Yeah, anyone
locked up behind bars and facing twenty years
would be glad to hear someone offering them a
way out. Still, I was cautious. After dealing with
Keisha and being stuck in this place, it made
sense that I was leery of this whole situation. I
didn't know what I was going to do.

"Hello? So are you in or are you out?" he said,
snapping me out of my thoughts.

My eyes locked on the guy in front of me,
and a frown etched its way around my mouth. I
guessed I had been zoned out. I'd already started
to get cabin fever from being locked up. So I
knew that I had to give him my answer, or else I
would remained locked up and would continue
to suffer.

"I'm in," I quickly responded.

Felt like I was floating out of my body at that
moment. There I was, putting my life in the
hands of some random dude. Instantly, I hated
Keisha's very existence because of my situation.

"Then I'll make it do what it do. We'll see each other again, Ms. Gaines," he said.

As he walked on out the door, I hoped that I wasn't being played. I prayed that I wouldn't live to regret the decision I'd just made.

Getting me out must have taken some work. By the time I got wind of the fact that I was being released, which was four days later, I had lost faith in the rescue. A huge part of me had been thinking that maybe something good would come my way for a change, that my mama was guarding me and sending blessings my way. The other part of me had felt like the whole thing was a setup. Had felt like it had to be, because I kept questioning how the guy had even known who I was. It had me anxious, and it had me leery.

However, when the guard called my name and told me I was leaving, I couldn't lie and say I wasn't geeked up. Being released felt damn good. All the while, though, on some real talk, I wanted to put my fists in Keisha's face.

But beyond that, I was just ready to go home.

I gathered all my things in my cell, and after glancing around it one last time, I clutched my bag of stuff and followed the guard. I was checked out, and all the belongings that had been taken from me were returned. Then I was free to go. I walked through the main gate of the jail and realized I could do me again and not be restricted. I wanted to party, wanted to have some fun. I'd been locked up for only a few weeks, but it had felt like years to me, a person who was used to being free. But as I boarded a bus, I realized that my freedom was all due to that Asian dude, and I felt worried.

I knew I had no job to go back to, so that meant I had to go back to the illegal work I had done that got me locked up in the first place. All just to pay the man back for bailing me out. I wasn't sure how I was going to get those fifty Gs, but I had to figure out something quickly. I knew he had said that he wasn't going to trick me, but I didn't trust anyone. Him having a dick wasn't the main reason not to trust him, but it was a good one. I took a seat on the bus and sat back, thinking about the little change I had from my thieving schemes and the legit money I had in the banks. Owing someone wasn't in my cards. I had had enough of that with paying bills and other crap. So, my mind was processing and ticking off things that I could do.

I finally made it home after walking for hours once I got off the bus. I cut through the back of several houses just in case I was being watched, and I made it into my house by going through the back porch. Everything was in place. I switched the lights on. Nothing. On and off, off and on. Still nothing.

Goddamn it!

I sighed and shook my head. Fuckers had been cut off. There was no gas, no nothing! Which meant that the little food I did have in the fridge had rotted. Luckily, I had some running water, but still! I needed to go. Needed to leave this place, but where I would go, I wasn't sure.

My mom had come from Cali, so maybe I could go there. Just change up my look and take on a new name. I could say fuck the man who had bailed me out. It was my life, so I could leave when I wanted.

I moved around my house, cleaning up, lighting candles, and taking stock of my things. I started packing, then sat down. I felt like a hot mess. I needed to retwist my lock extensions, but luckily, they weren't bad. Just needed a little refresher. Touching my low-cropped hair, I sighed. I needed a lineup, but for now, all I could do was take some scissors and trim the sides of my hair some. I smoothed down my hair with some Eco Styler olive oil styling gel, then continued to pack my bag and get ready to go.

"I'll be back, Mama. I promise you," I muttered aloud to her presence in the house.

I had stuffed an old photo album of hers and her small jewelry box with the things she had left me in my bag. I had also packed several pictures of us that had been sitting around in picture frames. I needed to go. This life wasn't for me, not with having to owe some dude I didn't know. I couldn't trust that he would keep the cops off me. So I needed to go and keep them off me by myself.

Gazing around one last time, I frowned. I planned on mailing the payment for this house as soon as I got downtown. I headed through my home, not knowing where I intended to lay my head down. There was an abandoned warehouse outside the trap that I liked to sneak into sometimes. It used to be where I'd temporarily store some of my equipment parts for my credit card–making machines. I had long since stopped doing that, but I knew the place was quiet, and I could hang low there without a problem, so that was what I planned to do.

I chain locked the back door to my house and exited the property through the backyard. It was quiet in the hood today, which wasn't unusual. Every day something was popping off, either something good or somewhat dangerous. So, many people would just chill in the quiet of their homes or on their porches, while some bold kids played or relaxed on the street. Back when I was little, I used to play double Dutch and learned some steps for fun with my girls. Now those days were long gone.

I sighed softly as I turned the corner in the back alleyway I had just walked down. A sudden stinging pain spread across my face as someone shoved me cheek first against a wall, then slung me backward. Stumbling, I held my hand back behind me to get my footing and tried to shake the sudden dizziness I felt.

"God damn it," I grumbled and rubbed my nose.

"Where you going, Mami?" I heard a voice say.

Tension and fear rocked me to my core. My eyes got wide, and I tried to inch backward. Damn it! I had just got out, and already I was being harassed by the cops?

A tinkling laughter came from behind me. I gazed up to see a tall Latino-looking brotha in front of me. Behind me, where that laughter had come from, was a female who was around my height, with a thick, curving body and crazy big breasts. I felt a little moment of jealousy over that, but I chilled out. My eyebrow rose when she waved my way like I knew her.

She sported two knotted ponytails on the top of her head, something I liked to wear myself. Piercing brown eyes that accentuated her caramel-brown skin stared my way. I noticed that she had a scar from a burn on the side of her bare stomach, and it made me flinch inwardly, as I felt for her. Only reason I had noticed the mark was that she wore a cropped top.

In front of me, old dude, with his sexy allure, studied me, while another equally fine chocolate brotha came from behind him, as if he were the guy's shadow. They both sported baggy jeans and matching open button-down shirts with black beaters. The chocolate brother had a set of keys in his hands. I saw him wink at me; then he pointed and motioned to me.

Wait, those were my keys. How in the hell had he got them?

"Ya might want to turn on around and head back to your place," he said with amusement in his voice.

This fool was on some ninja shit. Must have swiped my keys when I was stumbling, ran in my mind.

The chick behind me laughed again, then crossed her arms with a grin. "Mm-hmm, boss man is waiting for you, Smiley."

At first, shock rattled through me; then rage had my eyes narrowing and my brows dropping as I scowled. "I don't know none of y'all. So you all can get up out my way. I have business to handle."

That same light laughter sounded again, and Mr. Latino stepped forward, then looked me over with a smirk. "I think your business is ours, Mami. Especially since we're the ones who worked hard on getting you out. So, take our advice, because if you fight . . ."

"This shit won't be easy breezy for you anymore, and you won't like the end result," said Mr. Chocolate, who stood by his side.

He was equally well built, and I felt like a caged animal. There were three people surrounding me. Two males and one giggling-ass female. Mr. Chocolate had my keys, and I needed them back. I had to figure something out.

I quietly thought about my options. I could bust the broad's face with my elbow, then try to jet around the two big-ass niggas, but I could already tell from how they were spaced out that this wouldn't work.

"Yo, did her eyes just darken? She's up to no good," I heard one of the males say.

"Come on, sis. Let us introduce ourselves. Don't cause a fight and draw attention. We mean peace and not war," said the chick.

Considering how they all were dressed, it didn't seem like they were cops, but still, I wasn't trusting that, either. Fuck this shit. I turned around and was getting ready to go off when I felt myself being lifted up off the ground.

Tall Mr. Chocolate set me back down on the ground and then grabbed me by the back of my neck and pushed me toward my home as he spoke with his smooth, panty-dropping voice and started to annoy me. "Remember when you joined the team, Reagan? You tried to claw off my face. Shit pissed me off for days, Mami. I learned my lesson, though."

The chick he had called Reagan snickered again, then huffed, "Whateva. I just was protecting myself."

"Right, which is why I knew we needed three people to get this one. Given how she was moving down the alley, I already knew she might be trouble," Mr. Chocolate said while I struggled.

Swinging my hands behind me, I tried to dig my nails into his arms. But that didn't achieve a damn thing other than inciting him to grip the back of my neck harder and give me a shake.

"Chill the fuck out, and we can be cool, a'ight?" he growled against my ear.

My fist shot back into his eye, making me fall forward on my hands and knees. That position alone had me rising up in a sprinter's form, but it wasn't worth the effort. As soon as I tried to run, I heard a gun click, and I stopped fighting.

I held my hands up in self-defense. "Okay . . . okay . . . damn. I'm going!"

"Good call, because I don't want to have to shoot you, girl," the chick said.

I gazed behind me, and I saw a pink-and-black Glock pointed my way. I couldn't believe this shit. *When it rains, it pours*, I thought.

When we reached my house, Mr. Chocolate slid my keys in my hand. I worked the chain locks on my door. Fiddling with the keys, I unlocked multiple locks. Then, with a scowl on his face, Mr. Chocolate opened the door for me and pointed for me to go in.

I walked in. Darkness filled my home. "Sorry. The lights are out," I said sarcastically.

"Not for long, Mami. We're working on it. . . . Well, I am now," Mr. Latino said.

I turned and watched him disappear on the back porch. Tall Mr. Chocolate seemed to watch him intently before turning back to me and frowning.

"I'm sorry for hitting you, dude," I said, wanting to restore the peace and still thinking about how to get out of this situation.

"No you are not. Keep moving, shawty," he hissed, then pushed me forward.

He was right; I wasn't. They had messed up my plans, and now they were in my home, and there was nothing I could do about it. I headed in the direction of the living room. The sudden sound of the equipment in the house coming on made me jump.

"Wow, you have a nice place up in here, girl," Reagan said at my side. "We could kick it here for real during our downtime."

Kick it? In my place? Hell to the no!

"I don't know y'all from Adam and Eve. The hell you will," I spat out.

"You're about to know us, if you just calm down and chill out," said a voice from inside my home. It didn't belong to any one of the threesome who had kidnapped me.

The voice set off alarms of recognition in my head as I moved through the kitchen and into the living room.

The Asian guy who had spoken with me when I was locked up stood in the middle of my place. His hands were in his pockets, a toothpick was in his mouth, and he sported a black jumper that was unzipped enough for me to see his white beater underneath. He was built as if he was ready to be in some MMA fighting match, something I hadn't noticed before. I noticed his dark Tims, and I could tell he was packing heat from how the leg of his jumper was bunched up. He must have been moving around for it to pop up like that.

On his head was a big cap that gave him a sexy look, which was different from how he'd looked when he sat in front of me and played the lawyer. His long black hair rested on his shoulders.

"Can I get some water?" I heard behind me.

I crinkled my nose in frustration, then moved to drop my bags. "There're cups in the top cabinet. I don't have any food in the fridge."

"You got canned stuff, I see. We'll be good. Thanks, little mama," I heard Mr. Chocolate say.

From behind him, I heard the sound of Spanish popping off in my kitchen. That had me really confused. Something strange was going on between those two dudes. I could hear Mr. Latino complaining about how Mr. Chocolate always had to be rude and go through people's things, searching for food.

"That's why you got hit in the eye," Mr. Latino told him, which caused Mr. Chocolate to go off.

In the middle of their bickering, I heard their names, Lelo and Stitch, and it made me laugh aloud. "Seriously?" I asked.

"Seriously what, Nia?" Mr. Asian asked with a frown on his face.

Looking him up and down, I pointed behind me. "Who are they? Who are you? What the hell can I do for y'all? And their names . . . Are they really Lelo and Stitch?"

He cut his eyes at me and then addressed the chick beside me, who was grinning hard. "Go to the front and hit Seymore on the cell to see if everything is still clear in the neighborhood. Once it is, tell him to set up his security for this place. And you do your thing, like you always do, with setting it up, a'ight?"

"Already on it, boss man. He said it's clear," Reagan confirmed.

"Cool. Hey, Lelo. Since ya hungry, go do a solid and hit that corner store and bring back some grub for her. We're going to be a minute," Mr. Asian, their leader, said, not out of rudeness or harshness, but with a cool, light authoritative air.

"Sí, I'm on it. I'll give you the rundown when I get back, then," Lelo shouted back. Then I heard him jet out the back and slam the door behind him.

Banging could be heard in the kitchen, so I knew the other one was still in there, doing his thing and making my stomach clench from anxiety at these strangers taking over. I shook my head, and my gaze locked on my front door. I started to walk around Mr. Asian, but he stopped me by grabbing my arm.

Dark, almond-shaped eyes bore into me, and Mr. Asian gripped my arm tight. "Whoa. Where you going?"

Yanking my arm out of his hold, I sized him up. "Trying to see how you got in my place. My weak-ass pop put that bolt in. Made sure it was armored and couldn't be picked."

"Ah, well, I picked it. It is a good lock, but not anymore. I'll replace it," he said, then took two strides and dropped down on my couch.

I was speechless. I went to the door, turned the knob, and then sighed when I saw the bolt lock was broken. I slammed the door shut and used the bottom lock to secure it.

"My girl Code would have been here, but she had other things to handle, but to answer you, Nia—" he began to explain.

"Smiley. My name is Smiley," I interrupted, then crossed my arms while standing wide legged.

"A'ight, Smiley. In the back is Stitch, as you heard. He's my muscle, him and Lelo. Both are my IT and HR department. They are also useful with the rigging shit, which is why your lights are back on, and they're good with handling people. The little homie with the laugh is Reagan. She and my boy Seymore—you'll meet him later—are good with car repair, car detailing, and attention to detail when doing what we do with electronics and other illegal activity," he explained as he watched me. I heard the pride in his voice.

He sat up and rested his arms on his knees, then continued. "My girl, more like a sis to me in this game, is Code. She's the missing one. She is the money and finances. She's also my copartner in this. She's good with rides, as well, and, as I'm learning, other things, such as understanding the specifics of some weapons."

All of this was crazy to me, but I needed to know the specifics. "Okay. And you are?"

"Chill and have a seat, Smiley," the leader of this strange crew ordered with bass in his voice.

I shook my head, took a seat like he'd asked, more like demanded. I didn't want another gun drawn unless I was going to be the one doing it. Thanks to my crazy-ass pop being in the military, he used to teach me how to shoot. Two of the gifts he forgot to grab when he was leaving us were the shotgun under the couch and the 9 mm hidden upstairs.

"They call me Auto. I know it all, from tech to fixing up cars, to logistics and more. We steal rides, chop 'em up, and sell them wherever we want. We also go deeper, which is why we looked you up. Not only are you a beast in how you steal rides, but I've peeped how well you work with hitting up those ATMs too. Looked deeper, Miss Hacker, and I saw you got a PayPal account through which you route money you steal from online. Your coding is good, but we can make it better," he said, giving me the rundown.

I watched this guy speak with his hands and hit me with a spell so smooth that it had me almost believing the whole bullshit laid out in front of me.

Auto tilted his head to the side and watched me as he thumbed his nose. "How you jack rides is good, but again, we can teach you to do it better. We need you because we lost one of us already, and in this game, you need to have a banging team in order to stay ahead of the Feds, not just the regular cops. How we do things, how we groove is why we were able to get you out. We got people in high places, which is also why we can assure your freedom and make sure the shorty who set you up takes the fall. This is not a setup. This is family. We erase people's identities for a living and make extra dough with jacking rides. So we don't have time to play games. Do you understand me now?"

I sat and thought quietly. Watched him as he studied me. So there wasn't a setup going down on his end. All he'd said seemed to be legit. Some of the suspicion I had melted away. Enough to make me consider his offer.

"I think I understand you now. So out of this, I get my freedom and I gotta pay you back?"

"Yup, and if you decide to stay, this house you live in, you don't have to worry about paying no more. That job you lost because of your rookie behavior, you don't have to worry about it anymore, and if you wanted, that degree you were working on, you can finish just because. All of that and more is what you get for rolling with us. This all right here won't be gems and gold, and shit won't be some easy-peasy type of deal. But I can promise you won't be sorry with how the rewards come through, and with them, you got a team, a family that will hold you down and look out for you. So are you done running? Can we get to some real talk now?"

The scent of food cooking wafted my way. I heard the back door open and then the sound of Lelo's and Reagan's voices, and then a new voice chimed in about the ramp at the back of the house working out for him. I gazed at the dude who sat on my couch as if it were his, and then I looked around, feeling a weight lift off me. If I trusted them, that meant my life would be changing, and with this change, I'd have new people that, he'd said, would be like my family. I was unsure about it all, but, shit, anything was better than being locked up.

"I'm done running. I'm down. What do I need to know?" Exhaling, I relaxed and pulled my knees up to my chest, ready to learn more about a crew that until today I had no clue existed in the streets of ATL.

Chapter 6

Code

My cousin Frederick walked into the dining room. "Papa, we just got word the promised shipment has been delivered," he informed my grandfather.

All his grandchildren called him Papa. The old man sat at the head of the dinner table, dressed like he belonged in a corporate meeting. Food had been laid out: baked chicken, steamed green beans, yellow Spanish rice, and corn bread. The smell of apple pie contrasted with the other spices floating through the air. I'd barely touched my food.

The bloodred, tailor-made dress shirt Papa had on told of his mood. An array of colors seemed to swirl in his light brown eyes whenever his mood was iffy. The look in his eyes right now was redolent of murder. Something was bothering him. I just didn't know what. Though he was close to seventy in age, his body put those of some younger males to shame. The old man had always taken care of himself, and old age didn't stop him. It seemed only to fuel his fire.

I looked down at my phone to see a message from Auto telling me that they had gotten the girl and that she seemed to be on board. Apparently, she was a little jumpy, but he said she was willing. I nodded and then sent a response to let him know I'd gotten his message.

"Have you checked the merchandise, *mijo*?" the old man asked Frederick.

"*Sí*, Papa. All is in order."

"Then go make yourself presentable for dinner." Papa was big on presentation no matter what was going on.

My cousin Frederick did an about-face like the good soldier he was and left the room. The scar on his neck reminded us all of what would happen if you crossed our grandfather.

While the old man kept talking about plans and giving orders, my attention wandered, but when he started to talk about the man who'd supplied him with the merchandise he was excited about, my focus became riveted on his words. After all, I had been sitting around, trying to get information on this topic. With a little bit of info, I could know how I wanted to proceed.

Having that in my possession could work out well for my team.

"May I speak, Papa?" I asked, causing everyone to get quiet.

All eyes turned to me, including my mother's. She sat like the world belonged to her. Papa wasn't big on letting women run anything in his organization, but my mama had been his favorite daughter. In order to become the old man's favorite, you had to do something special. I didn't know what it was my mother had done, but because she'd done it, she had a lot of clout in our family.

People often claimed my mother and I could pass for twins. I begged to differ. It had nothing to do with the fact that she was darker than I was. Most people were often confused when she started to speak fluent Spanish. They oftentimes assumed she was a black American. But she had been born and bred in Cuba. Although her hair was thick, and you could clearly see the African part of her Cuban ancestry. Her locks were long and wild, cascading down to her ample backside. She lauded her own beauty. If anybody even hinted around that she was anything less than God's gift to man, she would likely kill them without a thought.

I didn't have her dark beauty or her long hair.
I mean, I had hair, but it was nowhere near as
long as my mother's. I had Papa's complexion.
I had his eyes. And if pushed to the point of
no return, I had the old man's temper too. Our
familia often claimed that was why I was his
favorite. I knew differently. I was his favorite
because at a very young age, I'd killed someone
no one else could for him. I was his favorite
because anything he asked me to do, I did without question.

Years and years of training with the males in
my family had made me as ruthless as they were.
I had had few friends while I was growing up,
because of who my family was. And those who
had befriended me had done so only because of
the status and rep it would give them. That was
why when I'd walked into Auto's shop that first
time, it had been refreshing to be treated like I
was just a regular person. No pretenses. No fear
behind the eyes of the people, no people who
were scared to even breathe out of fear of my
family name. No, Auto had had no idea who I
was or to whom I was related.

And he still had no idea. To him, I was just
Code. To our makeshift family, I was just Code.
They treated me like I was human, the same as
them. I'd told them enough so they could shoot

questions at me that I could answer easily. The team rarely trusted people they didn't know. So when they opened their hearts and doors to me, I walked in, knowing I would always protect them. I would always keep this, the true part of who I was, away from them.

Yeah, Auto knew the old man was rolling in dough, but he had no idea who my papa was. I intended to keep it that way.

"Speak, Maria Rosa," Papa told me, pulling me from my thoughts.

Old man had never given me a sobriquet. So he would never call me Code. He believed that a person should be addressed with respect, and that meant using the person's birth name. To him, when someone called you by a nickname, it meant he or she didn't think much of you. It was easy for the old man to feel disrespected.

I nodded, with a smile. "I wanted to know about the merchandise, Papa. What is it? Is it something I can play with?" I then smiled my most sinister smile, knowing it would please him to see the devilment playing behind my eyes.

"It's been a while since you've come to me as such. Your little friends at the auto shop not so much fun anymore?" he asked me.

I had to stifle the roll of my eyes. He looked down on the fact that I hung with what he considered to be such a low class of people.

"Does that mean yes or no, Papa?" I asked plainly. My voice clearly showed I wasn't impressed with his insult about my friends.

"Do you sass me, Maria Rosa?"

"Do you deny me the pleasure of new toys, Papa?"

At that moment Frederick walked back into the room. Took a seat on the left side of Papa. It wasn't lost on any of us that the woman who used to be Papa's mouthpiece was missing. I had to wonder where good ole Lilith was. Wondered where Papa had sent her sniffing off to. Lilith was one of Papa's trained bitches. I called her a bitch because Papa had her trained to act as any good guard dog should.

I could see my other family members watching us go back and forth, like we were playing in a tennis match. None of them would be fool enough to go head to head with the old man. His word was law. But I knew what line to cross and which ones not to. The old man regarded me closely. He sat back in his chair, back erect, eyes burning another hole in me.

I kept smiling as I sipped the wine.

"Do not forget where your true family lies, Maria Rosa," Papa said.

"I never have."

"That also means, don't forget where your loyalty truly lies."

"I know, Papa. May I see the merchandise or not?"

Frederick hadn't even been sitting down for a minute when Papa ordered, "Frederick, take Maria Rosa to see the shipment."

Without contempt, Frederick stood. I kissed my mother's cheeks, then did the same to my five aunts before making my exit. A few of my male cousins stared at me with disdain. Not even they could get away with challenging the old man like I did.

Frederick and I headed outside. Papa's estate was lush with green grass and meticulously landscaped shrubbery. If you looked close enough, you could see the camouflaged sentries in the trees and on the roof of the sprawling Spanish hacienda. The wind was blowing hard enough to almost knock me on my ass, and it felt hot, because the day had been sizzling. Trees rocked and swayed like a church choir. Dogs could be heard in the distance. Birds chirped and played about.

I looked at the watch on my wrist as we walked. I had to guesstimate the time it would take me to get back to Clayton County at this time of night. All I really needed to do was make sure the shipment Papa had was the same as the one we'd picked up in Vegas.

Frederick walked in silence. The stoic look he wore always tickled me. His bald head, perfectly aligned goatee, and onyx-black eyes were enough to drive many women mad. He had his share of them. Was a badass when it came to street fights and gun play, but he wouldn't stand up to the old man to save his life. Well, actually he had once. The scar decorating his neck proved he wouldn't do it again. Still, I needed him to talk so I could get the info I was seeking.

I asked my cousin, "Why don't you ever speak up to the old man, Freddie?"

"Not everyone can be his favorite, Maria," he answered, Cuban accent thick.

He had no idea just what I had to endure to be Papa's favorite. The paper cut–like keloids on my back started to itch in remembrance of the times I'd defied the old man.

"Judging by the scar on your neck, I'd say you are a close second," I teased.

"Fuck you, Rosa."

I smiled coolly as the man who towered over me in height glared down at me.

"Now, now, don't start to become like Uncle. May he *not* rest in peace. I'm not with that incest shit, Freddie," I said, then eyed him like I was considering it.

One of our uncles was a serious pervert. There was no limit to what his perverse nature would cause him to do . . . even to family.

"Fuck outta here," he spat.

I cackled. Freddie looked as if he was about to be sick. By then we had reached an old barnlike structure about fifty or so yards behind the old man's safe house. Freddie yanked the door to the building open.

"You're sick in the head, Rosa," Freddie sneered. "No wonder the old man dotes on you."

All I did was laugh. I liked to mess with people mentally. I got a kick out of seeing just how far I could take them out of their element.

"Oh, shut up, Frederick," I finally told him. "Show me the stuff."

My cousin shook his head as he walked over to crates that had been branded like cattle with the initials BK. I looked inside of one of the crates and pulled out a small clear box that was just like the ones the team and I had hidden.

I feigned ignorance and asked, "What's so special about these bullets?"

"You won't believe it unless you see it for yourself."

There didn't seem to be many boxes there, so I had to wonder if we'd taken the bulk of the supplier's orders. The supplier would have to be stupid to put all their eggs in one basket.

"Where did they come from?" I asked.

"Was at the gun show when ole boy who made these showed how they worked. These shits tear flesh clean off the bone and shit. The internal damage these motherfuckers do is loco, *bella*. He designed it, he said, to take out all vital organs."

"So if I aim this, say, at your heart, you're done?"

He nodded as he pulled a key from his pocket and opened the small box of bullets in my hand. I loaded my gun quickly. I had to keep up the façade. I walked outside and headed over to where test dummies had been set up. Papa always kept things about for us to use for target practice. Just for the hell of it, I let the gun roar. Aimed the first shot at the heart and ripped the fabric and internal stuffing from the dummy. I could only imagine what these bullets would do to human flesh.

"I want to meet the man who made these," I told Freddie.

He was already shaking his head and backing away. "No, *bella*. You know Papa don't like women in his business."

"All you have to do is point me in the right direction."

"Why?"

"Any man with a mind like this, I need to know."

Freddie shrugged nonchalantly. "Why?"

"He specializes in bullets. I specialize in using them. Match made in heaven."

He vehemently shook his head no.

I turned the gun on him.

He bristled, then drew just as quickly on me. The only thing I hated more than being lied to was being told no.

"You're going to shoot me because I'm trying to keep the old man off your back?" Freddie said calmly.

"No, I'm going to shoot you for having the audacity to say no to me."

He chuckled. "Spoiled bitch."

"Papa's do boy."

"Puppet."

We circled one another like warriors in a standoff. Neither of us would ever admit Papa pulled our strings like the puppeteer he was.

"You better hit me with your first shot," Freddie coolly stated.

"Look who you're talking to. I'll kill you without blinking."

"Not before I open your dome like melon."

"Stop playing and tell me what I want to know."

He smirked. "What's in it for me?"

"How much?"

"You take the fallout if Papa finds out."

I nodded. "Okay. Simple enough."

"And . . ."

"And?"

A slow smile eased over his face. "Yes, *and*. And I want the girl."

"What girl?"

"The dude who showcased these bullets had this pretty, dark-skinned, warrior-type chick with him. If I point you in the right direction, I want her."

"You want me to take her?"

"No."

"Then what?" I asked.

He looked off in the distance, like he couldn't make up his mind as to what he wanted.

Finally, he asked, "You going to kill this dude?"

I sighed, then put my gun down by my waist. "No. Hadn't planned on it."

Freddie nodded, then put his gun back in his holster. "Then, if you're going to talk business, take me with you. I can get the girl on my own from there."

I knew that look in his eyes. He was trying to find some normalcy. It was hard for us young-sters to do that when an age-old war was going on. No matter how hard we tried, as soon as we mentioned our last names, any hope we had of normality fled. So I agreed to let him tag along once I found out where the supplier was laying his head. Then I asked him what was so special about the girl he was so fascinated with.

"Saw her when Papa made the deal. I think she's ole boy's bodyguard or something. Mami's bad, like . . . like, she is unexplainable, *bella*. I want her."

"Like a pet?" I asked.

I gave him a look that told him I wasn't with that shit. The men in my family had a habit of taking women and using them as pets. I'd seen them break and bend women until they were no longer themselves. They were what the men in my family had made them to be.

"No, Rosa. Want to get to know her the way a man gets to know a woman. She's so fucking beautiful. Her name is Oya."

I rolled my eyes and shook my head as I headed back to the house so I could leave. Freddie had a goofy smile on his face, one showing all thirty-two of his perfectly aligned teeth, as he told me all the info he had on the cat who made the bullets. It was weird for me to see a man in my family smitten with a woman in a normal way. I didn't know how to take it, to be honest, but if it made my cousin this happy, I would oblige.

A few minutes later, I said my good-byes and made my way back toward Clayton County, to the auto shop. I drove down Mt. Zion, past the Park Apartments and the Magic Food Mart. Kept going until I passed Tara Elementary, the Wood Apartments, and the Pines Apartments. Passed Firestone. I waited to turn right at the light next to a big purple beauty supply store. The side street was dark as I crossed the abandoned railroad tracks, made a left at the stop sign, then pulled into the lively garage.

I saw Auto's black-on-black Ford Shelby GT500 parked haphazardly and knew he was in the shop. I didn't see anyone else's vehicle, but that didn't mean they weren't around. M.I.A.'s "Double Bubble Trouble" was blasting as I used my key to let one side of the garage up. I smiled when I saw the new girl. His arms crossed, Auto was standing behind her, in his signature wide-legged stance. He watched on in silence as she worked credit card–making machines like it was second nature to her. Equipment used to make fake IDs was out in the open, and so was skimming equipment with gas pump overlays and hundreds of counterfeit credit cards. The girl had the most comprehensive credit card–manufacturing lab that I'd ever seen.

"Damn, *chica*. This is all you?" I asked.

The girl looked up at me but didn't respond. She looked like she had half a mind to run. I guessed being sold up shit creek by someone you trusted had the power to do that to you. Auto only glanced at me, as he was keeping his eyes on the girl and her elaborate setup. If the cops rolled up on us, we'd all be looking at a long time on lockdown.

"This is all my stuff," she told Auto.

"Smiley, this is Code. Code, Smiley," Auto said, introducing us. His voice was mellowed out, like he was deep in thought.

Smiley only nodded at me.

I was curious. "What's all this for?"

Auto inhaled and exhaled, then unfolded his arms as he turned to look at me. "We're about to see if Smiley is really as good as her record says she is. Talked to Pascal back in Vegas. He contacted his people at Minot First National. They can get us some gen on the Vikings' bank account info. And we're going to hit them where they'll hurt. I want them to know it's us. They hurt our pockets, so we hurt theirs."

I nodded. "And then what?"

"You get to Vegas, to Chandler. Make him talk. While we're doing that, Smiley here will be transferring money from the Vikings' business account to a dummy account. Once that has the

Vikings' attention, Lelo, Stitch, and Reagan will
be on the Cessna. They'll wait for word from us
on what to do next."

I took in all he was saying. I trusted his judgment, but I wanted to make sure Auto wasn't letting his anger push him in the wrong direction.
Anytime we lost someone or came close to losing
someone on the team, Auto took it personally.
We hadn't lost Lelo or Stitch, but we'd come
close enough, and that had Auto bugging out. I
think that had him more on edge than losing the
money we had.

"You sure about this?" I asked him.

His pupils dilated and his eyes narrowed as he
looked at me. "Don't question me on this, Code.
There will be many things you can fight me on,
but this won't be one of them."

"Okay. Was only asking."

"You get that info on the supplier?"

I nodded. "Yeah."

"Same guy the old man was doing business
with?"

"One and the same."

"Okay. Take Smiley with you and scope him
out."

"Already planned on it, but you know I work
alone," I said.

He shrugged and averted his eyes. Then his gaze settled back on me. "And now you're working with Smiley until further notice. All you're doing is eyeing the man. Show Smiley around while you're at it. Let her know who our people are so if she's ever in a bind, she knows where she can run," he said. Then he began walking out of the shop.

"And where are you going?" I yelled behind him.

"I need to make sure the chick who sold Smiley out knows the tables have turned, and I need to make sure nothing else of ours ends up stolen," he said over his shoulder.

I shook my head and turned back to look at the girl, who didn't seem to be impressed one way or the other.

"You ready to ride?" I asked her.

For a while she just stared at me. She was pretty enough. I liked the whole "head shaved on one side" thing she had going on. She was what Seymore, Lelo, and Stitch would call skinny thick. Skinny, but her hips and ass had a thickness that couldn't be denied. I didn't know why she was staring me down, but I hadn't eaten any twat since I was in college a few years ago, and I didn't plan on doing it anytime soon.

I inhaled and exhaled hard. "We're not about to have a catfight, are we?"

She shook her head. "No. Was just trying to figure out what you are," she answered plainly.

"What do you mean?"

"You black?"

"By race."

"You gay?"

"Depending on my mood."

"I'm not with that."

"Good, because I'm not in the mood to be, either."

She picked up her backpack and threw the strap over her left shoulder. "Not trying to be your best friend, but I don't want any trouble, either, so if you prefer to work alone, I get it."

I chuckled lightly. "It's cool. The boss man has spoken, so I can't go against that."

"He said you were his partner."

I laughed this time. "Only when I remind him. Come on. We need to see if we can play I Spy with a bullet manufacturer."

Chapter 7

Boots

Even a guardian angel had a shadow. That meant that even those who protected needed protection. This motto of mine played in my mind as I leaned against my mirror-silver Ford Mustang. Ankles crossed, I popped Mickey D's fries in my mouth and gazed at the old-school-style brick brownstone building in front of me. I looked at the gentlemen's custom-fit suit establishment in front of me and thought about my obligations. I'd walked inside and handled a simple drop-off for my pops. The man I had been hoping to meet, unfortunately, wasn't there.

I was in a calm mood, and my attire added to that vibe. Black slacks, leather slip-ons with rubber waffle bottoms, so if I had to move out quickly, then there would be no issue. My white button-down was rolled up at the sleeves and was open at the neck, showing my white tank under it, and I wore suspenders attached to my slacks. My beard was trimmed so it was clean and looking good. I heard niggas on the street calling me André 3000, and I chuckled. I was fine with that. It helped put me in a category no one would understand completely.

I hopped in my Mustang, revved the engine, then hit ANSWER on my ringing cell.

"Did you get the product delivered with no problem?" I asked, then pulled off.

"Yup. No problem at all. They were thirsty for those five hundred cases, so it was smooth," Alize answered.

My mind kept ticking as I drove, whipping through the A. I was trying to decide if I was going to camp at my crib in the hood.

"Who's near you, Alize?"

Her soft chuckle sounded in my ear before she answered, "Shredder's here."

"Let me holla," I calmly stated.

Shredder came on the line. "'Sup, boss? I know what you're going to ask. The tracker blew out. There is no tracing where the bullets are at this point. We just know they are here in Georgia."

Grinding my teeth, I shook my head. "Tell me why the hell it blew out, Shredder? I designed it specifically for such shit. What up?"

"B-boss—" Shredder began, but I cut him off.

"Calm that shit down, fam! I'm pissed at the situation, not you. Tell me why the tracer blew out, please. Damn, son." Frustration had me pinching the bridge of my nose.

That cat was family, but damn.

"Yeah . . . so . . . sorry. It's like this . . ." He paused a moment, then began again. "We designed the tracers to track only the drop-off. They were created to stay on for long periods of time. After that time expires, their batteries become faulty, boss, which is why I was ordering new parts for that particular tracker . . . to update it. But the old tracker got put on the new product, and so, with it being on so long, it overheated and blew out."

Making an immediate right, I sighed. "That feels too damn convenient, but I remember you telling me that. Fuck, man. I should have switched it out beforehand. A'ight. Ain't nothing to do but deal with what we got. Have there been any whispers on the streets about our product leaking out?"

"Nope, nothing. Just the drop with the client last night, and that's it. It was smart not to give him the rest of the product we have, boss man." Shredder gave a husky, amused laugh. "Because he was foaming at the mouth with the small amount we gave."

"Yeah, wasn't my plan. Just fell that way. Our warehouses in Texas and Montana are just too far away to be giving him the amount promised in this small window of time. So digging into the smaller warehouses here and in Miami is quicker," I explained, speaking more to myself than to Shredder.

"Right, man," Shredder responded.

"Keep tabs. I'm heading to base two, but first I'm coming in to drop the Mustang off and get my Explorer," I said as I turned into the sheltered shipment facility, which was mixed in with empty airport factories.

I hit the button over my visor. Two tinted doors to the facility opened, allowing me to drive in. Shredder stood there, with his oversize geek glasses, blue jean overalls with one of the straps hanging down, and a goofy smile on his brown-bronze face. Like me, he had a beard, but his was wrapped around his jaw and disappeared under the beanie cap he wore. His lean, muscled build and his height often made me forget that he had a stuttering habit when angry. The stuttering made me forget the sharp intelligence of his mind. Shredder was one of those black kids on the streets who, if they had been born into privilege, would have gone to MIT. Instead, a degree from Texas Tech was all he had, just like I did.

Shredder locked his hazel eyes on me, then tossed me the keys to my ride. "We're producing more Blazers as we speak. Oya is overseeing the quality control, as Alize is in the streets, with her ear to the paint, reporting to Shango, who's at base two."

"All right, man. And what are you doing?" I asked, as if I really needed to know.

Shredder shrugged, a lopsided grin on his face. A deep dimple showed through the russet brown of his skin. "Eh, ya know me. Working on the coding of the new tracking system, moving our money, and talking to the fam in Italy about more shipments."

Though this was a small team, our reach was wide, even stretching overseas, thanks to old networking ties in my family lineage. While growing up, I'd learned never to put my eggs all in one basket. I never had, and I never would.

"Good deal, man," I said, commending him, then bumped his fist before I headed to my Explorer. "I'm out."

Massive boxes, storage containers, railroad shipment boxes, and more were all around us. Much of my work since coming to Atlanta was done here, but the rest, only a minor taste of my real work, was back at my place in the hood, which was where I was heading to. Word on the street was that there were new faces on the block. This piqued my interest, but as long as it had nothing to do with me, I was chill.

Riverdale was my hood. Twenty-five minutes later I pulled up in my Explorer and nodded to the "eyes" for my operation on this block: Pops Tank, or PT, as he made us call him, who was working without Shango today. PT was a real OG. Back in the day, the man had been a street king who brought people together, but he had also done his share of terror. Now the seventy-five-year-old man was my eyes and my ears, and he also collected the Gs I made by slinging minimal illegal contraband, weed, and hot products that people asked for.

After turning down my radio, I rolled down my window and kept my eyes on the complex in front of me as I spoke. "'Sup, PT? What's the biz?"

He gave a throaty laugh, and the scent of his favorite cigar mixed with weed seeped into my ride. "Twenty Gs in one hiding spot, another ten in my bag, and a bee in my ear talking about some hot new-new possibly hitting the streets soon."

I smirked from pride, then took the stack wrapped in idle mail, magazines, and other people's mail that PT slide in my window. "Thanks, Unc. You sitting okay?"

"Yes, I am, nephew. Got my baby loving the new gifts I got her. That new roof I put on the house is looking really lovely," he said with a prideful smile and a puff of his cigar.

I shifted in my seat, scoping my perimeter. "That's what's up. Let me know if I need to send anything to her in AL. You know I got you, Uncle."

"Ya know I will, nephew. Alize dropped in. She's in the courtyard, tearing up the grill. Ooh-wee, if I didn't know how good of a killer she was, I'd try to get some of that young snatch," PT joked.

PT was crazy in love with a lady, hidden in Alabama, who had held him down for decades and who had been the Bonnie to his Clyde back in the day when they ran the streets. So I knew the old man was talking smack, not that it mattered. Right now, he looked like a graying dopehead in dirty bum attire, but when I had need of him elsewhere, the man always cleaned up and appeared younger than the seventy-five years he was. I had always called him Mr. Colt 45, because he looked just like this guy I remembered seeing as a kid in the old *Star Wars* movies that my pops would have me watch.

I smiled at the tall older dude hanging on my car door. "So you want a fat plate? I got you, Uncle. Talk to me about the new faces you told Shango about."

PT shucked and jived. He inspected his area but played it off as swatting at flies in his face and talking to himself. I waited for him to hop in; then I rolled up the windows and pulled away from my complex to drive through the hood. I let the old man relax as the air cooled him off. He pulled out his Glock to adjust it so he could sit comfortably; then I took us to the local corner store.

"Ah, God blind me, 'tis hard work for an old man," PT said, letting his Barbadian accent come out.

"I know. Might be time to switch out and rest, old man," I told him.

I made a smooth right turn and pulled into the lot of the corner store.

"You see to yuh left? Right there, in di ride? Di new blood," he said with a nod of his bourbon-brown face.

My gaze scoped the modest car. I saw only one person sitting on the passenger side.

"Cops?" I asked.

"Nah, too green in how they move," he said with a chuckle as he lit up a new cigar.

"You said 'they.' How many?" I asked, keeping my eye on the car.

"Just two, nephew. Two beautiful girls. One looks unique and kind of scary with the way she's dressed, but there are just two. Doesn't feel like a threat, but we know looks can deceive," he said with a knowing tone of voice.

I gave him an amused look; then we both laughed. We knew what the other was thinking. Females running on the block, looking as if they had no care in the world, but once you walked up on them in a disrespectful manner, your life would be cut off. It was then you would know you'd just run into an African queen.

After parking the Explorer, I glanced back at the modest car. "They give you that vibe?"

"Not at all, nephew," PT said with a smug look, watching the women who moved in and out of the corner store. "Damn, that ass!" he exclaimed. He turned to me. "You going in? Get me an ice cream and a drink."

"Stop watching ass and maybe you could do what you do," I said in humor.

Though he wasn't my blood, it still felt like it. PT had been my first contact after I landed in Atlanta, and he always kept my business affairs in line here.

"I'm too old. Been in this heat too long. Treat an old man right, son," he drawled.

"I got you. Relax in the ride and keep watching. I'll make sure to get you a big plate and to ask for Alize to sit on your lap," I joked.

I hopped out. I slipped on my stunners, tilted my hat low, and slid my hands in the pockets of my slacks while I walked toward the store. All of ATL was alive and buzzing with life. I nodded at the young girls, who giggled and soaked up my looks. I licked my lips, then smiled at the ones my age whose eyes told me they wanted to fuck. After holding the door open for the girls to walk through, I gave my respects to the elders with a nod, then strolled around the store.

Bought two bottled waters, a forty, several quarter bags of chips and Cheetos, and a stick of gum. I spoke in code to the owner about the latest shipment of marijuana coming in, and then I walked out. The heat had me taking my hat off and running a hand over the waves on my head. I kept my eyes on the horizon and noticed that the person in the modest ride was getting out. She leaned against the car, fanning herself, then started jumping around. I realized she was running from a bug, and it made me laugh. The girl looked familiar to me, but I brushed it off when a shorty with a phat booty and a sexy gaze walked past me.

Girly appeared exotic, as other dudes would label her looks, but I knew she had the traits of a black girl with Latino ancestry. This chick was definitely a new face, I noted as she walked into the store. I walked back to my ride, handed PT his share of the food, then leaned against my ride and crossed my ankles. Popping Cheetos in my mouth, I examined my surroundings, paying close attention to the two new faces in the area.

"Those the two you talking about, right?" I asked PT on the low.

PT leaned to his right and waved his bag around. "Goddamn. It followed me in here," he yelled, putting on a show and living up to the "crazy old man" moniker people had labeled him with. "Yup."

I laughed and gave a nod. "All right."

Miss Cutie with the booty and the sultry eyes came out at that moment. She gazed across the lot, used the tip of her tongue to pull the straw in her drink into her mouth, then locked eyes on me. The way her lush lips parted in a grin, revealing only a little of her pearly whites, had my dick knocking on a hundred. However, the thinker that I was wouldn't allow me to fall for her ploy. I mean, unless I was going to get some good pussy and head out of the deal before tossing her out of my hood, but that was neither here nor there.

I kept my gaze on her as I popped chips in my mouth and chewed slowly, with a smirk. Chicks walked around, yakking it up, while brothers spoke about how thick the chicks were, especially Miss Latina. Though I kept my gaze on her, a team of young brothers in oversize white shirts and pants chilling around their ankles overtook my line of vision. And just like that, once they moved, she was gone.

There was something about the girl that had piqued my interest. My cell going off let me know that it was time to go back to my complex to check on my weed distribution and other illegal distributions I had going on.

"A'ight, old man. Let's go get your plate and get Alize to make it clap for you one good time. You know she'll do it too. It makes her laugh." I paused. "Remember that mixed-looking chick," I added before I hopped back in my ride and pulled off.

PT took a deep swig of water, then opened the window and poured some of his forty out. "Yuh, I will. What about that awkward-looking young girl at the car?"

"Watch her too. They could be scoping, or they could be some college kids trying to feel themselves. Either way, you know what to do."

Minutes later, we pulled up to my complex and then hopped out of the ride. PT shook my hand and stumbled toward the complex. I didn't follow him. As he went toward the courtyard, I headed toward the apartment building I occupied, giving a nod to Alize when I passed her.

"Hey, pretty young thang. Come give ya unc a hug, and get me a big plate of that barbecue, gal. Mi fin see how yuh work da grill!" PT yelled as the doors closed behind me.

I knew everyone in the complex, some by name, others by face only. Weed filled my lungs, and I knew niggas were getting blazed. Music thumped, babies cried, and kids ran past me as I went to the farthest end of the complex. PT had reassured me the cops were chill, so the next thing I had to worry about, outside of the new faces in my zone, was collecting my money, counting it, and working on my bullets.

I sat, hours later, in my apartment, going over figures and checking on the regions my products were traveling to. I liked to make sure no region was oversaturated with my products. Shango gave me the rundown on how the drop had gone with our client. I laughed when he told me about how he had almost shot a rat that ran past his feet as he was coming in from outside. I made a note to get a better cleanup crew in this cesspool.

"Laughing at my pain ain't cool, fam," Shango grumbled.

He kicked a chair in front of my desk, then put down the tablet he held in his hands. On the flat screen, I checked out the image before me of the whole hood.

"Oh, that shit is funny. Best believe it, patna. But the new faces . . . I couldn't see the other one's face that well, but her locks are distinctive. But the sexy Latina? Damn. She is banging. Has a body shaped like a Coke bottle. Looking at her, I already know she's trouble," I shared with Shango.

Shango gave a deep laugh, then stretched his long legs out on my desk while he watched the flat screen. "Then you need to stay clear, like your old man schooled us to do. The yoni can trick a nigga when he least expects it. He may think he got control, but the way that baby works, you will find yourself with a polluted mind, caught up, with your hands in the air and your money gone."

Popping a toothpick in my mouth to chew on, I gave a hearty chuckle. "You added that last crap to that phrase."

"Maybe," Shango said with a smirk.

I gave a nod, understanding what my boy was actually trying to say. My pops had really said, "Son, woman is the creation, the giver, the nurturer, and the truth, but if you fuck with her, she can be your pain, poison, or your death."

. Guessed that was why, with every lady I got with, I made for damn sure that I had the antivenom to that ass.

"Still pissed at you and Oya not working, huh?" I mused, then laughed at his scowl. "You messed that up, man. Your loss. Like I told you, should have left that alone and stuck with Alize. She compliments you, and you know it."

My boy gave me a look of death. I loved messing with the homie. Dude kept thinking with his dick, so being locked down to one female wouldn't happen anytime soon with him. He loved women too much. It was lucky for me and my team that the women on it didn't hate each other and didn't have that chicken-head mentality when it came to a brotha who they all knew just was not the settling down type of cat.

I laughed aloud, then glanced at the papers my right-hand gave me. "So this is a bunch of surveillance and blurry-ass pictures. What did the Scandinavians say about getting got? What else do you have, man?"

Shango gave me an amused grin. He swung his legs off my desk, then brushed a hand over his shirt. "I have plenty. I'm not your bodyguard and right-hand man for no reason. We have a little present. Check it out."

He headed to my bathroom, banged a fist on the door, then opened it. A bound and gagged body fell forward to the floor with a harsh thud. The man had gray duct tape over his mouth. He was sweating. His graying hair and a missing eye stood out to me. I chuckled in amusement.

"Oh, so we leaving bodies and shit in my bathroom now?" I joked, then stood.

"Pretty much, sir," Shango chuckled, getting in line with his role. "Allow me to introduce you to old man Chandler. The Scandinavians will be back later to pick him up. They want their own time with him for the drama that went down, but for now we get to squeeze a little juice outta the old rat."

The old man struggled and wiggled on the floor before me. I took two strides and dropped into a crouch to look the old pirate-looking cat in the eye.

"Ah yeah?" I rubbed my hands together, then gave a broad smile, with my toothpick in the corner of my mouth. "'Sup, old man Chandler? You and me are about to know each other very well."

I reached out to squeeze the old man's chin, then tilted it up toward me.

I made my introduction clearly. "You can call me BK. I know you're wondering why you're here, so let me help you out. You dicked around and let others take what was mine. So, my friend, who has it, and where the fuck is it?"

Rolling the toothpick around in my mouth, I assessed this nigga. I gave a slight laugh before all emotion drained from my face. Our eyes locked in a silent challenge. I wasn't the type of guy to get off on hurting others, but when pushed, I could make a nigga wish he was dead. I let my silence speak for me from that moment on.

It took time for people to understand how cold I could be when I was pushed to the limit or when I was fucked with. Chandler may have thought his time was running out, but what he didn't know was that we had all the time in the world. He was going to tell me everything I needed to know—by choice or by force.

Chapter 8

Auto

"This is Auto's Body and Collision."

I answered my phone with caution because I didn't know the number calling. Anyone who called me on that particular line was business. All that business was illegal. So for an unknown number to call me meant either the Feds were watching or someone was trying to set me up. Either way, I answered with trepidation. I could have ignored the call, but with all that was going on, I needed to be sure that whoever was calling didn't have my shit.

A mangled voice on the other end came through the line. "Auto," he uttered, then coughed like he was being strangled. "Th-this is Chandler. I . . . I need your help, man."

"Help with what? Your trucks giving you issues? I told you, you should have let me give you all new engines, but you're too cheap for your own good."

"This ain't about no fucking engines, man," he roared at me.

I could tell he was in a compromising position from the way his voice croaked. If I didn't know, I would assume he was in pain. My hand gripped the cell tighter. I could feel the muscles in my stomach coil, then release. Anger was riding me like a two-dollar whore. The fact that the motherfucker had the nerve to call me like all was well between the two of us made me want to kill him faster than planned.

"Well, what can I do you for? I'm not coming all the way back out to Vegas for some water pumps, though. You're going to have to get one of the locals—"

"Nigga, I ain't in Vegas no more. I'm in Atlanta," he screamed. "These niggas you stole that truck from done got me. I'm too old for this shit, boy. Give the man back his stuff."

I sat back in my chair and stared ahead at the busy auto shop floor before me. We hadn't brought in any new merchandise since the fiasco in Vegas. We were trying to lay low, see if the Vikings or the person who was missing his merchandise would come looking for us.

"Chandler, what the hell you talking about, man? I don't know nothing about no truck, or whatever the hell else you talking about. You getting senile on me?"

I hit the button underneath my desk. Red lights started flashing around the shop. Seymore was lying underneath a car. I watched as he used his hands to push the Craftman Creeper with the metal frame he was lying on. He quickly pushed himself over to his wheelchair. Used his upper-body strength to drag his feet behind him until he was in his chair. Dunkin and Jackknife, two other team members, ushered customers out of the shop, while Seymore ordered the rest of the crew to start locking the place up. The garage doors of the shop came down. Felt like I was in Fort Knox with the way shit was being shut down.

"Auto, stop playing with my life, nigga. Please," Chandler begged. "They're going to kill me, man."

Any other time, hearing the old man babble and cry like he wished for death instead of the pain he was in would have gotten to me. Chandler had been with us for a long time. He was close to old man Law too. That was one of the reasons I'd started doing business with him. But he'd betrayed my trust and my loyalty, and he had put the lives of my crew and our livelihood in jeopardy. I wanted to feel something for him, but with the way my stance on loyalty was set up, I couldn't. Once a snake, always a snake.

The phone beeped, then vibrated. I pulled it away from my ear, then hit the speaker button. There was a text from the same number. I clicked the icon and watched as Chandler's bloodied face and body took over my screen. He had only one eye to begin with. The patch that had covered the one made of glass was missing. Looked as if his glass eye had been taken out. He was naked. His pale body was bloody and covered with blisters and cuts. The nails on his left hand had been ripped from the beds of his fingers. His lips were swollen.

He kept begging, "Please, Auto. Please, man. Just tell him where his product is, or they going to kill me."

"Well, shit, Chandler. Just what the fuck you done gone and got yourself into, man?" I asked as I stood.

My voice held no emotion. I had detached myself from the situation so I could be sure my family was safe. I grabbed my personal cell and sent texts to Lelo, Stitch, and Reagan, telling them to abort the mission to Vegas. Good thing they hadn't gone the night before, as planned. Did the same to Code and told her to bring the newbie back. If somebody had gone to Vegas to get Chandler, then that meant the Vikings would be right behind them and would be showing up in Atlanta. We needed to make sure our home turf was covered.

The old man yelled at me, "Jesus Christ, Auto. Please don't leave me hanging like this, man. I'm sorry. I'm sorry, a'ight? I needed the money Mouse was offering me, man. I needed it. I didn't know shit about those bullets, I swear to the Most High."

I kept silent. So, he had sold us out for a few extra dollars and in return had got fucked up the ass with no lube because the Vikings had involved him in some shit that was bigger than him.

"Chandler, look, man, I don't know anything about no bullets. I don't deal in no underhanded shit. I don't know anybody named Mouse. All I do, all we do over here, is fix cars, man. I don't know what you done gone and got yourself into, but don't involve me and my family. Don't do that. You send anybody this way just to get heat off your ass, then what's being done to you will be nothing once I'm done. You understand me, old man? Don't do it. I will kill you and not think twice about that shit."

"Auto," he yelled. "Aww, shit. Ah, no, man. Nooo!"

In all my life, I'd never heard a man scream like Chandler did at that moment. Even with the juvie hall rapes, when young males took another's manhood, I hadn't heard a scream, a yelp of pain, like what I heard from Chandler.

I chuckled. "You just reminded me why I don't go against the grain. Good luck, Chandler."

I was just about to hang up when another voice came on the line. "Auto, is it?"

My spine stiffened. "Who the fuck wants to know?"

"I want to know only one thing, a'ight? Do you have my merchandise?"

I made note of the fact he had a drawl when he spoke. It was Southern, but it wasn't ATL Southern.

"I see Chandler ain't the only one hard of hearing," I muttered.

"Is that yes or no? You get only one time to make a wrong a right."

I frowned, then licked my lips as I loaded a clip into my gun, then pressed the barrel down into my desk.

"I really wish I could help you, my dude. I really do. Unfortunately, all I specialize in is the grease monkey business. But if I hear anything, I'll send you a pigeon message or some shit," I said.

"You sure you want to do this? Play this game? Run with the pack? A measly autoworker like yourself should just stick to what he knows."

I grunted at his slight insult. I took it for what it was, though. He was a man without his product, trying to shake his trees to see how many snakes fell out. But he didn't know who he was talking to. All my life I'd been adapting. My specialty was taking on whatever environment was around me. It was a nature versus nurture kind of thing. Everything that I was and all my knowledge had been determined by my experience.

"You must be shapeless, formless, like water. When you pour water in a cup, it becomes the cup. When you pour water in a bottle, it becomes the bottle. When you pour water in a teapot, it becomes the teapot. Water can drip, and it can crash. Become like water, my friend."

"Bruce Lee," the man on the other end of the line said to me, informing me that he knew where my words had come from. "If you're a fan of his, then you know that mistakes are always forgivable, if one has the courage to admit them."

A dangerous smile curved my lips. "Mistakes? I never make mistakes, like stealing another man's shit. You want to talk about mistakes, you talk to Chandler. You talk to those Vikings he was blabbering about. I didn't make any mistakes."

Feeling like I'd already said too much, I hung up the phone. I pulled my holster strap on, then slid my guns into the holders before pulling the top of my jumper on. I snatched open the door to my office and signaled for Seymore to keep the place locked down.

"Keep this shit on lock until I get back or send word otherwise. If some shit goes down, you know what to do," I told him.

He nodded, shotgun lying across his lap. "You want me to call in backup?"

I stopped, then thought about it for a second. "I don't know. I need to ride through the hood and see what I can find out."

I told him about the phone call I'd just gotten.

Seymore thumbed his nose, then said, "This shit's getting bigger than we thought. What in hell did Chandler get us into? All this nigga had to do was deliver some cars. How did we get involved in torture and bullets?"

I shook my head. "Your guess is as good as mine. But since we're too far in to back out, we have to make sure we keep our eyes and ears above water. If shit gets too hot around here, you can call an audible and make sure you bring in whoever and whatever is needed."

"I got you," he assured me with a nod.

Once I got to my car, I called Code.

"You get my message?" I asked when she answered.

"Yup. Watching something right now, anyway. Pascal called me. Said Chandler has packed up and moved out—"

"No, he didn't. He's in the A."

"How do you know that?"

"Just got a phone call. Whoever made those bullets got to him before we did."

I heard Code moving around. Listened as she told Smiley to stay down.

"You know how to shoot?" she asked her.

"Yeah, I can handle a gun. Daddy was in the military. He taught me," I heard Smiley tell her.

"Good. Then shoot to kill," Code said.

The hairs stood up on the back of my neck. "What's going on, Code?"

"We're being followed."

I could tell she was driving, speeding, trying to get away from wherever she was.

"Location," I yelled into my earpiece.

"Highway Eighty-five. Passing the Krispy Kreme, heading toward Fayetteville. Oh shit—"

When her voice was cut off and I heard bullets shattering windows, along with a loud squeal, I knew it was serious. It had to be someone new to the A. Nobody in their right mind would bring a firefight to the heart of Clayton County, where the police rode around like they were in a parade. There were three areas in Clayton County where even the lowest of the underworld steered clear of the police: Lake City, Forest Park, and Riverdale. Since Highway 85 ran through the heart of the city of Riverdale and was the main highway there, I knew only someone new to the area would be so brazen.

I did an illegal U-turn in the middle of Mt. Zion Road. Pushed my GT500 to the limit as I whipped a right out onto Tara Boulevard. Horns blared; brakes screeched. Still, I kept going. If Clayton County was going to come after me, they'd have to catch me first.

I quickly called the shop.

Seconds later Seymore's voice came through the line. "What it is, boss?"

"Code's in trouble. Get the team to Eighty-five, headed toward Fayetteville. Shots fired, so we don't have that much time."

I didn't give him time to respond. I dipped in and out of lanes. Ran the red lights at the criss-crossed four-way intersection where the Burger King sat. The black and yellow lettering of an abandoned Western Union and check-cashing place greeted me as people swerved to miss me. Luckily, the traffic at the next intersection wasn't so bad. I hopped in the third lane, like I was about to jump on 75 North, then swerved left to cut into the traffic heading down Upper Riverdale Road. Sped down that four-lane street like the speed limit didn't matter. Dipped into the far right lane to avoid rear-ending a school bus.

In my rearview, I saw three cars jump off Lamar Hutcheson Parkway. The blue Nissan GT-R was hot on my ass. The red Ford Taurus SHO and the silver Chevrolet Camaro ZL1 were right behind it. The lights flashed on the Nissan three times. They were my people. The Camaro slid into the left lane. I gripped my Glock as the Camaro's front passenger-side window slowly came down. Relaxed a bit when Stitch's slick smile shone at me.

"Reagan and Lelo behind us," he shouted over the roar of the engines and the traffic.

I only nodded. I could tell when he shifted gears in his car. He flew past me. Both he and I ran the yellow light to turn onto 85. It was easy to follow the trail Code had left. Cars had been sidelined on the road, with bullet holes decorating them. The McDonald's parking lot was full, with people staring down the street, cell phones to their ears. No doubt calling the cops. In my rearview, I could see that Reagan and Lelo were stuck at the light. All up and down 85, people had pulled over. I could see those who were victims of the melee as well.

I spotted Code's car and saw that the passenger- and driver's-side doors were open. Bullet holes had redecorated the exterior. The car had been abandoned in the middle of the highway. I slowed down to see if I could spot them anywhere.

If I hadn't been paying attention, the Ford F-150 truck barreling up Adams Drive would have T-boned me. My eyes widened as my feet instinctively hit the gas. The truck missed me by inches and crashed into the cars on a used car lot. I didn't have time to think about that, though. Suddenly bullets came down like hail, pelting my car. Stitch's car was riddled. I kept driving toward him, so I could flank him. We raced our cars into the parking lot of what used to be a Chinese buffet eatery. I crawled over to the passenger side of my car, then opened the door and fell to the ground. Stitch opened his car door, slid out, and crawled up next to me.

"We need to get to the used car lot so we can have cover," I told him.

He nodded, then pulled his gun out. He was sweating. Blood dripped down his shoulder. I could tell that it hurt him to breathe. In hindsight I could see how us running full speed across the small road to the car lot could have got us both killed as bullets rained down around us. We had no choice, though. Staying in that empty parking lot would have been a death sentence. Once we had got across the street to the car lot and had hid between two rows of used cars, which offered good cover, I breathed a little easier.

"Yo, Stitch, talk to me. You a'ight?" I yelled.

"Nothing that another set of stitches won't fix," I heard him groan.

He army crawled around a car as I pulled my guns out. In the process, he came out of his shirt, revealing the reason he had the nickname Stitch. His whole upper body was covered with scars, the result of being stitched up many times. He'd endured 95 percent of the stitches when he was seven years old. His mom's boyfriend at the time had thought it would be fun to take a blade to him. Had said he wanted to see how long it would take a little nigger to bleed out from thin slices across his body. Black woman with a white man who hated anything black and male.

We didn't have time to have a kumbaya moment, though. Gravel crunching under workman's boots alerted us to danger. We took off in opposite directions. I went left. He went right. Bullets followed us through the maze of cars like we were magnetic fields. I took cover behind a

Hummer. Positioned myself so I could take aim
at those aiming to kill me. I saw one of the men
hunting me. He was sloppy. Thought because he
had the bigger gun, he was in control of the situation. Not so much. The man had on a bulletproof vest, but he hadn't thought about the spot
under his arm that was exposed.

With quickness, I stood, fired one shot when
he raised his gun to fire at me. The bullet from
my gun tore through his armpit. He yelped.
Body jerked as he hit the ground hard. I rushed
over to him and put a bullet in his head.

One bullet from the chamber and his brains
scattered like the contents of a piñata. Shock
waves went through my system at the grisly
sight. I didn't know what I had been expecting,
but to see a bullet split a man's head like that let
me know the bullets we'd lucked upon were serious ammo. The demos on the bullets had been
impressive, but to actually see one put a man
down was something else altogether, especially
when the bullet tore through his skull and split it
from the inside out.

It was hot and humid. The smell of my sweat
mixed with the oil and grease from the shop
assaulted my senses. The Glock 9 was locked
tight in my grip. I dipped and ducked around
the back of the truck I had found myself next

to. Saw Stitch kneel down, army crawl around a car, and take out the Achilles tendons of two of the gunmen stalking him. Their yells rent the air as they went down. Stitch quickly got to his feet. When he let bullets off into their chests, the area exploded.

"God damn," Stitch yelled. "You see that shit? The nigga who made these motherfuckers—"

"Get down, Stitch," I yelled, cutting off whatever he was about to say.

He hit the ground hard as bullets rained down like hail. As I took cover, I did a mental count of the men I could see. Knew there were more that I couldn't see based on the direction the gunfire was coming from. There were too many of them. As sirens blared in the distance, I knew we had to get the fuck outta there. I wasn't sure if the Vikings had sent in the cavalry or if the man I'd spoken to on the phone when Chandler called had sent them after me.

"I see Lelo and Reagan," Stitch yelled at me.

"They gotta get out of here. We're outnumbered, even if Seymore and the rest of the team get here in time. We don't have the firepower to take these niggas out."

"I hear the burps and cherries song. What we gonna do, boss?"

Burps and cherries referred to the sounds the police cars made when in pursuit. Burps for the sounds. Cherries for the flashing red lights.

"These Vikings don't know this area. We can let them handle the cops," I said, then grabbed my cell.

I dialed Reagan. When she picked up, I told her, "Reagan, you and Lelo keep driving by. Make it seem as if you're just onlookers. Call Seymore and tell him to get back to the shop."

"What about you and Stitch?" she asked. "You know Lelo isn't going to leave without him."

"Don't worry about us. I'll handle it. You and Lelo get the fuck out of here and do it now. Tell Lelo not to question me or try no bullshit, either. We'll meet back at the shop. Y'all go there and wait for us."

"Okay. You find Code?"

I sighed. "Reagan, stop with the questions and fall back."

I ended the call, then looked around us for a way out. We didn't have that many options. They had us surrounded, and with the cops closing in on us, it looked like shit was about to go left.

"We can try to make a run for it back down Allen, but that leaves us open to the cops," Stitch said.

It was hotter than camel pussy. Felt like Satan had opened up all hell and had belched into the heart of the city. My palms had started to sweat, and my ears were ringing because of the bullets serenading the air. Those niggas didn't care what they hit as long as they hit us. Glass shattered and sprayed the area around us. Gray dust clouds from the gravel floated by like ghosts. I got down low to the ground and started counting feet. Twelve pairs of feet meant six shooters were to my right.

"How many shooters you see, Stitch?"

"'Bout three on my end."

"You know what to do."

Sometimes the art of war wasn't about how many kills you could get. It was about survival. You didn't always have to kill your enemy to survive. I reloaded my clip. Didn't have any more of the super bullets, but my old rounds would work for the time being. Behind me, I heard a growl, then a strangled yell. Stitch's low-pitched laugh told he had started cutting our enemies down by the ankles. That distracted the ones to my right. I watched as they all turned their attention in Stitch's direction, trying to see where the shots were coming from.

That gave me time to get up and move in behind them. The one thing the hood had taught me better than anything else was how to kill or be killed. I let off two rounds—one to the spine of a shooter and one to the head of a second shooter. The biggest dude fell to the ground in a heap. I ducked behind a Dodge Charger before coming up to take another shooter down with a bullet between the eyes. I went in for another kill, only to get punched in the head from behind. I hit the ground with a hard thud. My chin danced with the gray bits of rock and gravel. I turned over on my back just in time to see a boot coming for my face. I grabbed the man by his ankle, twisted it left, and watched him fall to the ground beside me.

He threw a wild punch that caught me in the jaw. With as big as his hands were, you would think he could hit harder. I angled my body, brought an elbow down into his sternum. I didn't give him time to recover. Although the hit to the back of the head had me dizzy, I was lucid enough to know what was going on. I quickly grabbed the hunting knife strapped to my ankle, jabbed the blade into his neck, then yanked it out. I watched in satisfaction as he futilely grabbed at his bleeding throat.

Another attacker came in from behind me, tried to grab me in a choke hold. I twisted my body, flipped him over my head, grabbed his right hand, and used his own gun to blow his brains out. Right as he went limp in my hold, a bullet grazed my ear. I quickly turned and fell on my back, with the body still in front of me as a shield. The man's limp body jerked as his teammate riddled it with bullets. The assailant rushed to stand over me.

"Tell Mouse he fucked with the wrong ones," I spat before I took his knees out with his partner's gun.

Once he fell to the ground, I threw the body off me, then stood quickly.

"Ahh, God, man! You shot me in my knees," the guy cried.

"No shit, Sherlock," I taunted him. "Now do me a favor. Tell your boss that he's gone and barked up the wrong fucking tree."

"He's going to fucking murder you—"

I took the butt of the gun and gave him a good blow to the head, which made him fall backward.

"As I was saying, tell Mouse to stay off my turf. If he wants back what was in that truck, then he's going to have to give me my shit back. Understood? None of this would have happened if he hadn't stolen from me first."

"Mouse ain't the one you n-need to be w-worried about," the man stammered. Then he laughed. He licked the blood from his lips, then spit.

My breathing was labored. I didn't like to be caught off guard. The whole situation had put

me in another frame of mind. Reminded me
of those days in juvie hall when the lights went
out. Made me feel like I had to sleep with my
back against the wall. Weapon always at the
ready. Clearly, we'd stumbled into some shit we
weren't used to. We didn't do the street fights
with bullets and weapons masquerading as
opponents. But since the fight had been brought
to us, we wouldn't back down.

"Who is it that I need to be worried about?" I
asked him.

All he did was laugh. He cackled in a maniacal
manner. Like he knew something I didn't know,
and like what he knew was of more value. I was
going to let him live, but since he had decided to
play with my mental, I ended his life with a kill
shot to the heart.

"We can take cover behind the dealership,
then see if we can cut down Allen, through the
trees, to get the fuck up outta here," I told Stitch.

He didn't put up much of a fight, since he
seemed to have been weakened by his injury.
We both took off at full speed. Riverdale and
Clayton County PD pulled in just as we raced
away. We knew they would be searching the area.
So we made a mad dash to NorStar Riverdale
Townhomes. We had a place there and could lay
low until the heat died down.

Once Stitch and I were safely inside the town-home, I had time to sit and think. We had two factions after us, and it was all because Chandler couldn't keep his end of the bargain. If whoever had him didn't kill him, then I surely would.

Anytime we had to do the murder-death-kill shit, it always reminded me of who we truly were at heart. It was innate in all of us. The thirst for blood. No matter how much we tried to deny it and fight it, the urban jungle always reminded us of where we were and where we had come from. So, as I had let my guns sing today, I kept hearing Mama Joyce in my head.

Those who live by the sword, Auto, die by the sword.

She always used to warn me about this. While I respected my mama a hell of a lot, those words had always gone in one ear and out the other. Besides, those who lived by the sword got shot by those who lived by the gun where I was from.

Chapter 9

Smiley

What type of fucking shit is this? ran through my mind while I ducked down, tried to shield myself with the ride I was in. Bullets rained down onto the car, shaking it. One had the nerve to make nice and graze my shoulder, which had the fear of God coursing through me. I glanced over to see Code popping off rounds. She was focused on our attackers and didn't look like she wanted to have a sweet conversation about what the hell was going on.

My mind went into overdrive while I gangsta leaned and tried to unsnap my seat belt so I could unlock the car door.

"This is some bullshit, Code. All of you are on some trife shit that I ain't sign up for. Stop shooting! We need to go. Because if we don't, we'll be dead, bitch. Let's go," I screamed. I found an open window to bail through and landed on the ground.

"And if I stop shooting, we're going to be dead. Go get cover and let me handle this," Code shouted back at me. She had gotten out of the car and had positioned her body behind her open car door just to get a better angle at the assholes gunning for us.

Every move she made seemed to be some guerrilla warfare crap. I didn't understand any of this at all. Before I'd been able to figure out what was going on, Code had known we were being tailed. She'd zipped through the streets like we were in *Grand Theft Auto*. All of it had made me think about the position I'd placed myself in.

I needed to get my life together and not be about a life of crime, which surely meant my imminent death. I didn't sign up for all of this. Code was on some *Scarface* shit, with her guns blazing, hair blowing in the wind, and taking down the assholes who were coming at us. All she needed was some grenades, and then everything would be like a Hype Williams music video or a Michael Bay film.

After we'd popped off shots and dodged those that came our way, it took some effort to pull her back and make her calm down with me. Homegirl seemed to be locked in a trance while she played murder-kill-kill, but I didn't have time to play Wonder Woman with her. I was on some "lookin'-ass nigga" shit and was using the military skills my sperm donor had taught me. I liked living.

Stress had me biting my lower lip. I turned on my back, then pushed up to point the Glock that Code had given me at my enemies. The powerful force of each bullet had this vibration traveling down my body. Letting several rounds meet the flesh of those who were trying to kill me had me suddenly amped up. I focused on those around me and vibrated with each ejection from the Glock.

Blood rushed to my ears. I dropped on my back, turned on my side, then crawled over gravel as fast as I could to a safe spot. Once I felt I was in the clear, I pushed up and ran my ass to a ditch on the side of the road, jumping over bodies of the fallen. It was then that a reality hit me yet again. I had never killed a man before. . . .

Wait, that was a lie. I had never *shot* a nigga like I was doing now. This was my first time, and

I wasn't too happy about it or geeked up. This was not a position I had ever wanted to be in. I wasn't a killer in this sense. What I had done before was commit cold-blooded murder, seek vengeance, and practice self-defense for my mama. This right here? This was just straight-up head bustin' and body painting. Self-defense, yes, but also plain ole murder. I'd just been released from jail; I didn't need to add murder to my record now!

Code's breathing let me know she had followed me, which was a relief, because old girl had that freaky look in her eyes still. We both glanced around, then let off more rounds when we saw that we were being followed. Code pushed me behind her as she pulled out another gun. I watched that chick shoot off some rounds, rush forward, then land several punches on a creepy tall blond with pale white eyes. Code's fist delivered a one-two punch to the throat, then to the gut, until she was able to gain leverage, push herself up, and wrap her leg around the dude's neck and squeeze, making him drop to his knees.

If my life had a soundtrack, while we were running through the trees, some crazy dubstep would be playing. I quickly looked over my shoulder and saw Code going in for the kill. While she battled, she took a knife out of her shoe and slammed it into her attacker's neck, slicing open his jugular. Red splashed down his body and onto Code's feet. After pushing him down to the ground, she knelt beside him, breathing hard and looking around with a lethal look.

She took his gun, popped up, and ran back my way, pumping bullets behind her. No lie, I stood there, shocked and freaking the hell out. Code was on some fucking Power Ranger shit, and I had no damn words to express how dope that was. All I could do was shake my head, then wave to her, letting her know that I was going into the thicket lining the highway.

"Those mofos just ain't quitting. What did y'all do, Code?" I asked when she caught up with me as I ran. My lungs burned from the exertion.

The chick at my side kept pace with me. She moved in a zigzag formation, using what she had taken off the dead bodies and sending it back at her attackers, as if we were in boot camp.

"What did *we* do? Fucking *culos* played us, and now they are coming at our throats! That's what *we* did. . . . Nada!"

My head whipped to the side, and I noticed how Code's eyes had narrowed. There was something more to this story. I didn't know what it was, but to hell if I was dying for a cause I hadn't helped set up. Twigs snapped and crunched under our kicks as we ran. I glanced up at the sky, then around us, and snatched at Code's hand to signal to her to stop. My finger rose up to my lips, and she gave a curt nod, letting me know she understood that I needed her to be quiet.

We had various guns between us. I had a 9 mm that I'd swiped off a dead body. Anxiously chewing on my lower lip, I listened hard and was rewarded—or cursed—to hearing more feet coming our way. Since I had used some rounds, I knew that I was running low. Panic had me looking at Code, who started digging in her pockets.

"I'm low on ammo, and they are still coming for us. Listen, I got us as deep as I can . . ." My hands were shaking as I spoke. "I see some lights, but if we don't take them out—" The pain in my shoulder had begun to act up, cutting off my words.

I tugged off my jacket and saw red running down my arm, soaking my shirt. Quick acting had me ripping the bottom of my tank, exposing my stomach. I wiped the cuts and scrapes on my body with the strip of fabric, then wrapped it around the cut on my arm that was bleeding, gritting my teeth through the pain.

Code bowed her head and checked her own body for injuries. "I didn't know you had those kinds of skills, newbie. Good looking out."

"Yeah, it was the only good thing my father ever gave me, I guess," I said, then stopped talking to catch my breath.

I watched as she finished digging in her pockets and held out her hand my way. Several small bronze shells sat on the flat of her palm. These babies spoke to the tech geek in me. It seemed like they had a marker of some sort, some kind of new tech that lined the side of the bullets like a vein. However, each "vein" was empty, so I could tell the bullets were a prototype of some sort.

"Take these. I have, like, six. Aim to kill, Smiley. Then get us out of these fucking woods," Code hissed through gritted teeth.

Old girl looked nervous too. All I could do was snatch what she offered, load up my weapon, then wait. I moved behind a big tree, and Code

did the same. We waited until we saw the whites
of their eyes, then let out rounds. A scream
almost ripped from my mouth as I stood in utter
shock at the gore before me. Each bullet literally
ripped through a body and blew that shit up
so that it looked like a cooked roast that had
fallen on the kitchen floor. I mean, flesh flew
everywhere, mixed with blood and bone matter.
I felt sick to my stomach, and I looked at the
crazy chick who'd given me that mess.

"What the hell is this?" I shouted.

Code jetted ahead of me into the woods, and
I followed. Behind us, the screams of those
men we'd gunned down stopped, and we then
knew that our aim to kill had worked. Still, we
doubled back, leaving some distance between us,
to check our kills. If I or Code found a wounded
person alive, we quickly took care of that nigga,
and we also left off shots to protect each other's
back. When I reached Code's side again, bodies
lay at her feet. A dark smile was on her face as
she threw a new Glock my way, then pointed
for us to go. Taking her lead, I now knew that
we had banished the enemy and were free to
trek through the woods, but questions still were
blazing in my mind.

"Wait, Smiley. Let me check out who these
culos are . . ." Code paused, stared down at the

bodies of the men who had been after us, then shook her head. "Scandinavians . . . fuck! What we used is what they were after. These!" She held up one lone bullet, then tucked it in her pocket. "Look, we need to get out of here."

A pulsing vibration drew our attention, and Code pulled out her cell. Holding her phone to her ear, she started talking. "They what . . . ? Okay. Okay . . . *Sí*, we're gone for now. The newbie, Smiley, is on some straight militant military shit. She's guiding us through the woods," I heard Code relay while we walked through the woods.

Memories of camping at Stone Mountain with my pops, and even visiting the parks, played in my mind. My father's paranoia was intense. I had never understood him insisting that I gain some tracking skills, which, he'd said, would help me not only in the woods but also on the streets. But now, in the aftermath of this battle, I was grateful, because those skills had been my ace boon.

"I'll tell her. Bye." Code glanced my way, then tucked her hair behind her ear.

Worry had my eyes wide while I kept a guarded stance. "What?"

Code tucked her cell away. Her face displayed various emotions. "Look, the guys who were coming after us are crazy as hell. We need you to go into our place and wipe out money. Start taking out whatever accounts you can and dump their money. Okay? Pascal gave me what you need to know to take care of this."

I was so confused in this moment. Ever since they had dropped me into their world, these fools had been making me choke and gorge on information on how they ran things. But erasing people? I knew I could do it. However, I didn't know their actual system. I knew they were trusting me only with their low-level computer system, but this . . . this was something different.

"How am I going to do that, Code? I've played with only your fake system. I don't know your real shit," I spat out.

Annoying laughter came from this chick. She smiled while she walked and shook her head. "You realized that, huh, *chica*? Okay, I'm about to give you some upper-level stuff. Pay attention, because this is your life in here too."

Time was not on our side, so everything she gave me—computer codes, passwords, and the names of the people who were after us—I had to soak up like a sponge. I'd have to play super-hacker and hone my skills and do things that I had only briefly played with. From what she was telling me, this was some serious money. It was up to me to make sure that the revenge was good and sweet for them fucking with us. I had almost died out there.

I led us out of the woods. We jetted down a hill, lost our footing, and slid toward the back of a major hardware store. When we came to a stop, I brushed off the mud on my kicks and pants, lost in thought.

"Did you get all of that?" Code asked, interrupting my thoughts.

Rubbing my temples, I inhaled deeply. Then I said, "Yeah . . ."

I spat out what she had said, using my memory as my tool. Passwords and money amounts I had typed on my cell so that I could review them and remember them for later. I quickly erased them now, then hurried around the building.

"So I have to go back to the place. Why again? Just so I hear you say it, because this shit is not for me," I said.

"You need to go because they don't know you. You have the benefit we don't. They know nothing about you," I heard her say.

All of this was getting on my last nerve, but I had said I'd do whatever to protect my ass, and I had meant it. My eyes focused on the surrounding area. We needed a car or some other sort of transportation to get the hell up outta Dodge.

"I get it. Just making sure," I said, still looking around.

"Here. Take my keys to the place and go handle business," Code ordered.

The weary tone in her voice had me raising an eyebrow while I took her offering. "I'm not going alone!"

"Yes you are. Don't worry about me. I got my out. You can disappear, and we'll contact you to meet up," she said.

I shrugged in disappointment. "Whatever then. I'll deal it and wait on y'all to hit me up."

"Good," was all she said while crossing the street with me.

We moved like twin bandits, scoping out the safest way to swipe a ride. I nudged Code with my elbow, then pointed out an old brown truck. I swore the thing looked like something from the movie *Cars*. I was unsure if I could break into this grandpa truck, but we both surrounded the car and worked the handles. It was nothing to pop one of the locks and get in. Code was the one who rubbed her hands together, then dropped down to rip the wires out and hotwire the truck. After I heard the comforting sound of the engine starting, I hit the gas pedal, then slowly drove off. It was only when we turned the corner that I hit that gas again and sped off.

"Drop me off near NorStar Townhomes," was all Code said as she began texting, then making calls.

I listened to her talk about someone she called the old man, then relay what had happened to someone named Freddie. Genuine concern and warmth reverberated in her voice when she spoke, though her tone also seemed guarded. Me, I just minded my business while I drove, acting as if I wasn't listening.

"Here! Here! Stop!" Code shouted quickly, tapping her finger against the car window.

The abruptness of her order had me slamming on the brakes. I then swerved the car and pulled up to an old gas station. As I sat there, gripping the steering wheel, the vibration of the car was all I felt and the sound of her speaking rapidly in Spanish on her cell was all I heard. I didn't know a damn thing she was saying except for a few words, but it didn't matter. I eyed a new ride to jack, a black 2008 Toyota Camry. Remaining incognegro was my priority here. It had me pulling my locks down, twisting them into a single side braid, and then pulling my jacket's hood over my head.

Tapping Code's arm, I gave her a stare. "I'm out. I'll hit y'all with a text," I said.

She told whomever she was speaking to, to hold on, then lowered her voice. "Don't fuck this up please, Smiley. We're counting on you. Besides, Pascal will be pissed if you don't get it right too. He worked hard on gathering that information, *chica*."

I gave a quick nod. "I won't, since y'all are trusting me." I gave a rare smile, then promptly climbed out of the car and headed across the street.

The black beauty before me had me eager to see if I could break into it, and luckily, I could. I hopped in, chucked the deuces, then sped off, heading back to the auto shop. My arm was throbbing from being grazed by bullets. My jacket was soaking up the blood that seeped through my makeshift bandage, so there was no problem, and the adrenaline rush going through me was like a hit of pain meds. I hoped that I wasn't leaving any DNA in this damn car. Once I made it to the auto shop, I took my time shutting the headlights off and drifted the car. In the big, unassuming building, I saw nothing. No one, and no disturbances.

I reached for my cell, then hit up Code. There was no answer, so I hit up Auto. As soon as he answered, I started speed talking. "It's no one's here. Like, do y'all have the capability to check the security, just in case?"

"No, Mama. We're working off burners. My people are injured. You have to check around and make sure it's safe. Can you do it?" Auto said with a gruffness to his voice.

My lips felt chapped, and nervousness had me gripping the steering wheel hard. Something didn't feel right. It had my stomach doing flip-flops, but if I was going to establish my reputation with this team, then I had to do this solid.

My slight uncertainty had me muttering, "I got this."

"You don't sound like you do," Auto quickly noted.

"I got this . . . ," I said solemnly, then sighed. "It's whatever . . . I'll try to do what I can with not knowing your system."

"Code gave you the rundown, right?" his deep voice asked in my ear.

"Yes, and I remember it all. She said she'll be okay on her own. Just wanted you to know. I dropped her off at some town house," I replied, reassuring the boss.

"A'ight. Good looking out," Auto grumbled.

There was a sadness and anger in his voice. When, back at my place, he had given me the limited rundown on the business and the team he had built up, I had heard the pride in his voice and had even seen it in his eyes. But now his mood had changed, thanks to the team being hurt like this. That sucked.

My Toyota and I quietly ghosted the lot while I listened to Auto's deep voice give me the phrases and numbers I needed. Once he finished, he cleared his throat. Then I heard silence.

"Hello?" I said nervously, not sure what was going on, on his end. When I got no answer, I kept talking. "I'll make sure to make this on point. Send the money to poor black folk wherever, and keep it steady and untraceable, of course," I said to let him know what was on my mind.

"Yeah . . . you sound like part of the team now. I like that," he replied, breaking his silence. He paused for a moment, then continued. "Now, listen, I know you're new, and I know you don't really have much loyalty to us, but on my word, once this is over, we got you, Smiley. Thank you for this. I knew you'd be someone we needed, a powerhouse. Handle that and watch your back. I have an old place in the trap, an auto shop where the info is going. If you need to hide—"

His tone of voice gave me the impression that he wasn't sure that he wanted to trust me with that info, so I interrupted him, feeling chill on that crap.

"It's good. Like you said, they don't know me. I can go home and stay low," I said, reassuring him.

"Still, just in case," Auto replied, then gave me an address.

It was familiar to me. I didn't know why. Then it dawned on me. I remembered following two young dudes to an auto shop when I was just a kid. They caught me and almost beat my ass, but they made me promise to forget it. One of the guys was the grandson of an old lady on my block who'd give all the kids sweet treats every Friday in the summer and some Sundays, after church. The other guy was some dude in a hoodie. His haunting, sexy eyes and his locks had made me interested in rocking locks myself. But that was when I was just a kid, and I had forgotten about the place until now.

"I got it. . . . Thanks for everything. My cell is on burner option . . . ," I told Auto.

"Another program of yours," Auto noted, sounding interested.

"Yeah . . ." I chuckled, feeling a slight blush.

"Be safe. Mama and I want the program," he said, then hung up in my ear.

I didn't want the car to trace back to the shop even if it traced back to me, so I quickly parked the ride in a hidden area near an abandoned building several blocks away. I took in my surroundings, then sprinted until I got to the shop. I quietly walked around outside the shop, and once I felt sure that no eyes were on me, I used the keys to open the door, then stepped inside the shop, closed the door, and quickly locked it behind me. I glanced around, then sprinted through the massive building and took the stairs that led up to where the geeks did their magic.

Relief hit me when I saw nothing had been disturbed. I quickly punched on the computer, then moved around the room in the darkness, waiting for the computer to boot up. Nerves had me tapping my hands on the counter in front of me.

"Come on. Come on!" I muttered, in a hurry.

The familiar sound of the computer finally coming to life made me laugh. I swiftly began typing, working the DNS codes. I put in the team passcodes. Images fluttered in front of my face, leading me to the Scandinavian file Pascal had. I checked the digits against what had been relayed to me. After shifting to grab my cell, I uploaded my coding program to take the money and swap it out. Liquid cash was what I turned everything into, from their property to their monies to more.

I changed everything and erased their claim to it. One quick call to the contact that Pascal had acquired by working closely with the banks where the Scandinavians had dumped everything, and I knew I was in. I transferred some of the money to various nonprofits, real ones, not the fake ones that had their CEOs sitting on the Dow. I then moved some money to an account for the team and sent a hacking code to alert the Feds about the Scandinavians' activity. I figured this would be the icing on the cake. I quickly worked my magic, erasing everything, sending new information out into the universe. Once I had completed my task, I went to hit END PROGRAM, but the sound of tapping drew my attention away.

My eyes widened with each tap, and I cautiously pushed back from the computer, holding my hands up.

"Well, now, isn't this interesting? I remember you, doll face," said the person before me. He gave a snap of the fingers, then chuckled. "Yes. Mama, I remember you. You were being handled by cops near Morton's. I was the one in the Audi . . . and curiously, you were on my block today. That was you, wasn't it?"

Butterflies in my stomach had me feeling fear, and I said nothing. Lights flickered on, and I saw a fine, tall brotha with the sexiest eyes and smile known to man staring me down. My mouth dropped open, and I realized who I was staring at. The man in the boots. The man both Code and I had been stalking. I thought the white guys with the creepy eyes and blond hair were after us, but it seemed like the crew I hung with had other enemies as well.

Ain't this some shit, I thought.

A second male dressed in all black with a spot of purple came into view. He, too, was fine, but there was a hard edge to his handsome dark face. His brown eyes looked me up and down as he strolled forward. One gloved hand held a Glock; the other suddenly reached out my way.

He gave me a pearly white smile, which belied his serious intent. His lush lips parted; then all I heard was, "Don't struggle."

I swallowed hard, then mumbled as I felt myself being lifted up. My arms flailed out, and I kicked erratically. I tried to use my father's moves to take this guy down, but it didn't work. This dude was too big, and his grip was too hard.

Pissed off and shocked, I glanced at the man in the doorway. He was dressed in simple dark jeans, a gray vest over a black button-down shirt, and one of those small caps dudes back in the day used to wear. He seemed interested in only me as he played with a familiar bullet in his hands.

Life was not a box of chocolates. Life was a bag of shit, and now everything fucking stunk. I stopped my frantic struggling, in realization that there was no getting out of this, and then I muttered, "Oh shit . . ."

Mister in the boots gave a smirk, walked up to me, then took me by my jaw. He locked his gaze on me, then chuckled. "Damn right, beautiful one. Now tell me . . . Where's my product?"

Chapter 10

Code

"Damn, *chiquita*," my cousin Mark said when he opened the door to let me into the old man's domain.

I was bloodied and battered. Hadn't expected to get into a firefight in the middle of fucking Riverdale. I shoved him out of my way and headed toward Papa's study. I needed to shower, but I opted instead to stop and grab a bottle of the old man's Cuban rum. He had had it made especially for him by an old-world rum-making family. It was the only rum he would trust to drink. I took the stopper out of the bottle and took some to the head. The spicy liquid burned my throat and chest as it went down and left an aftertaste of molasses and sugarcane in its wake.

"What the fuck happened to you?" Mark asked me.

Mark was Frederick's younger brother, but unlike Freddie, Mark was a monster. He lived up to the reputation most of the men in our family had. Mark had no heart. He didn't have that little voice in his head telling him to think about his actions. If the old man gave him an order, he followed it without question, and oftentimes with a smile on his face.

"Got into a fight," I told him.

Sweat rained down my face as I coughed, then spit up blood in the trash can. After sitting at the town house with Auto and the rest of the team for an hour, I knew I had to do something that Auto could never know about. But I had to be sure our asses were covered. No way, with all the damage done, we could keep the heat off us for long. So, I had to see the old man for another favor.

"Looks like you got that ass tapped," Mark taunted me.

"Fuck you."

"Say when."

I frowned and spat in his direction, "Sick motherfucker."

He only smiled as his eyes narrowed. Mark and I didn't care for one another. I'd always bested him in whatever task the old man had for us. Even when it was only for show and entertainment, I had been better than him. He had always detested me for that.

"No sicker than you, Maria Rosa."

I hated the way he said my name. It rolled off his tongue like venom in a snakebite.

"Fuck off, Mark, and tell me where the old man is."

"In his study. Let me guess . . . Was it you and your friends who caused the mess down in Clayton County?"

I ignored him, rolled my eyes, and made my way down to the end of the dimly lit hall, where the old man was holed up. On the wall was a floor-to-ceiling picture of a dark-skinned woman. None of us knew who she was. We just knew she was always watching us. Her 'fro was majestic, and her eyes were big, like a doll's, and the color of copper. She was built like an Amazonian warrior and dressed in the regal fashion of Khemet, now known as Egypt.

"Papa, I need to talk to you," I yelled at the picture as I looked into the woman's eyes.

I knew the old man was watching me. Through the eyes of that woman, he was always watching. After a few minutes, with no response from him, I sighed.

"Please, Papa. It's important!" I yelled again.

Finally, the picture clicked. Sounded like someone had unsnapped a button. Then it slid to the side to reveal a brass door. I didn't waste time; I pushed the door open and stepped over the threshold. Behind a red-oak desk, in front of a picture window sat the old man. His white blazer was neatly draped on the back of his Tudor-style wingback desk chair. Necktie hung on the coatrack, next to his Kangol hat. The top buttons of his black dress shirt were open, show-ing the top of his chiseled chest and his white wife beater. His curly salt-and-pepper hair was tapered on his head. His jaw was squared, and muscles ticked on either side of it, which meant he was pissed about something. I knew what it was since Freddie had already told me word had gotten back to Papa about the shoot-out.

He grunted, then growled low in his throat as he glowered at me. "You come to me filthy. What is this disrespect?"

I rolled my eyes. The old man's OCD had slipped my mind with everything else I had going on.

"I mean no disrespect, Papa," I said softly to him in his native tongue. "I just ran into a little trouble and need some help."

He kept eyeing me—up and down, then down and up—with a scowl, as if to ask why I was in his presence while bloodied, dirty, and smelling foul.

"You need a bath. You need to go and come to me like you know who I am. And not like I'm some *pinche pendejo* off the streets, Maria Rosa. Don't disrespect me," he spat out.

I walked closer to his desk and watched as he bristled. "Can you please, for once, overlook the mundane—"

"Get the hell out of my office before I toss you out on your ass. Come back with some modicum of veneration!"

I almost flipped the old man off, but I knew that would only set him off more. We stared each other down. Nothing in his office was out of place. Even the books in the wall-to-wall book-case were in alphabetical order by the author's name. The mahogany wood floor had been hand shined to perfection. Since I knew I needed a favor and could catch more bees with honey than with vinegar, I stormed from his office.

About thirty minutes later, I reentered the old man's study. This time I was dressed in skinny denims, a black button-down that tapered to my waist, and black combat boots. My hair had been pulled back into two French braids.

After he looked up from the papers on his desk, he gave me the once-over, then nodded.

"I need a favor," I said.

"Go on."

"We got into some trouble today. I want to know if you can make sure nothing falls back on me and my friends."

I was antsy. Needed to get back to the shop to see if Smiley was okay. Though she was new to the team, she had done her thing today, and I couldn't be mad at her for hesitating at first. I would have done the same had I found myself in her shoes. Still, in the end, she had come through. I needed to go make sure she had come through on the other end of things as well. Needed to make sure she was safe.

"Why was it wise of you to have a shoot-out so recklessly, *bonita*? Have I not trained you better than this?"

I nodded, still standing, so he could sense my urgency. "*Sí*, Papa, but my friends—"

"Eh," he spat out, then grimaced, as if he had something bitter on his tongue. "These people, these so-called friends of yours, don't know any better, then?"

"They know better too. They . . . We just had no choice. It was kill or be killed, Papa. You know the rules."

"Of course. I helped to invent them."

"Then you know it was imperative that we fought back."

"Tell me why someone would be so anxious to come after you in such a way, Maria Rosa." He leaned back in his chair, then laced together the fingers of his big hands as he studied me.

"They stole from us. We took the stuff back, then some. They felt they had the right to come for revenge."

"So simple?"

"*Sí*, Papa. It's that simple."

In the back of my mind, I was scared shitless that the old man would read through my half-truths. He hated to be lied to. Even more, he hated when his family lied to him. For a long while, he just watched me coolly. The look he was giving me would make most people, even the toughest of men, shit their pants. But it only reminded me that I had a Glock tucked against my spine. There was no way I could win a gun-fight with the old man, but I would wound him and would die trying. He knew this. That was probably why he gave a sinister smirk, pulled his gun from his desk drawer, and then laid it on the desk.

I took my Glock from its hiding spot and placed it on the desk, alongside his. A truce to show we were both thinking the same thing. My facial expression was still stoic. If I showed no feeling, there was no way my emotions could give me away. He clicked the phone on his desk. I didn't breathe a sigh of relief until one of my cousins, Officer Bryant, better known as Fuego to us family, picked up on the other end of the line. Papa put him on speakerphone and told him what he wanted. Fuego assured him it would be handled from the governor's office on down to the mayor, on down to the police commissioner.

"Tell Margaret I'd like it to be known that a new gang is trying to terrorize Clayton County. Make it look as if they started a turf war or something. We don't want it traced back to Maria Rosa or her people," Papa ordered Fuego as I stood there listening.

Papa and the police commissioner were on first-name terms. She'd been in his pocket since before she became the commissioner.

"Maria Rosa okay?" Fuego asked.

"She's here. You can ask her."

"You good, cuzzo?" Fuego asked loudly.

"*Sí*, cousin. All is well," I answered.

"You need me?"

"I'll let you know."

"No," Papa interjected. "Fuego will focus on the task at hand."

I asked, "What task?"

"You'll know soon enough," was how Papa answered.

A few minutes later all was done and I was set to walk out of the old man's office.

"Wait, Maria Rosa. Why in such a hurry?" he asked me.

"I need to see about my people."

He shook his head. Slid his desk chair back, then patted his lap. Nervousness settled in my spine and traveled up my back like a chill. To show that I didn't want to sit on my papa's lap would be to offend him. The last thing I needed to do was have him pissed at a time when my makeshift family needed him most. I put on my best smile, then walked over and sat on the old man's lap. I didn't flinch when he sniffed my hair, then rubbed a hand up and down my back.

In a quiet but serious voice, I asked, "What do you need from me, Papa?"

"You're my favorite grandchild. Do you know that?" he asked.

I nodded. "Of course I know this, Papa."

"And because you're my favorite, I will do anything for you, sí?"

"Sí, Papa."

"Will you do anything for me still, *bonita*?"

His voice was deep. The more he spoke, the deeper it got. Most people would be revolted by the tone he took with me, being that I was his granddaughter, but I was used to it. He used that tone with all the women he loved, including the ones he fucked for his sole satisfaction.

I dropped my head, then went to that dark place in my mind. "Sí, Papa."

He wrapped his arms around my waist and laid his head against my back. "Anything?"

My flesh started to crawl, if for no other reason than for the simple fact that I knew anytime I did "favors" for him, I lost a little bit more of my soul.

"Anything," I assured him.

"Then I need a favor in return for my favor to you and your friends."

I nodded. "Go on."

"You and your friends deliver and receive cars all over the United States, no?"

"Sí, we do."

"I need to employ your services."

I swallowed hard, then turned to look at the old man. His dark eyes gleamed as evil danced just behind his pupils. It was no wonder so many women got ensnared in his trap. His eyes hypnotized you.

"Tell me what you need . . ."

"I need you to transport a few shipments for me. I need them to come from the Port of Miami and to be shipped up to the Canadian border," he replied.

My heart thundered in my chest. I knew what he was asking me, and there was just no way could I put my family in jeopardy like that. Papa dabbled in illegal activities all over the place. From drugs to guns, he did it. No way I could bring that kind of heat to Auto. He was my brother. He trusted me. I couldn't do that to the empire he'd built.

"Papa, I . . . can't do that . . ."

His jaw hardened. "Can't or won't?"

"Papa, you're asking me to put my team's freedom in—"

"Their freedom? You don't think I will protect them?"

"If it came down to us and them, they'd be cannon fodder."

He chuckled. Leaned back, then took the time to light a Cuban cigar. He puffed, then put the cigar to my lips. To turn it away would be another slap to his face. I puffed, inhaled, then exhaled the smoke. The cigar had a very pronounced, robust, spicy flavor, and if I weren't used to it, it would be too strong for me. Papa's big hand caressed my waist as he held me on his lap.

"My Maria Rosa doesn't trust me," he declared.

"I do trust you. I trust you to be who you are, and since I know you, I trust you to always put you first," I stated matter-of-factly as I handed him the cigar.

He chuckled. "So is that still a no?"

I took his hand in mine, kissed the crested ring on his finger, then the palm of his hand before standing.

"Yes, Papa, my answer is still no. I can't put them in that kind of trouble. Tell me something else to do and I'll do it for you. Just not that."

If one didn't know me, one wouldn't be able to tell I was afraid. I'd just said no to the old man. Nobody said no to him and had all end well. So imagine my surprise when he scooted me off his lap, stood, placed that familial kiss on my lips, then smiled.

"I understand, *chispita*," he told me.

He'd called me his little spark, a name he hadn't called me since my first time handling a gun, the one he'd given me for my fifth birthday.

He ran a finger lovingly down my cheek, then moved toward the door. He placed the cigar back between his lips. I didn't know what scared me more, his calmness at my answer or the way he smiled at me as he left the room.

I didn't have time to dwell on that, though. I'd think of another way to handle the old man. I left the study, rushed out to my car, hit Smiley's cell, only to find out the number was no longer in service. I pulled my phone from my ear and looked at it like it was defective. I tried calling her number again, only to get the same message. I hung up, then called Auto.

"Hey, you heard from Smiley?" I asked him as soon as he answered.

"She was at the shop, taking care of that business. Why?"

"Trying to call her and can't reach her."

He chuckled. "Mama got this app that destroys her number after a certain amount of usage."

"Damn. She does?"

"Yeah. I told her I needed it. And apparently, she wiped out the Scandinavians. Pascal just got word from his person at the bank."

"Damn, she works fast," I commented.

"True."

"Everybody still at NorStar?" I could hear light laughter and mumbling in the background.

"Yeah. Laying low until the sky dogs and cops cool off."

Sky dogs were what we called police helicopters in the sky.

"Yeah, well, you need to find a way to meet me somewhere," I told him.

"I know. We need to get to the shop to make sure Smiley is okay. She hasn't called me back yet. She said she would. Last thing I want is to get her caught up in this shit. She has no idea what the fuck is even going on," he replied.

"I know. I'm going to swing by the shop, scoop her up, and then come back there. We can fill her in then."

"You do that, but don't bring her here. Take her to my place. She'll be safer. I'll be there."

"Any word from Chandler again?" I asked.

"No. Nigga's probably dead."

Auto said that with no emotion. Said it like he hadn't once held the man in high regard. Auto had a low tolerance for betrayal of trust. It didn't surprise me that he no longer gave a damn about what happened to Chandler.

"You know me and Smiley had eyes on the man who supplied the bullets," I said. "I talked my cousin into giving me info on who he is and where he is laying his head. The old man doesn't normally do business if he doesn't at least know where the supplier lays his head."

"So, what did you find out?"

"Not much. He lives in Copper Hills, on Garden Walk Boulevard."

"Get the fuck outta here," Auto remarked. "A nigga who makes those kinds of bullets? Ain't no way he's really living in a ghetto like Copper Hills."

"I'm telling you what I saw."

"Naw. That shit's got to be a front. Those bullets are too detailed and intricate. We need to look past what our eyes are seeing and scope beyond the lens. He can obey the principles of the hood without being bound by them. Same as us. We live in the hood, but that doesn't mean we're bound to it. We can all pack up and leave anytime we want to. That man is too smart to be in a Copper Hills frame of mind. Do your homework. Get Smiley and then meet me at my place."

With that, he hung up the phone. I had to admit, I had thought about the same thing. But I knew plenty of niggas who were too smart to be in the hood, but too dumb to do right with their money and get out of the hood. Mr. Bullet Man could be one of those brothers, I thought as I drove in the direction of the shop.

The hairs on the back of my neck instantly stood up when I pulled up in front of the shop. Something wasn't right. The doors to the shop had been left up. I cut my engine. Quickly exited the car so I wouldn't be trapped in the event of another gunfight. I ducked low, then rushed around to the side of the building. Looked right, then left, to see if the coast was clear. Once I was sure I wasn't going to get shot in the back, I quickly kneeled, then crawled into the shop. I pulled the door down behind me and locked it. Did a quick check of the shop.

"Smiley," I yelled as I ran around.

I felt sick to my stomach as I thought about what could be happening to Smiley. Started to feel like we should have stopped trying to save everybody.

I yelled out her name again as I ran upstairs, then back down.

I got no answer. I listened for even a whimper to see if she was tied up somewhere. Not a sound. The place had been tossed. Papers, parts, oil, grease, everything had been thrown around the shop. I let out an aggravated scream at the mess. I screamed because we had been found. Screamed because our computers and all had been snatched from the walls. All of what made Eraserheads who they were had been taken. Yeah, we had a real home base with backup files and all, but I had no idea how long our shit had been gone and no idea who'd taken it.

Just then my cell rang. A number unknown to me flashed on the caller ID.

"Who is this?" I answered.

"We have something that belongs to you. Same as you have something that belongs to us," a male voice said to me.

"Who is this?" I asked again.

My face was grim. Mind set to kill.

All I heard was her sniffles, then her shaky voice. "Code, help me," Smiley pleaded.

"Are you hurt, Smiley?" I asked her.

"Little bit."

"You get a good look at who took you?"

Took her a minute to stop sniffling. "Yeah."

"Tell me who."

"Bullets—" was all she said before the phone was snatched away.

"I can play this game all day, little lady," I heard the male voice tell Smiley. "Tell your boss I know he has my merchandise, and unless he gives it back to me, I'm going to keep taking and taking, until I get what's mine." Then the voice spoke directly into the phone. "Next move is yours."

The call ended before I could react. Next move was ours, he'd said. Then so be it.

Chapter 11

Boots

"Today on *ATL in the Morning*, vigilantes fight back against a brazen radical militia . . ."

A knowing smile spread across my face. Fighting gunmen with masks flickered across my flat screen. I sighed, with a smile, then swiped up my remote to hit MUTE, turned in my chair and dropped the remote on the desk.

"You see that, my sista?" I said, thumb pointing behind me. I grinned wide at my guest. "That right there is some powerful stuff. My people are tired of the bullshit and are not taking being stomped on the throat anymore. That's that shit that I like!"

My guest rolled her pretty bourbon-brown eyes, then pursed her lips. "Yeah, it's dope. I'd do the same shit if someone had stolen from me."

I liked this one a lot. She was a better guest than my past guests had been. Usually, they were all manipulating liars. I really couldn't blame them, but I hated liars. The majority were snakes from jump, and I was not a fan of that type of snake. But my new guest here? Shit, she was cool to the breeze. Holding her here had started becoming an enjoyment after she stopped cussing at me and trying to fight a brotha. I had taken her to send a message, and so far the waiting game was still going on. Which was why I was sitting back, just watching.

"So tell me, Smiley. What's it like to do what you do? I mean, what the hell do you get out of it, beauty, outside of monetary gain?"

Smiley sat in a La-Z-Boy with her arms clamped down by handcuffs. I had tried to make her as comfortable as possible. My man Shango had been the utmost gentleman after she stopped spitting on him. He had carefully changed her out of her bloody clothes and had swapped them out for one of Alize's jean overalls and a tank.

He had then carefully cleaned her wounds, right after he had got down and snatched her by her locks. The brotha was not about putting his hands on females, but he wasn't opposed to helping her understand that he would take only so much of her fighting him before shit got real.

His threat ice cold, I had just sat back and watched how quickly my guest got with the program, while at the same time, I had checked on my other shipment of items. After that, it had been mad smooth.

Right now, she was crunching on ice and watching me with an annoyed look on her face. Her nose was crinkled, she had a furrow in her brow, and her huge eyes kept rolling as she thought up some smart retort to release on me. It amused me. Made me laugh my ass off, because she reminded me of the shawties back in Houston.

"I get what I get for the moment," she answered. She shrugged, then tugged at her handcuffs in order to pop ice in her mouth.

After grabbing my Starbucks cup, I raised it slowly to my lips, took a sip, then locked eyes with her. "Yeah? Like my bullets."

"Nah, like my money! I don't know what your bullets are and don't know nothing about how they were taken, okay?" she sassed.

I ducked as a cup flew my way. Shango got ready to jump from his chill spot in the back of my office, but I held my hand up to calm him. "It's cool. She's still salty about being a guest here. But back to the discussion at hand. I believe you, Smiley."

"So let me go. I don't know a thing, and I can't help you any way it goes," she pleaded.

See, she was bullshitting. I already knew it from the tone of her voice, but I didn't care. I was enjoying seeing the sparks of intelligence going on in her mind, which was why I was keeping her. From watching her at her crew's compound, I knew she was a tech geek. I wasn't sure exactly what she'd been doing, because I hadn't been standing close enough to her at the time. But the coding she had done was quick and to the point, and it had me invested.

"Actually, you can help me out, little mama. Since you say you are new to the crew, I'm thinking that me and you can come to some type of arrangement."

Smiley's eyes widened; then she started twisting in her chair. "Hell no! I don't know shit about you, and I'm not about to be a ho for you or steal for you or whatever."

"Damn, doll face. Do I look like I want to fuck you? I mean, you're sexy in your own kinda way, but no. I'm not here for any of that. No need to force myself on pussy. Who I am is enough to get pussy willingly." I grinned, and I saw her eyes soften, then harden from emotion.

What an interesting chick, for sure. The sound of my cell phone ringing cut off our chat, and I swiveled in my desk chair to grab the phone. As I picked it up, I looked at her. "Shango, remind me later to approach our guest about a possible compromise."

"Speak," I said into the receiver and waited.

"We have a situation, a big one, *chefe*," I heard in my ear.

The voice on the opposite end of the line caused me to frown, sink farther into my chair, and pinch the bridge of my nose. "What happened now, Oya?"

"There was a weight problem with our truck coming in from Miami. Our man Dinzo had made it through all the truck stations without issue and had switched the load with Shredder. But once Shredder got to the weigh station leading into Georgia and tried to get through, he noticed a *problema grande*. Long story short, Shredder checked out and paid the weigh station to ignore it, and now I'm looking at something that could get us shook up."

The sound of Oya walking hit my ear. Every now and then she would pause, then mutter in the background, causing me to feel anxious at the moment.

"I'm so sorry, *chefe* . . . Boots. I don't know who is targeting us, but this is serious," Oya stated.

Whatever it was that had her on edge had the hairs rising on the back of my neck. I slowly stood and clutched my cell.

"What do you see?" I asked.

"I . . . You have to come down here and see for yourself. This . . . *merda* . . . Just come to our drop spot," she urged.

"I'll be on my way." I quickly hung up.

After walking up to Shango, I muttered in his ear, "Bring our guest. Oya said something has gone down, and we need to check it out now."

"A'ight, boss. I'll move her to the back and get the car ready," Shango replied.

Heat crept up the back of my neck. Tension had me rolling my shoulders.

"Well, Ms. Smiley, looks like we're going on another trip. You might be able to help with this one. I think your crew is fucking with me."

"Yeah? Well, you did snatch me," she spat, with a haughty look of pride in her eyes.

Her loyalty amused me, but right now I was too pissed off to care. I grabbed her by the back of her neck and hunkered down low to look in her eyes. "If you fuck around and fight, do understand that my man Shango has no issue with fucking you up for putting your hands on him, feel me?"

Smiley gave a slow, fearful nod.

I exhaled. "Get her up and out. I don't have time to waste."

After stepping out of the back room that was my office, I told Alize to hold down the fort and make sure that PT was nearby. I took several strides to the exit of my complex, shifted my hat to cover my eyes, and then slid into the waiting car, which contained both Shango and a bound Smiley. We headed out of the hood, and I leaned against the window, with my finger against my temple. The majority of my work was making sure these bullets got to where they were going. The fact that I kept having problems with just one shipment was surely screwing with my vibe.

"Tell me again what you know about your crew, Smiley . . . Eraserheads, as you say."

Smiley's eyes were wide, and her plump lips spilled over the simple gag in her mouth. My boy pulled it down, then offered her some water, which she greedily drank before speaking.

"Nothing . . . From what I was told, they just work the auto shop. That's it. And they do what people do who want good rides. Steal 'em," she rushed to say.

"So tell me why they are called Eraserheads, then?" I asked, keeping my temper in check.

"Shit if I know! I guess 'cause of how smoothly they swipe rides and wipe out the identity," she said, rambling out of fear. "Please don't kill me."

"If your people had anything to do with what I'm dealing with now, trust me, killing you will be the very last thing I do after I get done shipping your parts to them, understood?" Anger made my voice deeper and gruff.

Shango watched me from the corner of his eye, and I shook my head, stopping him from speaking. "Just keep driving."

An hour later, we were at our drop-off spot outside Atlanta. Trees surrounded the open concrete carport. The heat of the Georgia sun beat down on us, and although the AC was blasting in the ride, outside I could see waves of heat drifting in the air.

Oya was pacing back and forth in her black leggings and bulletproof corset vest, which was wrapped around her lilac button-down shirt. Agitation and frustration showed on her appealing face, which was apparent from the way it was scrunched up. The moment she saw our car, she waved a hand and turned, causing the brown fishtail braid on her head to whip over her shoulder. She stood side by side with Shredder, who was near the back of the truck, with a pissed-off look on his face. He muttered something.

"Handle her, Shango," I said, getting out of the car.

After slamming the door of my black Explorer, I walked toward Oya, but then Shredder stepped up to me and started his stuttering. "I . . . I . . . I . . . did shit right."

"I trust you, man. Just calm down and explain it slowly. What's going on?" I said.

Shredder glanced at Oya, who had moved over to where he was standing when we pulled up. I followed while Shedder walked in her direction and took care with his words. "Dinzo said that before taking the cargo, the big bosses were holding him back talking about issues with his truck, but when he checked it, nothing seemed off about the shipment."

"Okay, so it's not his fault. Continue," I said.

"These motherfuckers were playing with us. . . . They . . . they . . . switched our shit on Dinzo!" Shedder spat out.

"How?"

"We don't know," he said.

Frustration had me almost shouting, "What did they switch out to cause the weight change?"

Oya opened the back of the truck. "Take a look, *chefe*," she said as she motioned for me to peer inside the truck.

Glancing inside, my mouth dropped, and anger had me ready to kill. Before me were stacks of white blocks lining the walls of the truck's trailer. I could see where either Dinzo or Shredder had yanked back a false wall, which was now slouching. Though that had me pissed off, the shock came when my eyes focused on the teenage girls and boys who were lying on their sides, the plastic ties that had bound their arms lying beside them. From the looks of things, many were only a few years younger than me and my crew, while the rest were preteens. Fear was in their eyes, and I knew . . . knew that my crew and I were being set up for some fucking drug and human-trafficking shit.

"You got to be fucking kidding me!" I spat out and flung the doors of the truck wide open. "So, where the fuck are the bullets?"

Oya and Shredder both shook their heads, then dropped them in disbelief.

"Call up, Dinzo! The fuck is this?" I shouted, then punched a fist into one of the doors.

Every kid in the truck whimpered, then shrank back in fear. They all seemed emaciated and exhausted. Bruises were on their bodies, and some of the girls had blood staining their thighs. I already knew what this shit was about with them, and it sickened me to my spirit.

"Dinzo is taking another truck to Texas, since this one is hot, boss. We manipulated the records as usual to say it was signed off," Shredder said quickly, clarifying matters.

Oya spoke up just then, because she knew Shredder was equally pissed and was about to spaz. "Shred and I spoke to Dinzo. He broke down everything that he could recall and that felt shifty to him. It was a group of biker-looking white guys who rolled out from the trucking station and went to different trucks. He didn't think anything of it, because he was doing what we pay him to do," Oya explained.

"They have something on them that made Dinzo think it was them?" I hastily asked, the wheels turning in my head.

Shredder stepped forward, tucking his hands in his overalls. "Yeah, he said he saw some similar ones at the weigh station, watching his load—"

"Sounds like those same-looking niggas that came after me and my crew," Smiley interrupted.

I turned and narrowed my eyes at Shango, who was holding her arms. His hold got tighter, and he started to drag her back to the ride, but she began bucking and tugging yet again.

Panic was in her eyes as she stared at me and yelled, "You wanted me to tell y'all if we had something to do with this. Well, I'm telling you, Boots. We didn't have shit to do with this. I don't know nothing else going on, but I know those niggas you just described is who was gunning for us over in Riverdale. I promise you on my life."

"Who is this, *chefe*?" Oya asked, her voice chilly, after she walked up into Smiley's face, then stared her down with a lethal gaze.

"Looks like she's an ally for now, Oya, and an asset to us when we all go after the niggas that are playing foul with my bullets and stealing from me," I replied.

Rubbing my jaw, I pulled myself into the truck and looked around. "Did you talk to these kids?" I asked, sticking my head out of the truck.

"Shredder tried. He couldn't understand them, which is why he called me to the drop spot," Oya explained. "They are Haitian."

I jumped out of the truck and slowly moved around it, eyeing it. The flat of my gloved hand ran over the outer surface of the truck, then connected with the hitch. I pulled open the door near the hitch, and I looked inside. Molly, meth and other bullshit were nestled in the compartment. My bullets were nowhere in sight. No crates, no nothing! Blazing anger had me going all the way off. I returned to the back of the truck and addressed the children. My language changed to French, and I asked them all the relevant questions.

"Tell me what the people looked like who took you," I spat out.

Many didn't know a thing. Some were just immigrant children who were walking home from school in either Miami or the surrounding area and were snatched up. The ones who could provide some details gave me descriptions of cars, which I spat back to the crew to take note of. As the kids spoke, some in broken English, I smiled. After many minutes, I was finally able to get to the meat that I needed. Physical traits.

An older boy laid out that a tall man had taken him. Another said his captor was blond. Other kids mentioned that they'd been kidnapped by someone with blue eyes. All of them said the people spoke weird, and many said they were forced to stash drugs on their bodies. They all woke up after being drugged and found themselves hidden in the truck. The loud sobs of some of the girls chilled me to the bone. The older boys made their way over to them and tried to shield them.

I pushed up to turn my back on them and look at my team. "The Scandinavians . . . and Mouse! Motherfuckers turned their back on me and flipped the script."

Oya and Shredder both hopped into the back of the truck with me. They both glanced at each other for a moment, then went to help the kids. Oya knew French as well as Portuguese, so she was able to communicate effectively with the children.

"We are here to protect you. Their blood will spill for bringing harm to you, I promise," I heard Oya gently say as I climbed out of the truck.

The pain in her voice, I knew well. This all hit home with her, as she had been snatched from her home in Brazil and was also a survivor of human trafficking. Chills ran down my spine.

"We'll gather what we can from the truck, scrub it out with my kit in the trunk, and try to get these kids back to their homes," I muttered while walking toward Smiley.

Smiley's eyes were rimmed in red as she watched the others. I didn't know if she was really telling the truth about her people not being involved, but I knew I was pissed off at the thought of being played.

"Was there a tracker to set us up?" I asked Shredder, who had jumped down from the truck and followed me.

"Yes, boss. I left that shit on the side of the road once I left the weigh station and took a U-turn in Daytona," Shredder explained, quickly moving to my side.

"Good call. That gives us a little more time here." Thinking of what to do from here, I paused next to Shango and stared at my guest.

"So, Smiley." My hand rested on the small of her back while I worked to remove her cuffs. "Today we both have an understanding. Your team's things will be returned. My point was made, but with the wrong people. I'm a man with mine, so I'll speak—"

As soon as I said that, cars zoomed up, and a door flew open. All I saw was a long braid, shapely, exotic eyes, and a lithe female's body.

Behind her, from the second car, was a male. I frowned. I didn't have time for this shit. The Scandinavians were gunning for me, fucking with my livelihood, and I needed to understand why before I pumped iron into their skulls and blew smoke through the openings.

Moving Smiley behind me, I stared down little Miss Latina, whom I recognized from the convenience store. Something about the power in the way she moved had me wanting to give her mad respect and to fuck her. But at the same time, I was ready for whatever fight she wanted to throw.

"You said it was my move, so here we go." Her gun lifted; then she rolled her shoulders. "Give me back my homie."

An amused smile spread across my face, and instantly, I wanted to mind fuck the shawty. "Who? You don't even know this girl to be calling her homie."

Little Miss Latina gave me a snarl that reminded me of the many pics online of my Caribbean sistas with the red lipstick giving me heat. The sound of her gun going off near my feet had me slightly annoyed. I moved to the side, and I saw Oya move the kids farther back, then hop down from the truck and come my way.

"You want gunfire, we can do that, Mami. But you need to listen to what I have to share with you in this moment in time," I spat out, locking my steely gaze on her from under my cap.

Smiley tried to push from behind me, but I kept her in place and growled low, "You move and don't let me handle this, then you'll get hurt, you understand me?"

"I don't care. You know we didn't—" she began, but I interrupted her.

"Yes, I know. Let me communicate that shit."

Agitation rode me. Females could do the utmost sometimes. I was trying to show my hand in respect, but here we went with the bullshit.

I turned my attention back to the woman with the guns. "I know you're pissed, and I extend my apology, but listen. I have more guns on you than you have on me. If I wanted you dead, I could do so. As for my death, I don't really give a shit. But if I go down, so does your homie. So put the gun down."

A cold smile spread across her face. She gave a fake laugh, then laid the gun down. "Okay, truce."

I wasn't feeling how easily she laid her weapon down. Something in her mannerisms, as well as those of her boys, had me on edge and told me to keep my distance.

"It seems we have a common enemy. You got played, and I got played. Whoever the puppet master is, he or she wanted us to go out and wipe each other out. Now, both of us so far have been operating on smarts in this whole thing, and I want to keep it that way. Do you hear me?"

My gaze stayed on the chick. She pushed her hair to the side, then gave a shrug. "Yeah. Now do you hear me?" With a snap of her hand, two other people came out of the cars, holding guns. "Now we are equal with the gunplay. . . . *Dios*, wait . . ." She pulled a gun out of her jacket, then pointed it my way.

I sighed. The broad was clearly crazy as fuck. Here I was, offering an olive branch, and here she was, playing G.I. Joe.

The irritation was too much for me, so I let Smiley go and tilted my head. "Tell your friend to chill. I want peace. We might be able to help each other, okay?"

Smiley glanced up at me; then she looked at the kids in the truck's trailer. I could tell the wheels in her mind were turning, because she then gave a frown and gruffly said, "Fine. But for them."

As she pushed Shango back and brushed past me, she rolled her eyes. She jogged to her friend and held her hands up. "He's talking truth, Code. He's been played. Look in the truck."

Smiley motioned behind her, and the kids peeked their heads out to look around. Little Miss Latina's eyes widened; then she slowly dropped her weapon.

My team and I stayed still and watched, keeping our distance. I realized that one of the men behind the woman I had learned was named Code had been my client's bodyguard. Oya stepped forward, and so did Shango, both of my guards revealing the heat in their hands. I could see the recognition in their eyes, and I knew I wasn't tripping then.

Something like an irrational anger hit me. I signaled my people, and our guns pointed straight ahead. Someone had a fucking secret, because some foul shit was going on here. I didn't know completely what it was. But fuck this shit. If I was going to die today, then so be it.

Chapter 12

Auto

Time was on my side. At least that was what the song I was humming told me as I calmly scaled the side of a house in East Atlanta. Too much had happened for me to ignore everything, and with the taking of Smiley, I was no longer going to sit back and be on defense. I tried as hard as I could not to tap back into that mentality of surviving by any means necessary. I figured, if I stayed off the drugs and the guns side of things, me and my family could do our due diligence without having to worry about retaliation from gangs, cartels, and other bullshit that came along with the gun and drug trade.

Stealing credit card information, cars, a little money here and there; wiping out bad credit history; wiping out identities wouldn't put my family in peril. I never wanted to lose another member of my family to the streets. Had, by happenstance, lost a friend of mine to a street king by the name of Damien Orlando. Kitty, our resident credit-card skimmer, had been killed in a drive-by that had nothing to do with her. And now Smiley was missing. Yet again, for something that had nothing to do with her.

I tried hard—only the gods knew how hard I tried—not to go into that place where I saw the hood as the jungle it was. But since motherfuckers wanted to test me and thought they could just come in my house, stick their hands in my refrigerator without asking, just straight disrespect me and mine, I had to become a predator. And at this point, that was fine by me.

The fact that the Vikings were posted up in Southeast Atlanta, in the Lakewood area, told me they had some serious backing. No way could their pale faces, blond hair, and blue eyes survive in an area ranked number nine on the list of worst neighborhoods in America unless word had been put out that they were not to be touched. Good thing I didn't give a fuck about that, though.

I adjusted the backpack I had on my back and hopped down from the wall. Signaled to Lelo and Stitch, who were casually sitting in a delivery car nearby, that I spotted six men in the house. Two were watching *SportsCenter* in the messy living room. Two were in the kitchen, taking shots from the big bottle of tequila sitting on the old, worn round table. One had made his way to the bathroom, and another was posted up by a window, with a MAC-11 on his lap.

Reagan sashayed down the street in six-inch stilettos. Her hair fell down her back in twelve neatly done cornrows. Lip gloss called attention to her lips. The earrings she had on looked as if they were covering the whole lobes—they was really her earpiece so she could communicate what was going on without having to say much. Her beautiful brown skin glowed in the sun. It was rare that we got to see Reagan in something that showcased her femininity, so the ass-short skirt and the black mesh halter top showing off her thirty-six Ds gave me pause for a minute. Hell, they even gave Lelo and Stitch pause. While they may have been a couple, they weren't blind. And since they both shared the same baby mama, they weren't ignorant to the wiles of a woman, either.

"Damn," Lelo remarked.

We all had on earpieces and could easily hear what the others were saying and doing.

"When Reagan get all that ass and those tits?" Stitch wanted to know.

I chuckled. Couldn't lie and say that her ass and thighs weren't working everything male in me, but we had a job to do. Besides, she was the little sister, and we all had to remember that.

"Why don't all you niggas stay focused on the task at hand and not my ass," Reagan snapped. "Fucking pervs."

"Kinda hard not to pay attention when it's sitting out there like that, baby," I told her in a low tone so my voice wouldn't carry and give away my location.

Lelo chuckled. "And you know I'm an ass man. I like ass. Don't matter if it's male or female. If it's sitting pretty, I'm on it like stank on shit."

"Really, bruh?" Stitch said, cutting in. "You're going to go with that analogy while talking about ass?" he asked his lover.

Reagan cackled loudly. I wanted to laugh, but I had to keep my voice low.

"Shut up, man. Don't start with me today. I'm already pissed at you," Lelo responded.

"Pissed at *me*? For what now? You know, if I didn't know you had a dick, I'd swear you were female. Always nagging me about some shit," Stitch fussed.

"Because you always doing stupid shit, nigga. Like drinking all the fucking milk, so when I go to fix me and the kids some Cap'n Crunch, we can't eat the shit."

"I didn't drink the milk. Carmen did."

"When was Carmen at the house?" Lelo asked.

"Yesterday morning, fuck boy."

Lelo smacked his lips. "I told you about calling me that shit . . ."

"Oh Lord. Here we go," Reagan groaned.

I just shook my head and chuckled as I pulled out my black biker gloves. The fingers had been cut out. Thumbtacks had been pushed into the inside so that the pointy parts were sticking out on the back of the gloves.

"Hey," I snapped. "Desi and Lucy, chill out. We got action. Reagan is going in."

I watched as Reagan walked down the sidewalk, passed the window the one Viking had been guarding. For any man, to see Reagan strutting by was neck-breaking action. Didn't take long for the Viking to stick his head out the window.

"Where you going, baby?" he asked Reagan.

"Why? You offering to take me?" she replied in a voice coated with innuendo.

"I got something you can ride on to get there," the blond male told her.

She smiled wide, then licked her lips. "Yeah?"

He nodded and smiled like he knew something she didn't. Didn't take long for a few of the other males in the house to take notice of her. The two in the kitchen rushed around to see what all the fuss was about. Since the kitchen was separated from the living room by a swinging door, I snuck around the back way. I jiggled the doorknob and found that it was unlocked. I pushed the door open, then closed it quietly behind me. The front door opened and closed. I could hear Reagan talking as I quietly examined the items on the counter. Pictures of me and my crew were lying about, an indication they had been watching us.

Some of those photos were from weeks ago, and that puzzled me. Had they been watching us the whole time? Was the hit on us not as random as I had once thought?

"How much for all of us, baby?" I heard a gruff voice ask Reagan. He was already growling and groaning.

"Well, that depends, suga. What you boys trying to get into?" Reagan cooed.

"Well, you, of course, darling."

Laughter echoed around the living room.

"I need you to send one of them to the kitchen, Reagan," I told her. "Need to get the numbers down. You keep an eye on the one you think would be easiest to make talk."

"As you wish," she answered, but she did it in a way that made the men think she was talking to them. "Somebody get me a drink and put some music on. I'ma show you white boys how we do it in the A. Anybody ever tell you, you look like Eric Northman from *True Blood*?"

The chorus of "Round of Applause" started to beat through the house. I heard Reagan ask what they knew about that. They eagerly spoke up, each one trying to outbrag the others about being down.

"All the time," one said as he pushed the door open to the kitchen.

He was so busy looking over his shoulder at Reagan that he didn't see me standing behind the door. Once he closed it, I swept his legs out from under him. His forehead hit the kitchen table hard, knocking him backward. His eyes widened when he saw me. The recognition in them let me know he had been watching us long enough for him to know who I was by my face alone.

He went for the gun in his waistband. I grabbed his wrist and twisted it. Sent my fist flying into his face, drawing blood instantly because of the thumbtacks on the back of my glove. I grabbed the black hunting knife from the back of my waist and shoved it into his neck. Sliced him from ear to ear.

"I got one down," I told my team. "Lelo, you ready to go? Be careful, though, and try to hide your face as much as possible. These mofos got surveillance photos of us."

"I'm on it, boss," I heard him say.

"Stitch, cover him."

"You already know I got him covered," Stitch told me.

While I waited for them to make their move, I looked at the dead man on the floor and grunted when I saw he really did look like ole boy from *True Blood*. Waka Flocka blasted in my ear. Reagan was laughing and inviting men to touch her nipple piercings. I pushed the door open to the kitchen only enough to get an eye view of what was going on. She had the biggest one on the couch and was straddling his lap, with her top off. The skirt she had on was up around her waist, and her perfectly rounded brown ass was on display. Two of the men were kissing it, while two more looked on in eager anticipation.

There was a loud knock on the door, which jarred them out of the lust-induced trance Reagan had them in.

The big one Reagan had been sitting on tossed her to the side as they all grabbed guns. He jerked his head toward the door, silently telling another dude to answer it. The one who raced to the door had a scar on his face; it looked like someone had branded him.

He snatched the door open, gun aimed.

"Whoa, man," Lelo said. "Y'all ordered pizza, right?" he asked, with a Domino's carrying case in one hand and a receipt in the other hand, which was up in the air.

In the movies this scheme normally worked. But since this wasn't a movie, we really had had to intercept a call they'd put in for pizza. Since I didn't want to risk one of my people being killed by these trigger-happy motherfuckers, I thought that would be the best thing to do.

Lelo nodded at me from the door. He was playing his part so well, one would think he was actually a Domino's delivery guy. He had on the khaki pants, a Domino's uniform shirt, and all. Red and blue cap was pulled down, shielding the top half of his face. Scarface snatched the pizza from his hands, then threw money at him.

Lelo frowned. "Damn, homeboy. It ain't gotta be all that," he said as he kneeled to pick up the money.

"Shut up and get the fuck out of here, fucking spic," Scarface said to Lelo.

"Yeah, whatever," Lelo said as he shook his head. He counted the money, then sarcastically retorted, "Thanks for the tip." Lelo turned to walk away, then turned back around. "Oh yeah, you forgot something."

Before Scarface could say anything, Stitch came around the corner with two Desert Eagle .50 caliber pistols aimed at the man's face.

"Who the spic now?" Stitch asked Scarface. The man tried to aim his gun but thought about it. "Nah, homeboy. I wouldn't do that if I was you. Back on up."

The rest of the men in the room looked on in silence. Lelo walked in behind Stitch, slammed the door behind him, and then kicked the radio over. Waka's voice croaked out as Lelo snatched up the MAC-11 that had been left on the coffee table.

"I told you we shouldn't have holed up in the hood," Scarface said to the big man.

He spat out the word *hood* as if it were something foul he needed to get off his tongue. They'd been so busy trying to get in Reagan's goods, they hadn't even noticed their man hadn't come back from the kitchen yet.

"Now, this can go good or bad. It all depends on you," Lelo explained.

Stitch still had his gun aimed at Scarface. There was a scowl on Stitch's face that said he was anxious to take the man out. More than likely it was because he'd insulted Lelo.

"Not nice to call a man's lover a racist epithet, you piece of shit," Stitch said coolly.

One of the men made the mistake of moving. Stitch moved his right arm underneath the left one and blew a hole in the man's chest. Another of Reagan's ass kissers tried the same thing and met the same fate. Reagan jumped over the couch like she was on some *Mortal Kombat* shit. Sent a flying kick into the sternum of one dude—who was smaller and had been quiet in the corner—when he tried to tackle Stitch.

I moved from the kitchen just as they realized what was going on.

Big man snarled at Reagan. "You set us up, bitch."

She sent her heel into his face. "I'm nobody's bitch, fat boy."

I grabbed the smaller one, the one Reagan had kicked in the sternum. Scarface's eyes widened when he saw me do this. I shoved the man over to the couch, where the big man was.

"Now that we have your attention, we need to have a conversation. Now, this is going to go one of two ways. You're going to talk, or we're going to kill you," I informed them. "It's that simple."

"Fuck you. I'm not telling you shit," Scarface spat.

"Shoot him," I ordered Stitch.

Stitch gave a crooked smile. "Gladly."

It was safe to say the bullet to the heart at close range killed the man, but I guessed Stitch wanted to make sure by adding a bullet to his head.

"Anybody else not talking?" I asked the two who were left.

The big man grunted and then chuckled before saying, "You have no idea, no fucking idea, who you're toying with, man."

"No? Why don't you tell me," I said to him.

I had Lelo and Reagan tie both men down; then I grabbed a chair from the kitchen. I placed it in front of them and just stared for a moment.

"All I want to know is, Who sent you after us?" I finally said. "We know Chandler gave you our routes and delivery times, but y'all got photos of us from weeks ago, almost eight weeks back, because I remember what I was doing on the day of some of the photos. Who sent you?"

The big one spoke up first. "You may as well kill us, man. The people who put you in our sights are going to kill us, anyway. So, do it and get it over with."

I shrugged, then signaled to Stitch to give the man what he wanted. A kill shot to the heart ended that discussion. Reagan nodded at the small dude. Standing at least six feet tall, he was the runt of the group. I grabbed my knife and cut the shirt away from the man's body. I wasn't in the mood to give him the option to choose death. While he looked around with a cocky disposition, I slammed the hunting knife down in his jean-clad thigh. He yelled so loudly that his voice gave out at the end, and all he could do was whimper. Before he could come down from the high induced by that pain, I put my fist into his jaw. For good measure, I ground it there, just to hear him squeal. The thumbtacks were making a bloody mess of his face.

"Arrrgh! Fuck, man!" he squealed.

I pulled out my other hunting knife, the one that was strapped to my ankle, and slammed it into his other thigh. By now, he was sweating. Tears had rolled from his eyes, and piss had soaked the center of his jeans. Once that was done, I pulled out "the kit," as Code called it, from the backpack I had. I didn't know exactly what she had in the white bag, but I was sure it wouldn't be to the Scandy's liking.

I rolled my shoulders, then clapped once. "Since I'm sure you don't want to talk to us, I'm just going to use you as bait, you feel me?" I asked, taunting the man, whose eyes had gotten wide as saucers.

"Damn, Auto. You on some other shit," Reagan said.

I looked up at her, expecting to see a frown. Instead, she was smiling, as if she had just won the lotto.

"Been wondering when you was gone go ham on these niggas for real," Lelo quipped.

"If I were you, man, I'd start talking. I seen what's in that bag, and I assure you, you don't want it," Stitch gibed as he glared at the man.

I pulled a blowtorch and a jar of Blue Magic hair grease from the kit. One could only guess what Code did with this shit. I unscrewed the top on the Blue Magic. Dipped my hand in the jar, stood, then spread the grease all over the man's chest. Then I lit the blowtorch, took a seat in front of him.

"Fucking aye, man," he sobbed. "Wh-what you doing?"

"About to see what burning flesh smells like," I told him.

His eyes widened again, but it didn't bother me in the least. When the fire hit the grease on his chest, it sounded like his skin was sizzling, then popping. The sound reminded me of when fries hit hot oil. By the time I was done, we had Mouse's personal cell number, the place where he was holed up, and a lead on who had really paid Chandler to sell us out.

***

Two hours and a phone call from Code later, I knew where Smiley was and had found out we had placed ourselves into another little situation, which annoyed the fuck out of me.

Reagan pulled up, and from my spot in the back seat, I beheld a scene that looked something like a standoff at the O.K. Corral. Code had gotten Smiley back, but she also had the man I'd come to know as Boots, the bullet manufacturer, in her sights. Reagan swerved our ride to a stop. Lelo and Stitch hopped out before she even put the car in park. Although Code was older than all of us, we protected her like the sister she was. I think Lelo and Stitch babied her a little too much, but it was their thing. Dressed in fresh baby blue jumpers that boasted the name of our auto shop, they rushed up to flank her. Reagan hopped out next, then did the same.

Seymore and the rest of the team were in a truck behind me. Keeping a lookout on the road. Ready to go, if need be. And me? I'd tapped into that part of myself that I hadn't wanted to. I hadn't wanted to wake up the sleeping monster inside of me. But as always with the ways of the hood, it was a dog-eat-thug world. You just had to decide if you were going to be the dog or the thug. I personally wanted to be neither, but if you pushed me, I could become both. A hybrid of sorts.

Dressed in a black suit, with a white, collarless shirt underneath the black blazer and a bloodred rose in the breast pocket, I looked like I'd just stepped out of a movie about triad crime syndicates. I stepped calmly from the back of the car. I walked over to where Code was. She was dressed in all white. The white-on-white Ford Mustang she had driven here had been parked haphazardly. I had my left hand clasping my right wrist loosely as my gun rested against my thigh. I took in the tense standoff. Saw that while Smiley might be a little shaken, judging by the Glock in her hand, she had no problem with getting down. The phone call I'd gotten from Code had rattled me. You could turn only so many cheeks before being taken out altogether. And I had no intentions of being taken out.

"Smiley, you okay?" I asked her. "They hurt you?"

I saw the faint bruising around her wrists and neck. The thought of her being harmed for something she had nothing to do with made me roll my shoulders to release some tension there.

"I'm okay, but there is some freaky shit going on," she spat quickly. "He said you stole some bullets from him, and they got kids in the back of that truck."

I looked over at Code, and she nodded once. There was a look on her face I couldn't read. Men whom I didn't recognize flanked her, but that was Code. I figured she'd called in help from the old man. That was something I'd have to question at another time. I looked over at the nigga in the cowboy boots and frowned.

"I'd like to know why you felt you had the right to come into my home and take a member of my family," I said to him.

There was a look of disdain on his face as he spoke. "When I'm wrong, I have no problem admitting my wrong action, but there is some shit going on here that doesn't make sense to me."

I shrugged. "None of this shit makes sense to me, so I figure we can take a few minutes to try to square shit away to both of our likings before we leave a trail of bodies and a truckful of fucking kids." I frowned hard and asked out of curiousity, "Nigga, why do you have a truck full of kids?"

I regarded the man with caution. There was once a time when the hood was shaken because of all the kids, especially young girls, who had gone missing. If the nigga in front of me was on some "selling kids" shit, I would kill him myself and not care about the consequences.

"You have the same questions I have. Tell your people to lower their guns," he said, then scowled at Code. "For real this time, so we can talk. And my name is Boots, not nigga. Address me as such."

Judging by the drawl in his voice, I knew he was the one I had talked to right after I spoke with Chandler on the phone. I told Code to lower her guns. She told her men to do the same. I watched as Boots kept his end of the bargain. He lowered his gun, and then his people did the same, although begrudgingly.

"Okay, Boots. Let's start with the Scandinavians. You send them after my shit?" I said.

Boots chuckled. "Homeboy, I don't even know you. Why would I send them after what? Some cars? I specialize in weaponry, not auto parts."

"That's good and all, but they took not one, not two, but three of my shipments. You mean to tell me this is random? Don't piss on me and tell me it's raining, man."

"You want to talk about random? Let's talk about why your girl over there is flanked by men from my client's cartel?"

I cast a glance in Code's direction. We both knew that it was the old man who'd made a deal with Boots. We'd known that the moment she laid eyes on the bullets. I didn't have to tell him that, though.

"That's not important to me right now," I said. "I would like my shipment back."

"That's the thing, my man. I don't have your shit. I don't know where your shit is, but I do know you have my shit, and I want it back."

It was my turn to chuckle. I shook my head before answering, "Now, why would I give you back your merchandise—if I had it—without a return on my investment?"

"Why we doing all this talking, Boots?" one of his men asked him.

Homeboy looked like he was straight out of the Zulu Nation. Tall, with Dove chocolate skin. He was so loaded with muscles, I bet even his personality was on steroids.

"Because somebody is playing us toward the middle, and until we figure out who's pulling our strings, what the fuck are we fighting for? We're going to kill each other and, in the end, still not have our shit," Boots barked at him.

Clearly, the man was just as annoyed as I was, and I was really in no mood myself to "talk" the shit out. But since we were at an impasse, it was all we could do.

Boots looked back at me and kept going. "Not only am I a businessman, Auto, but I'm a business too, man. Do you get me? I put blood, sweat, and tears into my merchandise. You're a businessman yourself, so you know how I must be feeling right now."

I gave a slight head nod. "I do."

"Then you have to know I'm not bullshitting you, right? I got a truck full of kidnapped kids and drugs. This ain't my business. I don't do this kind of shit here. Now, both of us, as of this moment, have a common enemy, the Scandinavians. Now we need to figure out who's behind the scenes, giving them orders. My shit was supposed to be packaged and shipped through legal means. How you got involved is anybody's guess, but here we are. And quiet as kept, judging by the way your girl is looking, I'm going to guess that she knows a little more than she's letting on."

"You can kiss my ass," Code blurted out.

"If you survive this, maybe we can arrange that. Until then, start talking." Boots nodded at one of the dudes behind Code who had a scar running from ear to ear on his neck. "Homeboy was with the man I was supposed to deliver those bullets to. I find that eerily coincidental. Especially since your boss's merchandise is missing, and now you have mine," he told Code.

"I paid a little visit to our Scandy friends," I interjected. "Now, you had a deal with their leader, Mouse, right?"

Boots nodded.

I continued. "Well, seems like Mouse had a little deal with somebody else. All this time we thought it was Chandler who had betrayed us on his own. However, someone pulled his strings, right along with Mouse's. So, looks like we both got played, my man."

"So, Mouse played me?"

"Pretty much. Looks like he made a deal to sell your bullets to somebody else. Now you're after me, and whoever you made a deal with to buy your merchandise is going to be after you for not being a man of your word."

"You're basically just a casualty of this thing, then, a pawn?" Boots asked.

"To them, me and my team are the weakest link."

"But you proved to be more."

I smiled coolly. "And now we're here."

Seymore yelled in my earpiece, drowning out whatever Boots said next. "Got about ten black Hummers racing up the back way from Fulton Industrial. Dunkin and Jackknife can hold them off only for so long."

Judging by the urgency in Seymore's voice, it was safe to say the people in those Hummers weren't our friends. All I could think about were the kids in the back of that truck.

I looked at Boots. "You got another way outta here?"

I could tell by the way his eyes went to the kids that he, too, knew if we let those Hummers get any closer, we would have a problem.

He nodded. "Shredder, you and Dinzo get this truck out of here. Take the kids as far away from here as you can. Then call our contact at the Atlanta PD to see if we can get some help in rectifying this problem on the low." He turned back to me with a stern look on his face. "Meanwhile, it looks like you and I need to put our heads together to get this heat off our backs."

I agreed with him. We agreed on another location at which to meet; then we all got ready to head out. I was truly tired and didn't feel like getting into another fight of any kind. I glanced around at my crew. Noticed Code was acting strange.

I asked her, "You okay?"

"Yeah," she answered a little too quickly.

"You sure?"

"Yes, Auto, I'm sure."

I studied Code hard. Had known her long enough to know when she was lying or not being all the way one hundred with me. The fact that she averted her eyes from mine, then glanced around before meeting my eyes again told me she was lying to me.

Code said, "Let me take Smiley, to get her cleaned up."

I shook my head. "Nah. She's coming with me. I need to make sure she's safe. I'll call you later, and we'll go from there."

Chapter 13

Smiley

Standing between a rock and a hard place, I glanced at the guy who'd held me as collateral and then back at Auto. Getting kidnapped had been a fucked-up deal for me. Yet it hadn't been as bad as I thought it was going to be, because Boots's main agenda hadn't seemed to be about hurting me. I had soaked up a lot of information while I was with his team. Had made sure to remember every little thing he had in his office, especially the pictures he had on his desk.

Dude was weird to me in a crazy but cool kind of way. He had that kind of personality that reminded me of an old dude, but at the same time, he had that young dude quality to him too. His style of dress was important to him. He'd even gotten his face clean shaven and his hair lined when he was holding me hostage. Had talked to me about the news, and to Shango about sports and hip-hop. He reminded me of an old-school gangster. I just wondered if he'd be able to live up to that role. With how niggas were gunning for him, his life count was ticking away every day.

A flash of light came from the truck and drew my attention away from Boots and Auto. The flash was followed by a sharp chemical odor, something akin to bleach and ammonia, which oversaturated the air. I could see Shredder and Oya, the pretty, tall chick with the long, dark, crinkled hair, working the truck. Oya had stripped off her top, then had put it on one of the girls. I watched her take strips of clear plastic material from Shredder and put them in a case while handing him spray-type cans.

"Lelo, Stitch, go help them out. Make this go quicker," I heard Auto say in a low voice.

Boots shifted his weight from one foot to the other. He put his weapons away, then brushed off his arms.

He spoke to Auto. "Now, for our arrangement, how will we do this?"

Code moved forward, cutting off Auto before he could even begin. "I'm going with you. That's how we are going to do this. We want back what you took, and, frankly, I don't trust you, *culo*. So I'm keeping my eyes on you. Fair exchange."

I got ready to open my mouth to protest, but Boots laughed, then gave a curt nod. "Yeah, no doubt it's no robbery. I'll be gamed for that if your boss is gamed."

Auto's hand snaked around my arm, then pulled me back sharply. "If you harm her . . ."

"Yo! Look, again, I'm not that type of guy. Respect is given even when it's not earned from me. She'll be safe, and it'll be like she's one of my crew. Unless she acts a fool . . . By the way, Smiley, if you ever need a team to call your own, call me. I like your skills, Mama, especially those tech skills. If we survive, I could use you with something," Boots said with smooth authority.

He turned his back to us. The *click-clack* of his black, scratch-free boots as he moved was like a song. Boots slid a hand in his pocket, pulled out a toothpick, and stuck it in his mouth. Then he turned back around and addressed Auto. "Once we all are settled, your partner . . . Code? She can hit you with a call to get this shit handled. That sound good to you, friend?"

There was a quiet anger going on behind Auto's eyes while he watched Boots. Judging by how he and Code had spoken to each other in hushed tones just minutes before, I knew that they had some deep connection. It worried me for a second, because I thought Auto was going to pop off. But I was shocked when the color of his eyes changed, as if he was adapting to the situation, and he gave a slick smile.

"Code can handle herself. We'll speak in due time, my brotha," Auto said in return.

"Just to be clear here, what I did was done to ensure a response from you," Boots told Auto. "There's no love lost here. I could be a good friend, because we are dealing with the same shit, but I can also be a better enemy if you turn on me. I figure, in time, we can work on that ally thing—if this works out first."

The toothpick in Boots's mouth wobbled back and forth, only to pause in its dance when he gave a megawatt smile. "Besides, I have a feeling that you and your crew can also be good friends but a formidable enemy as well, and I'd rather have a crew like that on my side than start a war over some manipulation going on. Makes good business sense, yeah?"

Something like a smile played against Auto's light almond skin. He gave a slight chuckle, then nodded. "To me, the thing that is worse than death is betrayal. You see, I can conceive of death, but I cannot conceive of betrayal."

Boots walked closer to Auto and extended his hand. "Let's be diplomatic in what we do," he said. Then he thought for a moment. "I'm not your enemy," Boots added for good measure.

I saw Auto look down at Boots's hand before taking it in a firm grasp and giving it a shake. "It is what it's going to be for now. I'm down with this peace for what it is for now. We have bigger fish to gut and fry, so we'll have this convo later. I hear the trucks coming. Let's get our people moving faster with that cleaning, then burn that bitch while heading our separate ways."

Auto gave a cool smile. Walked off with his hands in his pockets, but then he paused and turned back around. He tilted his head, as if in thought, and said, "Code . . . don't kill this dude before we all can talk about our plan."

Code rolled her eyes, crossed her arms, and frowned, then said something in Spanish. I noticed both Auto and Boots shaking their heads. Boots crossed his arms over his broad chest. I understood only a little of what she'd said; she'd commented that you had to thank a man for taking something that was already his. The rest was lost in translation.

When Code strolled my way with her head held high, she gave me a hug. The way she controlled the show had me chuckling at the power she was throwing. Her arms hugged me tightly, and then she spoke over my shoulder, and in my mind, I knew she was giving both dudes a defiant, heated gaze. "If this *culo* treats me right,

we'll have some peace . . . for now. Let's ride out.
Take care of yourself, *chica*. I know you can."

I felt the corners of my lips tilt up into a smile;
then I gave a nod. "Ask for some of Alize's peach
cobbler. It was dope."

I heard Boots grumble to Auto, "Is she always
like that?"

"Like what?" Auto asked.

"Crazy and bossy as fuck?" he asked while
taking his hat off, then running a hand over his
deep waves.

Auto sucked his teeth and blew out wind.
"That's her being nice. You saw her pissed off,
slightly. So yeah, maybe. Have fun . . . friend."

"Shit . . . Might be the type of venom in that
bite that I like," I heard Boots mutter while Auto
guided me to his ride.

I swore Boots was watching the way Code's
ass seemed to sway to its own rhythm while she
walked. He moved past her to open a back door
to the Explorer, with a scowl on his face. Once
she was inside the vehicle, he turned to give
orders to his team while putting his hat back on.

"Did he touch you?" Auto asked, cutting through
my thoughts.

Hopping in his ride, I shook my head no. While
putting my seat belt on, I said, "Seriously, he
didn't."

Auto closed my car door. Moved around his car with purpose. Then both teams divided the kids up among the cars. They all waited on Boots and Auto to head out. Once Auto got behind the wheel of his car, he stuck his hand out, gave a signal, and then Boots turned his ride and pointed for us to go in the opposite direction of the cars coming our way.

"Did any of the others touch you? Physically? Sexually?" he asked.

I noticed a slight icy chill to his tone, which caused the hairs on my arms to rise up. I shifted in my seat and looked him over, wondering what had him dressing as he was. He had a serious scowl going on, as if he was at war with his thoughts. His hands clutched the steering wheel, and it made me very anxious all of a sudden. I didn't want him to worry about me or try to turn around and start shooting.

"No . . . well, yeah, but it wasn't like anything crazy. I was fighting him, and he was holding me back. What got me bruised was the handcuffs . . . and when Shango had to hold me down by my neck. I was kicking him . . . so he, like, held me down, that's all."

"Don't lie to me," he said, turning slightly to watch me while he drove.

"I'm not. I promise. No bullshit went down. I was scared. They were on one with scaring me. Thought he was going to kill me, but, I mean, it was weird. He treated me good, fed me, got me these clothes . . . stuff like that. I mean it. Why do you look like you're ready to go off? I mean, I know why, but it's like there's something more there," I said, concerned.

"Nothing, Smiley. I'll trust your word. It's good to have you back. I'm going to take you to my place so you can rest your head and we can start planning what to do next. You sure he's worth trusting on this level?" Auto replied, looking me over and giving me a smile that his eyes didn't reflect.

There was no hesitation in me when I answered. Anytime I felt like I couldn't trust someone, I felt a knot in my stomach and an ache in my head. This time, there was nothing, and I gave a quick nod and answered, "I'm sure. He was mainly wanting his bullets back. That was all he wanted. Then everything flipped." Pausing, I kept trying to read Auto's face but got nothing. "Um, you're freaking me out, Auto."

"I understand that . . . and it's nothing." Auto tapped his Bluetooth speaker in his car, then began to elaborate while shifting gears. "I'm not feeling him coming after you and trying to offer business with you, but it is what it is." He paused, then addressed Seymore over the Bluetooth. "Hey, Seymore, ride out! Thank you for stalling them. Y'all good?"

I was a nosy chick. I was not about to just sit there and not find out what was really going on. So I was going to ask as soon as he got done talking.

"Yo, we got these mofos trying to juke us up, but we good," Seymore said as I heard shooting going off.

"Get out of there," Auto ordered.

"Will do," Seymore shouted, his voice breaking up from what sounded like his car shaking.

Auto shifted gears, glanced into the rearview mirror, then added more juice to the gas. "Good. Make sure they don't follow. You know the deal. We're going off grid. Go to your zone, and I'll connect later."

Only the sound of Seymore driving, then a loud bang was our answer. Auto ducked his head as he glanced behind him.

"Oh shit! Did y'all just make some shit explode?" Auto said to Seymore.

I quickly turned in my seat to see a plume of smoke fill the air behind us. "Damn . . . They weren't playing."

Auto drove faster, merged onto the expressway as I gawked at what was behind us.

"We can neither confirm nor deny," Seymore
said, then chuckled. "How's the new girl? You
get her back? Code chilling?"

I smiled, appreciating that he had asked about
me.

"Code is good. She brought some of her family
as backup. She went as collateral and to get our
computers back. As for Smiley, all seems to be
well. I'll hit you up soon, man," Auto said, then
turned off his cell.

"Welcome to the family, Smiley. Fuck Boots's
proposition. You're an Eraserhead now," Auto
said with authority and pride in his voice while
he gave me a slight smile.

My shoulders slumped a little from exhaustion, and I gave a chuckle.

Auto drove us to his place hidden in a cool-ass
warehouse away from the trap but close enough
to the city to get around quickly. I wanted to go
home, but from what Auto had said, it was just
safer this way.

"You could have taken me home. I just need to
get some clothes," I said as we got out of his ride.
I just wanted to see if he'd be willing to take me
home.

"Nah . . . It's better that you're with me." Light
washed over us both as he walked toward the

building. "They won't look for me or you where we are. Besides, I want your home to be a safe spot for you, and I do not want to have trouble come your way. I'll send someone over there to get you your stuff. In the meantime, you can chill in Code's room here. You'll know it when you see it once we get inside. You can put on some of her stuff. She won't mind."

"Okay, I guess . . . ," I said, giving up.

Auto unlocked a steel door, and then I slowly walked into his place. He followed me, then closed the door behind us. I looked down at the floor in the foyer, and under my feet was something I had seen only on HGTV when I used to watch it with my mom in the hospital: bamboo flooring. It covered the foyer floor and the long set of steps that led to an open den. In this room there was fly modern-style furniture. A large cream-colored L-shaped couch faced an expansive glass panel, and this window provided a view of everything. However, from the outside, you couldn't tell if the structure had any windows at all, and so you could see inside, so how this glass panel was designed was too cool. He also had plush chairs for seating in the den, and a dark mahogany table sat in the center of the room. Behind the seats on the left side of the table was a granite-tiled fireplace. A large abstract painting hung above it.

A large mahogany bookcase stood behind the couch and served as an additional wall. I moved around it and saw Auto kick his shoes off, then go left. Once I looked that way, I saw a huge chef's kitchen that had me dropping my mouth. Shit was like a gold mine. Everything in this place was, actually. I could lift quite a bit and make some serious street dough off it. However, I wasn't going to do anything like that, but I couldn't help the thought.

Uncertainty had me biting my lower lip and tapping my nails against the sides of my legs. I wanted to sit down, since I was tired, but given how clean and nice his place was, I didn't want to mess it up in any way.

"Hey, today was a crazy day. Did you see them crazy-ass boots dude had on? They were cool, but let me tell you a secret. He always has them shits on. Different pair every day," I said, laughing, as I tried to find somewhere to sit that I wouldn't dirty. I ultimately opted for a simple ottoman by the fireplace.

"You're wild, Smiley, for real. I said you're a fit on our team, but trust me, in the beginning I wasn't sure. I saw how you were fighting in jail. Was thinking that maybe I chose wrong."

"Wait now, dude. I was fighting like *The Hunger Games* whateva! Let you get locked up and watch how fast you'd be scrapping to keep your ass safe," I said in all seriousness, but I found myself laughing with him.

Auto turned on his feet to watch me for a moment. I noticed his gaze lingering on me for a second before he turned his back to me and began unbuttoning his shirt. "I've been locked up before, and . . . you're right, Mama."

"Yeah?" I asked just to ask, because considering his line of work, I wasn't shocked.

He paused in the middle of his crib, then crossed his arms over his chest. "Yeah. Part of the hood, right?"

"Yeah, right it is," I muttered, then yawned. "Thank you for bringing me here. It's cool that you feel I'm part of the team."

"You are. I mean that. Like what you do . . . the tech skills. Shit coming up with wild-ass apps," he said with a smile on his face. "Like there's fucking potential in you. I just hope that you stay and let us see how you grow." He paused for a moment. "Let me show you Code's room, Mama, so you can get cleaned up and go to sleep," he added, then looked me over, humor visible in his exhausted eyes.

In that quick moment, I felt a big shift between us. Respect and trust had just been given to me, and I appreciated it. I got up and followed him

down a hallway. Halfway down, he pointed to
Code's room. I nodded.

My life had changed drastically, but it was
cool to be held down, I thought as I walked
into Code's room. Like Auto had said, I was an
Eraserhead now. I guessed that it was time to
act like it.

Chapter 14

Code

"I'm going to just go ahead and hypothesize that it's safe to say by now you know that I'm not stupid," he started off. "I need to know why the man who was protecting my client is also a part of your goon squad."

We had been driving for about thirty minutes. I could only assume that we were headed back to his place of residence. The woman he'd called Oya was driving the truck we were in, and of course, I had had to bring along Freddie as part of the deal I'd made with him. As we cruised down I-20 and hopped onto I-75, the traffic was moving at a steady pace. I regarded the man they called Boots with caution, as I didn't trust him. I must say I was relieved to see that Smiley had come to no harm.

We'd had to follow Boots for a few days, longer than expected, in order to find out where he'd taken Smiley. It hadn't been back to Copper Hills. He'd moved like he was in a hurry, and while he had still taken precautions to cover his ass, I'd been doing this criminal shit for way too long not to know how to tail someone without them knowing it. The man was smart. He'd covered his tracks well, until today.

However, what I hadn't expected to see was a truckful of children and drugs. My heart was beating. Set to jump out of my chest, because I didn't want to believe the old man had a hand in it. By the way Freddie kept glancing at me, it was clear he was thinking the same thing as I was.

I didn't want to give in to that coiling in my stomach that was telling me Papa was pulling a double cross. That would mean too many things. Things that I didn't want to have to ask about. Things that would open another can of worms. For as long as I'd been old enough to understand the inner and outer workings of my *familia*'s crime syndicate, the one thing I had never wanted any part in was the trafficking of humans. I'd shipped drugs and guns. I'd even tortured a few men in the name of Papa as he looked on. But the fight between him and me had always centered around the trafficking of children and women.

I sighed and shook my head as my stomach started to free-fall. If Papa had been able to intercept Boots's truck like that—I sighed as the thought ate away at me—that meant that he'd been working behind the scenes all along. Admitting that would mean I would have to admit that he had something to do with the Eraserheads' missing cars as well.

Boots took off the gray ten-gallon hat that made him look like a black cowboy. His impatient movement brought me back to the matter he'd asked me about. He crossed his right leg over his left thigh, making his legs look like the number four, then folded his arms across his chest. I sat to his right as Oya whipped in and out of lanes. Shorty was driving like NASCAR was in her blood.

"Since you're so smart, maybe you can figure that out on your own," I responded to him.

"You're related to my client? If so, how? I need to know these things if I'm going to be doing business with you and your crew."

I asked, "What does one have to do with the other?"

"I just need to know who I'm dealing with in all aspects."

"Let's just say the man who's your client is also a client of mine."

Boots grunted, then glanced out the window before looking back at me. I could tell by the way his eyes watched me that he wanted to keep interrogating me, but something stopped him. His boots stood out to me. Made me remember a story Papa had told me about a man and his boots. I remembered that story because it was connected to all the other stories the old man would tell me about a war that had left a lot of people dead in its wake. I'd never seen a black man in cowboy boots in person, and with a cowboy hat to match. Still, I had to admit that Boots wore the look well. Not to mention that his Texas accent worked me anytime he spoke. It made me feel like ice was creeping up my spine, only to be chased by a fiery heat that made me take notice of the man in ways I shouldn't.

Shit, I needed to stay focused on the task of killing those who were trying to kill me and my crew. I didn't need to be thinking about the spicy, musky smell emanating from a potential threat if things went in a different direction. Boots was everything the woman who had birthed me had warned me to stay away from. Men like Boots were good for only one thing, I thought, my mother's words echoing in my mind. They were good only for fucking and breeding. Nothing more.

My eyes took in the bulge in his pants. I chuckled.

"What's funny?" he wanted to know.

"Nothing. Nothing at all."

I sighed, folded my arms, and turned my attention to the passing exits and billboards. We passed the JCPenney Outlet, the farmers' market, the automobile auction house, and more before we got to exit 235, where we left the highway. Took a right onto Upper Riverdale Road. Made a right by Southern Regional Medical Center onto Garden Walk Boulevard. Passed a firehouse, then Riverdale Elementary and Drew High School. Kept going until we made it to Copper Hills Apartment Homes.

If you had ever seen the hood, Copper Hills Apartments on Garden Walk was it. The Dumpsters looked like they hadn't been emptied in over a month. Trash littered the parking lot. Dirty little kids ran about, making as much noise as possible. Men, and boys pretending to be men, walked around with their pants hanging off their dirty asses. Women, and girls wanting to be women, strolled about in clothing that made them look like they should have been down on Metropolitan.

Loud music banged from car stereo systems. You could smell someone had a barbecue grill going. If you paid close enough attention, you could see the ever so subtle drug deal going down. If you looked even closer, you could see the old man paying the fifteen-year-old for pussy as they walked into one of the abandoned apartment buildings. It was when Smiley and I had done our stakeouts to find information about the man staring at me now that I had got to hear the whispers about the nigga who lived in building fifty-five. No one else lived in that building. All four apartments in that section belonged to him. Nobody liked him, but nobody would step to him about their disdain for him, either.

I could see now that how he ran things was all a front. He had to keep up a certain appearance. Had to make people respect him enough to fear him all at the same time. As we turned into the complex, I could see some people rushing back inside their apartments, the looks on their faces saying they'd been doing things they shouldn't have been.

Once Oya parked the truck, Freddie hopped out. He'd been trying to make conversation with her the whole time. She'd been giving him the short end of the stick, though. She would say only enough to keep him guessing. I had to laugh at the effort Freddie was putting in. He was used to women bowing at his feet. He'd never had to work for a woman's attention a day in his life. I had serious doubts that he would get far with the regal beauty.

Freddie opened my car door for me as Oya did the same for Boots.

"What can I say to get her to give me more than two words?" Freddie asked me in a whisper as he closed the door behind me. "I've tried talking about everything, from guns to sports. She won't say too much shit to me."

"Don't try too hard, *niño*. The best way to attract bees is to leave a flower for them to pollinate. Give her a reason to talk to you, *sí*?"

He only nodded as we walked up to building fifty-five. Boots pushed the door to the building open. He and Freddie allowed me and Oya to pass through first. We went by the first two apartments on the left and the right—C and D—and headed up the five money-green carpeted stairs to the next two apartments. Oya went through door A, then came back out to open door B. Once I saw that Oya would be in the apartment across the hall from us, I told Freddie to go with her.

"You sure?" he asked me as he eyed Boots.

"Yeah. You know I can handle my own."

"If something happens to you, Papa will have my head."

"Freddie, who am I?"

"She who fought in white clothes while riding upon a white horse, with divine inspiration to guide the way."

I nodded. "Exactly. Now go. I've got business to handle."

Once Boots and I got inside the apartment, I just stood there for a second. Didn't know what I'd been expecting, but it wasn't the mundane scenery before me. There was one mocha-hued oversize sofa. A sixty-inch flat-screen smart TV had been mounted on the wall. The carpet wasn't clean, but it wasn't dirty. It was nothing that a run-over with the vacuum wouldn't fix. An empty Chinese container was on the round glass end table, along with a Corona that was half full. Roaches—smoked blunt tips—laced an ashtray. The breakfast bar had little black chef statues sitting about.

Someone named Alize had left a message on the small menu chalkboard for Shango to kiss her entire black ass. Another message, this one from Oya, told Shango to go fuck himself. I quirked a brow. The place may not have been as clean as I was used to things being when I dealt with the old man and his OCD, but oddly enough, it smelled like bleach and Pine-Sol.

Boots tossed his hat on the coatrack, then started to unbutton his shirt.

"Take a seat," he told me.

"Nah. Where are my computers first?" I said.

He tossed his shirt on the coatrack with his hat, then glanced over his shoulder at me. Now, I was a lot of things, but blind wasn't one of them. Boots was a man's man. He had a laid-back personality that reminded me of André 3000, but his build said he would have sold for top dollar on the slave auction block. The long beard and waves on his head set him apart from most of the dudes walking around the hood with locks and fades. He was dressed in a black wife beater and jeans that sat grown-man low on his hips and were held up by a thick leather belt with the initials BK on the huge buckle, but what stood out the most was his boots. I'd never seen a nigga in the hood wearing snakeskin cowboy boots, and I couldn't get over that. I smiled. I was sure the twinkle in my eyes gave away what I was thinking.

It took me a minute to get my thoughts together, because he wasn't what I had expected on the grand scale of things. He stood well over six feet tall. Without my heels, I would have to strain my neck to look up at him. It wasn't his looks that got to me per se; it was the scowl he carried as he looked down at me that rattled me.

"You're so paranoid about trusting me, when something tells me I shouldn't be trusting you," he remarked.

I was of no mind to split hairs with him, not when he still had our property in his possession. "So now that we have that understanding, where's my shit?"

"We'll get to that. I had a chat with Chandler, as you may well remember."

I nodded and watched as he poured himself a glass of amber-colored liquor.

"And?" I asked.

"Since I figured it was him the traitors had to go through to get this ball rolling, I also thought it was only right for me not to kill him and to let you have your time with him."

I folded my arms across my breasts. I watched the way he licked his lips after taking a swallow of the drink in his hand. I didn't want it to show, but I had to admit that finding out they had gotten to Chandler before I did made my ass itch.

"So, where is he?" I asked.

Boots drained the rest of his libation. Inhaled as he watched me, then nodded toward the back room. Anxiously, I made my way down the hall. I pulled the Sig Sauer 9 mm from the back of my pants, where it had been tucked away against the small of my back. I wanted Chandler dead, but not before he told me what I wanted to know.

I opened the door to find Chandler hog-tied in the middle of the plastic-covered floor. The windows had been covered, so the only light came from the hall. He'd pissed himself, and the smell of it almost burned my eyes. There was no sign of defecation, so it was safe to assume they had been taking him to the bathroom while they were here. I barely recognized the man. For as big as he was, he had been seemingly reduced to the size of child with the way he was whimpering from obvious pain.

He looked like he'd dropped a few pounds. "Damn. Did y'all even feed the man?" I yelled.

Boots answered cryptically from the front room. "We don't fatten frogs for snakes."

I sighed and shook my head and turned back to the shell of the man who'd once told us stories about how he could trace his ancestry back hundreds of years ago to pirates.

The hole in his head where his glass eye had once been unnerved me.

Seeing the blisters, burns, and cuts on his body up close gave me a sick satisfaction. There wasn't much more I could do to him at this point. His mouth was taped shut, but with the way he was trembling, eyes wide, and mumbling, I knew he was deathly afraid of something. I knelt down beside him, then yanked the tape from his mouth. The man was sweating, and I couldn't tell if it was electrolytes or puss from the blisters on his face.

Tears streamed out of the corners of his eyes. He was trying to catch his breath, but it seemed as if it pained him to do so.

"Just tell me who paid you to be a turncoat on me. Then I'll kill you and put you out of your misery," I coolly explained to him.

"Co-Code," he stuttered. His eyes kept darting around the room, like he was seeing ghosts or some shit.

Just what in the hell had they done to the bastard to have him so afraid?

"Chandler, stop playing with me. Tell me what I want to know, and all this shit will end," I demanded.

I could hear footfalls behind me. Boots was watching from the hall. I could tell by the way Chandler glanced over my shoulder. But he also looked at the corner of the room behind me, like there was something there. I slapped the man for bullshitting me around. Stood up and kicked him in his nuts for playing with me. Was set to blow his fucking brains out when I heard something hissing, then rattling in the corner behind me.

I swiftly turned, only to be confronted by the biggest fucking diamondback rattlesnake uncoiling that I'd ever seen before in my life. Those shits weren't found in Georgia, so it told me that someone had placed it here. For a second, I was frozen in fear. Nothing in life scared me more than a snake. For mere moments I was seven years old again. In the basement of Papa's sprawling Spanish estate in Cuba, ten snakes lying before me. I had to overcome my fear of guns and snakes in order to survive.

The old man sat there and watched me damn near piss myself as the snakes slithered around me.

"Papa, please," my seven-year-old self begged.

"Chose life or death, Maria Rosa," he taunted me.

I looked around for my mother and found that she was staring at me without blinking. There was no emotion in her eyes. The one thing I knew for certain was that I'd better not disappoint her, or there would be hell to pay once we got back to her wing of the mansion. She knew I was afraid of snakes, so it didn't take a genius to figure out she'd told the old man what to use against me. One snake in particular seemed to stare at me head-on. For minutes it seemed that snake and I stared one another down, and then it leapt out to strike at me.

Just like before, I had seconds to react. But when I did, I chose life over death. The first bullet blew the rattlesnake's head into pieces. I screamed out, almost in a delirious panic, as more and more hisses and rattling joined the fray. I started shooting blindly into the corners of the room, sure I'd hit some and missed most because of my blind rage.

I backed out of the room quickly, leaving a terrified, yelling Chandler behind, and then I slammed the door closed. I screamed as I jumped around in a circle in the hall. My chest heaved up and down rapidly. Sweat beaded at my temples and in my armpits. I kept screaming like it would help my frightful state, until my eyes turned to Boots. It was my turn for my eyes to turn to slits. Heated breaths exited my nose. He'd known the fucking snakes were in that room. He probably didn't know I was afraid of snakes, but he'd known they were in there. He'd sent me into that room, knowing another threat was lying there in wait, one that I couldn't see, and *that* angered me.

I flipped my gun so the barrel was in my hand, knowing that I was out of bullets, or I would have killed him, then pitched it at his head. He dodged it effortlessly. I charged at him like a madwoman. Tried to send a punch to his mouth, but he blocked it. He caught my wrist, spun me around, then shoved me back down the hall. I kept my footing, then went at him again. I swung high. He ducked low. Left his body open, so I used my wedged-heel pump to make him regret leaving his body open. I kicked him so hard, trying to crack a rib and puncture a lung.

The kick pissed him off, because he returned the favor. Sent a meaty fist into my ribs that knocked spit from my mouth.

"What the fuck is wrong with you?" he yelled at me.

The fact that he was feigning ignorance of what he had done turned my anger up a notch. There was a pull-up bar in one of the doorways in the hall. I took a running leap and grabbed the bar, then sent my heels into his chest. He stumbled backward, fell to one knee, then growled low, like the fight was annoying him. While he was off balance, I tried to run and knee him in his face, only to be speared like he was Roman Reigns from WWE.

We both went flying into the table in the middle of the front room, with me taking the brunt of the blow. The front door to his apartment swung open. The dude I remembered him calling Shango came barreling in. That didn't stop me. I saw my gun was just within my reach. I could hear Freddie yelling my name as he came running across the hall. The handle of my gun in hand, I aimed the barrel at Boots's head. I mean, it was empty, but they didn't know that.

Shango's gun was on me. Freddie had pulled his gun out, only to have Oya's and Boots's guns aimed at him.

"Just what the fuck is going on in here?" asked Shango, his voice booming.

"Boots, is this how you get women to have sex with you?" Oya chimed in.

"I swear to the saints, if shorty takes this gun off me, you're dead," Freddie threatened Boots.

I heard feet stampeding on the stairs. A chick with micro-braids, denim booty shorts, brown cowboy boots, and a Cowboys midriff on came barreling around the corner. She took a look at us all, with her guns pointed at me and Freddie. We were outnumbered. Behind enemy lines. I was so hyped off adrenaline that I didn't realize Boots was between my legs. My shirt had been ripped open. No bra on, so my golden breasts and brown nipples were on full display. I could taste the blood in my mouth.

Boots was in no better fashion. His wife beater had been torn. Blood trickled from his eyebrow the same as sweat trailed down his face. His face held the same look as mine. We both wanted to kill one another.

"I'm going to need one of you to explain before we kill somebody just because you two on some other kind of shit when it comes to fucking," the girl in the booty shorts spat.

"This nigga tried to kill me," I blurted out.

"I did not," Boots countered.

"Bullshit. You sent me into a fucking room filled with fucking rattlesnakes," I said through clenched teeth while swinging at him again.

Shango rushed over to grab my hand with the gun in it, while Boots grabbed my other one before standing. He got up and yanked me up with him, then shoved me away. I tried to swing on him again, only to have Shango body block me.

Boots yelled, "I told you we didn't fatten frogs for snakes! What the fuck you thought I meant?"

"You asshole," I screamed.

I didn't even realize I was crying. Actually, the situation would have been funny had I not really been scared out of my mind.

"I need to talk to my people," Freddie said with his hands still in the air, like he was being stuck up.

"Naw, you just chill right there," Shango told him.

Freddie ignored him and looked at me. "There are really snakes in the room, *chiquita*?"

"Snakes. Fucking big-ass rattlesnakes!" I answered.

Only Freddie knew my pain. He knew what it was to have what you feared most used against you just to do the old man's bidding. When we were younger, I had had to watch on in horror when he was tossed into the deep end of the pool. Being that Freddie was deathly afraid of water, Papa had made water his specialty when it came to hired killing.

It took a good twenty minutes for me to calm down enough to get Boots's people to take their guns off Freddie. Another twenty to get things back to normal. Between Chandler's yelling and me cursing Boots to hell, it had turned into a circus. Boots said he'd told me snakes were in the room, but how the hell was I to know snakes were *really* in the room? I wasn't used to the riddles shit. So, the fact he'd used one annoyed me.

By the time they got back to the room to check on Chandler, he'd been bitten six times. His death was slow and painful, but no more than he deserved.

Chapter 15

Boots

Some women know how to test a man's resolve. I had such a woman in my apartment. I was fighting not to wrap my hands around her lovely throat and land several blows against her skull. All in the desire to give back to her what she'd done to me. Yeah, I had sent her into the Garden of Eden without a clear layout of what exactly was waiting for her ass. However, I *had* told her there were snakes in that there room. Not my fault she hadn't listened or understood.

Rocking back in my chair, I rubbed the side of my face, then tented my fingers in front of my lips. Everything I'd done was all her fault. She'd chosen to come with me and my team, while acting like a boss bitch. Believing that the world was hers, when in fact it wasn't. She held secrets. One of which wasn't hard to break down and determine when I saw her right-hand, a

dude she called Freddie. That fool currently was
testing my last nerve with how he kept trying to
holla at my sister-at-arms, Oya.

However, being who I was, I couldn't just
bring her into my world, my second apartment
in this city, without testing her. I mean, I wasn't
going to even do that much until I overheard
her conversation with Freddie. I mean, who was
she? *She who fought in white clothes while riding upon a white horse, with divine inspiration
to guide the way.*

Ah yeah, right there, that one phrase signed
the deal for me. See, in my training and growing
up, I had listened to a lot of stories about my
pop's past. Specific long tales, myths, histories,
additional intel, and then the truth to it all.
These specifics were necessary for me to understand in order to survive with the legacy I had
inherited.

Wiping a wet towel down my face, then over
my chest and abs, I shook my head in thought.

Maria Rosa.

Yeah, I had known her name the moment she
exited the Garden of Eden and came at me like
a crazed bull seeing red. I had had to listen to
my pop's informant speak about all the people
associated with her *familia*, including her old
man's gang of wives, sons, daughters, grandkids,

other relatives, and more. Her name was revered in the underworld circuit. Not many knew her face, but they knew her name, because she was named after a fifteen-year-old Spanish warrior.

The one thing we knew about her that not many other people knew was that she was afraid of snakes. That was what had given her away. Pop's informant had given him all the names of those in her family who were most trusted. Because of that information, I had had to not only train in the way of my pop's lineage, but I had had to train like the enemy trained. I had had to experience everything they all did, just to get into their heads and understand the psyche of the man who made it his mission to birth and educate killers.

I had never known a face, had known just the names, sex, and ages. I was getting closer to my agenda. I knew what I wanted to do with all of it. I couldn't kill them. No, I had to keep getting close, but the funny thing about it all was my dick.

How my dick was set up had me wanting a dip in the venom that was between the thighs of a woman who had tried to take me down like another nigga in the street. In other words, I wanted to fuck a crazy chick, and that right there was something I had never expected to happen—to have desire for my enemy.

If I didn't know my history so well, I'd say
my ancestors would be rolling in their graves at
this desire. A man with my bloodline wanting a
woman of her bloodline would always mean war.
Our two families didn't mix. The man sitting on
the throne of the empire that had created the
woman I desired would see me dead first, just as
I wanted him to be. So, as long as I kept my focus
on that, then the rest I'd have to chill on, and I'd
have to say, "Fuck it. I'm young, and I enjoy the
crazy."

Days later, after dealing with my crew clowning me and talking about all the ass, titty, and
hard dick that had been on display during the
wrestling match going on, I received a call
that changed the nature of the agreement that
my crew and the Eraserheads had made. Joy
Lake, an actual lake in Lake City, was where I
was told to meet up. I gathered my people, and
we headed out. I decided to drive my ride this
go-round, and Shango sat to my left, with my
new guest and ninja master, Code, in the backseat.

Her cousin Freddie and Oya, Alize, and Shredder
were in the second ride and were following us.
Foliage, trees, and the typical scenery that was
found in Atlanta passed us by as we headed to
Lake City. Joy Lake was a known place where the

locals fished and threw the occasional birthday party. It was nothing to brag about, but it was a good place for the business that was about to go down. There was a narrow road that led to a tiny shack at the entrance where you could buy or rent fishing rods and purchase bait, such as worms and chicken livers. That shack was also where you paid a fee to get in and use the place. It was open from seven in the morning until eight at night. We all arrived there after hours.

Chilling in my old Chevy Caprice, I waited for the person who had arranged this meeting to show up. Just as thoughts about this meeting hit my dome, I watched a black Lexus pull out from a shaded spot in the parking lot, a spot covered by trees. The loud slam of a car door closing had me giving Shango a nod as we all got out of the ride to meet our host.

Auto stepped my way. Behind him was his crew, and my former guest Smiley was at his side. The leader of the group had a serious look in his eyes, his jaw was square and tight, and his gloved hands dug into his pockets, then pulled out some ducats. He turned and approached a wily old man who was coming his way. I watched as Auto peeled off a few bills and gave them to the white man who ran the place. The old guy stood there and counted the money, nodded, then turned the lights off in the shack. I waited until he had locked up and disappeared through the trees before I walked around my ride, then opened the trunk to the old-school Chevy Caprice. A menacing smile spread across my face when I saw what my crew had been able to catch and place inside my trunk. The Scandy known as Mouse.

A low chuckle came from me. See, the people I was slowly aligning myself with, for now, had hipped me up to the lifestyle that Mouse lived. Mouse loved black women. I figured that a man like him, who had a love for all things with a fat booty, a twerking pussy, and beautiful black skin, would stay posted in a place like Magic City. It had been decided that while we all were on temporary downtime, we would scope out Mouse. Funny thing was that Mouse had made things happen faster than planned, which was no sweat off my back.

Now here he was, bound and gagged in the back of the trunk, on his side. Since I was really in no mood to mess around, I stepped back, then stared down from under my wide-brimmed black cowboy hat at the woman I was doing my best not to go deep into our beef with. I waved a hand for her to step forward, and I crossed my arms over my chest, then got down to business.

"Get him out of the trunk," Code ordered her crew members Lelo and Stitch.

Once they had taken the big Viking out of the trunk and had dropped him on the ground, I watched her kick him and stomp on him until she got tired. She combed her fingers through her curling hair, then quickly braided it as she glared down at the rat lying at her feet. A smirk played on her lips. Her heels had left holes in his chest, arms, and legs, but she didn't seem to care.

Hell, I didn't care, either, so it was all good in the hood, which was why I stepped forward, assessing the bastard.

"Are you going to leave him alive so we can ask him some questions, or are you seeing snakes again?" I asked sarcastically.

A large grin spread across my face when I saw her eye twitch. The twitching stopped as soon as she spit at my feet. Auto shook his head in my peripheral, because I could hear Freddie going over in detail what had happened at my apartment. No doubt, I was very heated for how she had attacked me. But on another level, I recognized that she was no more pissed than I was about being thrown into a den of snakes. I still chuckled at it, though. It was what she got.

Still, she knew I was right. There was no need for her to kill the man before getting the info we needed. Which was why I backed off. I used this time to calmly take several strides toward Mouse, who was writhing in pain.

"You keep that crazy Cuban black bitch away from me," he told me. "Why do you have me here, man? I work for you!"

I tsk-tsked him in amusement and gave a disheartened sigh. "Nah. See, something isn't right with the cheese in Denmark, my man. A little pirate told us that it was you who came to him with the idea of selling me out. Now, what I want to know . . . is, Who paid you?"

Mouse looked shocked. "I do not know this of which you speak! I swear to it. Why would I betray you? What have you ever done to me to make you think I'd do such a treacherous act?"

I shrugged nonchalantly, then crossed my arms over my chest. "I don't know. That's what I want you to tell me."

Playing the game, I snapped my fingers. Oya came forward and pulled out a tube from the case she had been carrying. After taking the transparent tube, I popped it open with my thumb and slightly shook the contents within. Making a show of it, I held it out for Auto and his team to see. "This here is what I like to call truth serum."

Auto walked over, took the tube in his hand to examine it, and then handed it back to me. "Why do you call it that?"

I didn't answer at first. Well, not verbally. I tilted the tube over Mouse's right hand, and we all observed how the liquid pooled on the top of his hand. Bubbles began to form, then eat through flesh, burning a hole, eating away at his skin like fire burning through paper. A vapor rose, and the funk caused me to crinkle my nose. It smelled like burning bacon and charcoal. Mouse's shrill yelps disturbed the wildlife around us. For our benefit, like a domino effect, any lights that had been on in the houses surrounding the lake began to flicker out. All we had to see by, anyhow, were the headlights from the cars, which shone directly on the little man before me.

"Ah God. Fuck, Boots! Please, man!" Mouse begged.

His pleas fell on deaf ears as my boy Shango placed his foot on Mouse's left arm. We watched his palm open, and I grinned while I treated his left hand to the same fate. More screams ensued, and Mouse began to struggle. Once I was done with his hands, I looked toward Oya. She came my way, and with her own wicked power, she dropped down into a graceful squat, balanced on

her heels, then took one gloved hand and patted
Mouse's bulge. She laughed as I gave my nod of
approval for her to strip the man of his pants.

"Oh, hell naw," Smiley said from behind me.
The girl had a screwed-up face while she shook
her head. "This nigga is dick slanging. On some
real shit, do niggas not wear drawas? Where y'all
from?" she quipped.

The two men I knew as Lelo and Stitch chuckled. Auto grunted. My own shit started to shrivel
from the knowledge of what I was about to do
next. Every brother in the place stopped laughing when I leaned my hand over and started to
pour the acid dangerously close to the man's
dick. By the time the acid had burned his thighs,
Mouse had passed out from the pain. Shortly
after, the scent of alcohol-laced piss and shit
saturated the air.

I ordered Alize to go into the case for me and
grab a syringe with a long needle from it. Always
happy to get her hands dirty, she gave me an
enthused nod and then did as I'd asked.

Looking at my girl, I slid back on my haunches
and scowled. "Wake this bitch up."

Happily complying, Alize hauled back and
left a red handprint on Mouse's face. In her left
hand was the hypodermic needle. When she
didn't get the response that she was looking for

from Mouse, she shrugged her shoulders and forcefully stabbed the needle into Mouse's chest. It literally took less than a minute for this fool to jerk up with a loud gasp and look at us with wild eyes full of awareness.

"Now that we are done with that shit, all I want to know is where my property is and who paid you to pull that trickery shit on me. This is my last time asking nicely," I told the man who'd pissed and defecated on himself minutes ago.

"Okay, okay," Mouse said breathlessly, trying to hold his hands up in self-defense. "There was a dude who came to me a few months back. Said he wanted me to take some cars that Chandler was having shipped through Vegas and Cali. Said for me and my men to intercept the cars and make sure they got to the Canadian border. There we were to leave the cars, and his people would take it from there."

"That's when you started taking my shit?" Auto inquired while dropping down into a squat in front of Mouse.

Mouse flinched, then licked his dry, peeling lips. "You know cars have to be shipped as open cargos. Can't be shipped in closed trailers."

A flash of annoyance hit Auto's eyes, and he reached behind him, pulled out his Glock, and pointed it toward Mouse, taking the safety off. "No shit. Keep talking, dickhead."

Fear was spilling from Mouse while he stumbled on. "Once we would get the cars to a certain point near the border, these dudes would come through, strip the cars, and take all the drugs and money out."

His words had me thinking. I stood up, then backed up to look down at Auto. At that moment, as he looked up at me, I think he also was feeling and thinking like I was.

"Drugs and money? Fuck you talking about, homeboy?" Stitch spat out, with constrained anger.

Lelo then shook his head while adding, "Yeah, we don't ship no drugs and money, nigga. You fooling."

Mouse took a deep gulp. "Look, man, that's what was in the cars. All my crew did was pick them up from Chandler."

"And my cars? They're gone?" Auto asked.

"You can kiss the cars and the money spent for them good-bye," Mouse responded, with a hint of arrogance in his panicky voice.

Irritated, I rubbed my neck. The math was not adding up, and it was pissing me all the way off. "How did my bullets come up in this situation?"

Mouse nervously looked my way; then his gaze shifted to that of pleading with his eyes. "Boots, look, man, I know you're going to kill me, so at least make sure my family knows where the money is I left them—"

His words ticked something off in my brain. Before he could finish, I slammed my boot down and crushed his already injured left hand. I dug the heel of those black cowboy shitkickers so deep into the already seeping wound, it seemed as if his hand was going to split in two.

"Listen to me, Mouse. I don't give a fuck about nothing you fucked or sired at this point. You fucking with my livelihood and my money. Speak up, nigga, or forever hold your peace," I snarled.

"When Shredder came to me about a shipment he needed to be handled for you, I spoke to the man who'd made a deal with Chandler. Told him I didn't know what you were having shipped, but that it was a big deal, because you would be at the gun show in Vegas. He was interested. Paid me up front," Mouse started to explain.

"How much?" I asked.

"What?" he asked, his eyes fluttering from the pain that was going through him.

"How much he pay you to sell me out, nigga?" I repeated in a heated tone.

"A quarter mil," he finally told me.

If we'd had a DJ in this shit, if it were music or a record, it would all suddenly scratch to a halt. Did this motherfucker say, "A quarter mil"?

Looking around me in amazement, I scratched the side of my jaw. No, this motherfucker did not just say, "A quarter mil"! *Where they do that at*? I thought. I smiled. That smile quickly turned into a snarl, and then my boot slammed back down on that bitch. The sensation of bone crunching under my foot made me grin in pleasure. I stomped Mouse's hand, then kicked him in his face so hard that teeth and spit flew across the fallen leaves and grass.

"Nigga, I paid you double that to ship that shit for me, and you sold me out for less?" I spat as I kicked Mouse's ass all over the ground.

At that moment, I did not give a fuck about how I was being seen. All the smirks and laid-back banter and demeanor were all gone. This motherfucker had just fucked with my livelihood and my plans. *A quarter mil? Oh hell no*.

Mouse was on his knees, hands limp, coughing up blood, by the time I got tired of kicking his ass.

Taking a moment to get my breath, I adjusted my hat and looked down while thumbing my nose. "Motherfucker got blood on my good pair of boots. Ain't that some shit?"

I then rubbed the soles of my boots on this traitor-ass bitch's battered body and watched as he attempted to look up at me.

Glassy-eyed Mouse began to stammer. "I . . .I . . . I . . . had to split what you gave me between my crew, man. That quarter mil was all mine. Had debts and shit to pay so my family wouldn't—" he said, but I quickly cut that shit off at the pass.

"Fuck your debts! That wasn't my problem, motherfucker," I yelled, then pulled my heat from the small of my back and pointed it at this cunt.

Code's voice cut through my heated rage.

"Whoa. Hold on," she said, rushing in and holding a hand up. "The man . . . Who's the man, Mouse?"

Curiosity danced in the corners of my mind. It was a gut feeling I always listened to, so I took a moment to calm down and listen. We all had to wait until Mouse had finished coughing before he turned to look Code in her eyes.

His voice was low and even when he said to her, "Now, we both know why I can't give you that. So just kill me. I got a family, and he'll kill them all with no question."

Interesting, flashed in my mind. I knew when I glanced at Code that it was also the confirmation that she needed. A tension seemed to form around her while she fisted her hands by her sides. I could definitely guess that she was feeling some type of way. A nervousness appeared for a hot second over her face before she backed away from Mouse and trekked back toward her crew's car. I saw her cousin Freddie stop his stalking of Oya only to follow closely behind Code.

Getting back to my business and forgetting the rest, I handed my hat to Shango. Then I glanced at Auto, and he stepped back, knowing what was about to go down. Two rounds of bullets sliced through the bastard's dome. The asphalt under him became an abstract art painting of blood and brain matter. I looked back down at my boots, then wiped them off again on Mouse's legs.

Shango reached for my warm Glock, then handed me my hat, which I placed on my head and adjusted. While my right-hand man made sure everything was back in place, I noticed Smiley jogging toward Code and Freddie. From the body language going on and the movements of her mouth, I could tell that she was asking something. I also noticed that Freddie was purposely keeping his gaze away from Smiley.

It was another secret, another story going on between Code and Freddie, and it had my interest. However, this was something that would probably be discussed later, and I really had another situation to deal with. No, we *all* had another problem to deal with, and something in my mind said it had to do with the woman who was now pulling off in her crew member Lelo's truck. I glanced at Auto, while he looked in the direction in which Code had sped off. Dude's jaw was clenched tight again, and I knew that he had hella questions on his mind too. As the saying went, "What's in the dark always comes to light," and now my ass needed new fucking shitkickers. God damn!

Chapter 16

Auto

I thumbed my nose as I sat in the office of the auto shop. Regular business was going according to normal. The shop was buzzing. Seymore was giving out orders. Lelo and Stitch were arguing, as usual, but were working in tandem to put the transmission back into a 2002 golden PT Cruiser. Reagan was prancing around in a cut-up jumper, her ass distracting Lelo, Stitch, Seymore, Dunkin, and Jackknife, as she worked under the hood of a Ford F-150. Yes, all was well in the auto world.

The same couldn't be said for the illegal side of things, though. Owing to the money we'd lost due to our shit being stolen, we couldn't move ahead in copping the new machines we needed to stay ahead of the law when it came to our illicit activities. Just like we had to stay ahead of the law when it came to credit theft, skimming, card clones, and so on, the law tried to stay one step ahead of us too. And we'd lost way too much money to put stock into new machines.

We'd been so focused on recouping our losses from the last shipment being taken that we hadn't had time to see the money we were losing on our other venture. I was feeling it now, though. In just a couple of days, we'd lost clients and hundreds of thousands of dollars. We could still do stuff like make fake IDs, passports, Social Security cards, and so forth, but pretty soon we would run out of the material needed for doing things like making new credit cards. We never used the same machine for too long, because in no time the Feds would get wind of the activities of the digital criminal underworld and all the gadgets. So we always liked to be ten steps ahead of them.

"Hey, can I talk to you for a minute?"

I looked up from the computer screen, which showed the numbers in the bank account for the auto shop and the other accounts. Smiley was standing in the doorway, a backpack on her back and another hanging from her right hand. Her spiraled locks were pulled to the side, exposing the shaved half of the head. Eyes sparkled, even though the look on her face was stoic. She had on baggy clothes that reminded me of girl groups of old. Back when a girl could be a tomboy without being labeled a dyke. She wore an oversize sweatshirt repping Howard U, the bottom cut off, showing her belly. Baggy jeans sat low on her hips, showing off Hanes undershorts. Trinkets decorated her locks, giving her a hippie-like appeal.

I'd left her at my crib, with instructions for her to stay put. It was clear that she wasn't one for taking orders. I nodded. She walked in. Dropped both backpacks on the floor, then took a seat, moving stealthily. Whatever scent she was wearing wafted under my nostrils and teased me. Anytime a woman wore something that smelled like fruit, it tickled my senses.

My office needed cleaning. Empty oil containers were strewn about. Gas cans sat idly in the corner. It smelled of an auto shop: oil, grease, gas, and grime. The heat in this place was sweltering. But it was something I was used to. Only the waiting area in the front for customers was cool. We always wanted our customers to be satisfied on all fronts.

"It's hot in here," Smiley complained, then looked around like she was looking for something. When she spotted the fan, she stood up, walked over to it, and then turned it on high.

She sat back down, then looked at me.

"Why didn't you stay in the house, like I told you?" I asked her.

She quirked a brow, then fixed her mouth so it looked as if she smelled something that stank.

"I'm grown. Nobody tells me what to do," was her response.

"It was for your safety."

She made a show of looking around. Stood up and checked her body for what I could only assume were injuries.

"I look fine to me. What about you?" She was being sarcastic.

I grunted, then leaned back while I looked at her. There was still something about the way she and Code had been speaking secretly as of late that bothered me. Since the night we'd seen Mouse's demise, they'd gotten closer, it seemed. I'd walk in and find them whispering. Code would seem to be fussing at her about something. Smiley would be adamantly trying to get her point across.

"Don't be facetious, Smiley. You know shit is hot around here for us. Especially since we don't know who targeted us in the first place. I need to know all my people are safe. Is that so hard for you to comprehend?"

She sighed, then picked up a backpack from the floor. The black backpack had a small lock on the zippers, locking them together. Smiley reached up in her hair and pulled down a small trinket made like a key. She then took her time unlocking the lock. Once she was done with that, she stood and dumped the contents of the back-pack onto my desk. Rolls of money fell out of the backpack so fast, it looked as if the backpack didn't have a bottom. It was never-ending. Once she had emptied the backpack, she looked at me.

"The Vikings owed us, right? Well, when you sent me to wipe them out financially, I took the liberty of wiring some funds to myself. Been doing it over the past few days so it didn't seem suspicious. What I don't have in cash, we have in Visa debit cards. There is a limit of three hundred a day on each one for fifteen days, max. Figure if we disperse enough of your people around the city and some in Vegas, where you say you have more people, we can recoup a big chunk of what y'all lost."

"How many cards in all?"

"About thirty."

I did quick calculations in my head.

She kept talking. "The Vikings had an elab-orate setup. According to the info your boy Pascal sent over, they had accounts in their kids' names, deceased grandparents', wives', and other faceless people's names. They must have had someone inside the bank too, so tell your people to be careful."

I locked my sights on the money covering my desk, then gazed back up at the criminal-minded spitfire in front of me. After taking a wad of the money that was rolled and bound with red rubber bands in my hand, I popped the bands. In the roll was about fifty ten-dollar bills. I took another roll, saw it consisted of twenties. Saw rolls of fifties and hundreds.

"When in hell did you have time to do all of this?" I asked, wanting to know.

I knew she had been with me for a few days, and while I hadn't kept track of her twenty-four hours a day, the times I'd gone back home to check on her, she was there.

"You weren't always home. First day I timed your movements. Was easy to slip out when you weren't around. Most times you stayed gone for two hours or so. So, it was easy to cop that over the past five days. All I had to do was make sure you weren't going to double back, and then I slipped out to handle my business for the team. Code came to check on me from time to time too. Got her to take me around. And you're welcome," she responded.

I didn't know how I felt about her timing my comings and goings like she had. It made me feel like somebody else could easily do the same thing if they happened to find out where I lived.

"What's in the other backpack?" I asked her as I nodded my head at it.

She looked a bit uncomfortable. Her eyes darkened a bit; she scowled. Then, just that fast, her stoic look was back.

"Nothing," she answered blandly.

I looked at the way the backpack was bulging. It was clearly overstuffed with something. "That's a whole lot of nothing."

She didn't respond. Just picked up the backpack and put it on her shoulder. I could see that she was still behind that shell. She didn't really trust me, even though she was trying to earn her place on the team. Which was weird to me, since she had opened up to Code, when I was the one who had kept her out of prison. It had to be a female thing. Or Code could have called dibs on her. It was no secret that Code could pull women better than any dude I'd been around. Yeah. Maybe that was it.

I didn't press the issue, though. If she didn't want to talk to me, I wouldn't force her. Didn't want to make her recoil even further. I clicked on the security cameras and checked our surroundings. I'd been a bit paranoid as of late. I couldn't front about it. Having somebody with

no name and no face gunning for you had the
tendency to do that. I'd always been the one to sit
back and think before I acted. Bruce Lee was the
reason for that. He'd been the only figure that I
had looked up to at times when I was a kid. I'd
been so thirsty for knowledge about my mother's
origins, about where she had come from, that I
had latched on to anyone and everything posi-
tive that resembled me. He had taught me that
a quick temper would make a fool of you soon
enough.

I had to learn that at an early age and still
took it with me everywhere I went. So as I
watched the screens and pondered our next
move, I kept the need to kill a motherfucker
in check. I hadn't heard from Code in almost
twenty-four hours and had to wonder what she
was up to. Last time she'd gotten this quiet, the
old man had forbidden her from leaving the
house. At least that was what she had told me.
When she had finally come back around, she'd
been despondent. She'd been closed off and
hadn't said much to anybody. It was always hot
as hell in the shop, and yet Code had walked
around with her workman's jumper damn near
zipped to her neck, and that had told me the old
man had struck again. I didn't like what he did
to her, but since Code would never let me speak
out against him, and since I didn't know where

he laid his head, there was nothing I could do about it.

That thought brought me back to Smiley. She was now sitting at my desk, doing a search of eBay on one of the computers, as I'd asked her earlier to look on eBay to see if there were any new skimming machines she could use. It was easy to see she was in her element when it came to stealing credit card information. She was like a geek at a nerd convention.

"You heard from Code?" I asked her.

She glanced at me, scratched the shaved part of her head, then answered, "No."

Something about the way she averted her eyes told me she was lying.

"You sure?"

"Yeah. I ain't heard from her."

"You're lying," I said.

She smacked her lips. "How you gone tell me I'm lying?"

I sat back in my chair and looked at her. "I'm good at reading people, Smiley."

"Or so you think."

"So I *know*. Just like in the interview room at the jailhouse when I came to visit you, you avert your eyes when you're lying. You scratch your head and bite down on the corner of your lips too."

"That doesn't mean anything. I do that all the time."

"Which means you lie a lot."

She looked offended. If she'd been a snake, her eyes would be in slits, as they narrowed and she shot daggers at me.

"You got a bad habit of acting like you know me," she spat.

"And you have a bad habit of lying."

"Kiss my ass is what you can do."

I chuckled. Logged off the desktop, then stood. "I'm heading out to lunch. You should join me."

"I'm not hungry."

"Come with me, anyway. Need to keep an eye on you."

"Why?"

"Need those cards you talked about."

Since I saw she still wasn't willing to put her full trust in me, I'd be a fool to put all mine in her. There was a reason she was so standoffish, and until I found out what it was, I'd be keeping a keen eye on her.

We hopped in my old pickup truck, a 1958 Chevy Apache. The only thing new in it was the engine. The red paint wasn't new, but it wasn't old enough to draw attention, either. There were many ways to get caught when doing illicit activity. If distinctive body markings or scars didn't give you away, then your vehicle might. If your car was too new or too old, you would be ripe for the picking.

People remembered vehicles with fresh paint, rims, and other prominent features. Those same people remembered old cars. Cars that made a lot of noise or looked to be rusting and falling apart. People rarely remembered a vehicle that was neutral: No color that stood out. No rims spinning and reflecting the sun. No distinctive noises, and no booming system.

Growing up in the hood was like being in a jungle. As always, you were either going to get with the program, or the program was going to get you.

Once Smiley and I crossed over Mt. Zion, we hopped on Southlake Circle and made our way around to Southlake Parkway. We drove down Southlake Parkway until we got to the empty building where a Bally Total Fitness used to be. Next to that building was a shopping center that housed something called Monkey Joe's, a temp agency, America's Best Contacts & Eyeglasses, and the diner I was headed to.

Colleen's Diner was a cheery restaurant that sold traditional soul food in a family setting. That was what they boasted. In reality, it was a little hole-in-the-wall joint, but it wasn't run

down. There was a small seating area outside,
surrounded by a wrought-iron fence. About four
round wrought-iron tables were there, with pale
chocolate-brown umbrellas that shielded you
from the sun. It wasn't that hot out. Wasn't cool,
either. It was the kind of weather that Georgia
was used to. An equal mixture of hot humidity
and wind. You either wanted to stay inside
or out. The parking lot surrounding the area
wasn't that full. Most of the cars belonged to the
families at Monkey Joe's, which was an inside
play area for kids.

I walked inside the diner, with Smiley trailing
behind me. The green-, brown-, and cream-colored décor kind of made you feel as if you'd
stepped into an episode of *The Mod Squad*. The
square tables on the right side of the room had
chairs turned upside down on them, as if the
diner would be closing soon. In the buffet-style
serving area on the left, steam rose from most of
the food. On the same side were six green and
brown booths.

Employees rushed back and forth between the
front of the diner and the back like they had a
full house. The place was empty, minus the few
people sitting outside. That wasn't unusual, and
I often wondered how they stayed in business.
Still, the food was good, price was decent, and

it was a good place to handle business. I got turkey wings, cabbage greens, sweet potatoes, and corn-bread flapjacks. Smiley got the same, minus the flapjacks. I paid for both our meals, said a few words to the cashier, and then took a seat in one of the booths.

Smiley sat across from me. She kept that backpack close to her.

I looked at my phone to see if any of my runners had gotten my message. Thirty cards times three hundred dollars times fifteen days would give me one hundred thirty-five thousand untaxed dollars. We had never been hurting for that kind of money. Just a few months ago, that would have seemed like chump change to my operation. Now it would be a godsend.

Smiley's phone kept beeping. She kept checking it, then looking at me to see if I was watching her.

"That Code?" I asked her.

She pulled her curly locks to the side, then gave me a look that said she wanted me to mind my business.

I said, "Tell Code she needs to check in with me and let me know what the fuck is going on. Otherwise, the lines between enemy and friend will start to get blurred."

Smiley wiped her mouth, then looked down at her plate. "I ain't talking to Code. Told you I ain't heard from that girl."

I thumbed my nose and went back to my food. I placed my issues with Code to the side for the moment, then started to pay attention to my surroundings. Three white guys and a black girl walked in. The males sported Confederate flag tattoos and bald heads. They were dressed like they had just come from the backwoods of West Virginia. Dirty coveralls and brown boots. The black girl sported a 'fro with a black power T-shirt. Green, red, and black tights covered her thick thighs. The girl sat behind Smiley, while the males sat in a booth on the other side of the wall opposite me.

I looked at the cashier. He nodded at me. I went back to my plate. Five more people of different racial backgrounds walked in. Each time one took a seat, the cashier nodded. That went on until I had finished my plate of food. All those people were in some way a part of my crew. They would keep the cards for fifteen days. Draw out as much money as they could, then drop it at an undisclosed location for pickup.

Once all the people who had come in had exited, Smiley and I were left alone once again. For some reason, I found myself attracted to the girl physically. But I'd never been one to let my dick guide me. Hadn't been in many relationships, but I prided myself on not being one of those niggas who thought the more pussy he got, the more man it made him.

There was something about a woman who had some mystery to her. I liked that shit. Liked the fact that while I sat with her, although mostly quietly, she gave me peace. It had been a long time since peace had been my friend. So I'd take the little bit, even though I could feel it would be interrupted soon enough.

Smiley looked up at me like she was about to say something. Then something she saw behind me gave her pause. Her eyes widened. She got the "deer in the headlights" look right before she snatched up her backpack and the empty plate. She made a beeline to the trash can in back, then rushed into the bathroom.

I always sat with my back to the door when I ate at Colleen's, as I was in a friendly zone. Even still, you could never be too careful or too comfortable. I gripped the butt of my gun and then slowly stood. I turned to face the entrance just as an elder male—couldn't really tell if he was black or not—walked into the establishment. He was tall, well over six feet. Gray suit had been tailored to fit his broad shoulders and muscular frame. The salt-and-pepper hair was tapered on his head. Gray beard was shaped to fit his square jawline. And a fresh pair of square-toed dress shoes added to his diabolical appeal. Something about the man's stony gaze told me the gun in my hand should have the safety off.

Flanking him were two males of equal stature. The one on the left had an eerily similar look to the dude Code had called Freddie.

"Auto is it?" the man said to me.

The air in the place seemed to get cooler. My throat had tightened with tension. The possibility of an imminent threat had me on edge.

"Who wants to know?"

"My name isn't of importance at the moment. All I want to know is if I can talk business with you, *sí*?"

"I don't do business with nameless people, my man."

The man chuckled. It wasn't a chuckle that showed he was in a happy mood or that something was funny to him. His chuckle was demented. Put ice in my veins. The fact that he had the same Cuban accent that Code mimicked when she was upset told me I might be in the presence of the old man.

"She said you would say that," he commented.

I squared my shoulders. My legs were shoulder width apart, and I had no qualms about not hiding the gun I held at my side.

"Who the hell is *she*, and why does she think she knows me so well?"

For a few tense moments, he simply gazed around the restaurant, his lips turned down into a frown, as if something had offended him.

"Maybe if you do business with me, sí, you can afford to eat in cleaner eateries than this one, no?" he asked. "No more time for bullshit. I am a businessman, sí? As are you. I come to you with a proposition that will benefit us both. Word on the street is that you specialize in a business I can use. Those same lips whispering about how good your business is also tell me you've been experiencing some difficulties."

I kept quiet. *To know oneself is to study oneself in action with another person*, I thought.

He continued, "Those difficulties I can help you with, but only if you help me, sí?"

I started to think about all the things Code had told me about the old man. I'd asked her why she stayed under his thumb so much. Asked her why she still worked for him but was dead set against anybody else doing so. It was around the time when she and I had first met. I had been a green nose in the game, a rookie. So when I found the old man had power, I'd toyed with the idea of asking Code if he would be good to do business with.

"He's not somebody you want to go into business with because the money looks good. You can't trust him, and he isn't to be taken lightly. His only true loyalty is to family. When you're not family and you do something he doesn't like, you're done. Once you go into business with him, he owns you. He owns your family. He owns your friends. He owns your kids. You will never be able to walk away," she'd told me.

I'd never forget the passion and fear mixed in her eyes. It was then that I'd figured out her weakness. She loved the old man and loathed him all at the same time.

"I don't know who you've been talking to or why they would tell you such bullshit, but I assure you, I don't need your help. Didn't ask for your help. Don't want your help," I said to him.

"So assured of yourself, sí? You do know I can pretty much make this as difficult and as easy for you as I please? It would take nothing for me to crush you like the Asian beetle you are. I can make your shop, your friends, all of it disappear."

For the first time, my features hardened. One of the things I'd grown to hate more than anything was for someone to make reference to my race as an insult. Another thing that made my ass itch was to threaten my family.

I stepped closer to the man. The men flanking him drew their guns on me, but I didn't give a damn. If he was going to kill me, then I'd go to hell dragging one of the men in front of me with me.

"Tell you what," I said with a cold, distant voice I didn't recognize. "You do what you have to do, *me entiendes*? But if you come near my family, I'll come back for you in ways you won't be able to comprehend. Don't let this baby face and this calm demeanor fool you, old man. Fucking with anybody who I consider family is a sure way to expedite your journey to hell."

I could feel my nostrils flare. I was so angry, heated breaths escaped when I exhaled. The old man didn't seem fazed, though. He only smiled coolly. For as long as I lived, I would never forget the callous look that old man cast at me. If the prelude to death had a face, it would belong to that old man.

"I like you. It's really too bad you decided to turn down my offer. A boy like you would rise through the ranks in no time. Would make a good right-hand for the one stepping in to take the throne," he stated plainly, then clapped his big, rugged hands once. "Still, too bad you would rather your family starve and lose their livelihoods than swallow your pride and make a good business decision."

I had nothing else to say on the matter. I watched in silent rage as he and his watchdogs did an about-face and left Colleen's. I ran a hand through my hair, then down my face. Hate coursed through my veins. I tucked my gun back against my spine, then remembered Smiley was still in the bathroom. I rushed to the back, pushed the door to the women's bathroom open, only to find she wasn't there. The big square window in the bathroom was open.

I shook my head, annoyed. Her reaction to the old man told me that either she knew of him or she knew more than she was letting on. What in hell was going on with her and Code? It was Code who had picked her out for us to save. It had me wondering just what the hell was going on. For the first time in a long time, I felt lost. I experienced a feeling of panic and alarm that I hadn't felt since that night at Mama Joyce's when the police raided her house. I sent out a text calling a meeting at the auto shop tomorrow. I made it mandatory that everybody show up. It was time to get our house in order.

Chapter 17

Smiley

Long ago, I got away with murder. I traveled up to New York, sniffed out where the man who had created me laid his head. During this time, I stayed in the streets, living as a homeless person, being an invisible kid, just to watch the patterns of the man who was my father. Why? Because a well-laid plan could work only with perfect timing. So, I watched him. Followed him while he walked the streets to go to his VA meetings. Watched him buy his favorite drugs from some people in a populated area of Harlem that had people who looked like him. There was one house in particular that he would always visit. I'd watch him be greeted by people with light eyes. I'd observe the wicked yet alluring smirk he always had plastered on his face while he spoke in Spanish. Those people shared the same blank, cold darkness in their gaze that he had often had as he beat my mama and me.

I watched him. Picked up a little of the Spanish he spoke frequently now. Learned his movements and knew when he was carrying a lot of heat and when he wasn't, such as when he was at his VA meetings. He kept only a knife hidden on him when going to his meetings.

In my short time up in NYC, there was one day in particular, the day before I assisted in killing my pops, that had me reflecting on some shit. I had broken into my father's house and had waited in silence for him to come in. Hadn't been hard to pick his lock and make sure that I did not move one single item. He had taught me how to hide in plain sight and how to work in strange environments.

As I'd waited, I'd checked out a picture he had near a stack of old magazines that were coated with weed and white powder. In it, I saw a huge family. Behind them were palm trees and a crystal-clear blue and green ocean. In the middle of that perfect scene was my pops in his military attire, with a huge lopsided grin. He had that crazy look in his young eyes, but he seemed happy. Seemed like he was ready to take over the world, and it was all for his *familia*.

As I studied each face in the picture, one drew my attention. An older man. I had never, ever heard my pop's talk about his family except the final time he put his foot in my mom's face.

"You're still an African queen, bitch. Worthless and useless to me. Just like that twin of hers. I should have killed Nia right along with that ugly infant who wasn't mine. You whore. Only a whore would be pregnant with two men's babies at once, but you're lucky. Nia had my blood, unlike that baby who looked like that Goose nigga you loved so much. There's nothing you can do to stop me from taking her. She is mine, not yours. La familia will learn about her soon here. All you have to do is die first. Once you die, I can be free. I played by the rules by watching you and fucking the enemy. It's now time to get back to mi familia, mamacita."

The hatred in his voice put a fear in me. I could hear the bones crunching while he beat my mama. Saw the blood decorating our floor, a floor my mama and me used to clean with our own hands while we listened to her favorite Boyz II Men songs and other cuts. She now was part of that floor. Her bright red essence was seeping into the foundation of the house.

I hated him because of this. He always hurt her and always hurt me. I hated him. I didn't want to be with my pop's. Didn't want to go with him. I didn't like the words he was saying. Didn't like this new information that was coming my way. I used to be immune to his crazy attacks. Thought it was his military stuff, but now this was something different. This was impending death, and with everything he spat out, confusion lit up my mind. I had a twin? Who was Goose? Why wasn't this Goose nigga here to protect my mama from this devil?

All these thoughts ran through my mind when I rushed my father to protect my mama. I watched strength enter my mama the second she saw me. She shielded me. She kept her promise that she would always protect me. She turned into a warrior I had never seen before as she landed blows on my father. Fist to his jaw, to his perfect, handsome face. Hit his chest, stomach with a swift kick that had him stumbling backward from the force. She used whatever was around and slammed it into him, inflicting the same pain he had put on her.

In her sickness, she fought like she had superpowers, until he slammed his fist against her temple. I watched his foot come up and knew that if I didn't block it, my mama would die that day. So that was what I did. I rushed forward again and threw my body over hers. I watched my pops look at me with disdain while he held his bleeding jaw. He staggered backward, smelling of liquor, then lunged forward to grab me by my long, thick hair.

I screamed with all of me, kicking out at him and pleading for him to let me go. By then, my mother was so tired, so weary that she was on her knees, emptying her stomach. By the time we both realized what was about to happen to me, it was too late.

"She's mine and part of my family! They will know. They will all know!" A hot kettle began whistling. Next to it, I saw through my tears, was his tool kit. I thought he was going to grab something in it, but he didn't.

Instead, as I struggled, he pulled out a glove and put it on. "Stop fighting, mija!"

But I didn't, couldn't. My mom screaming at him to stop was taking over my senses, but it didn't matter, because my father was on a mission. He pulled out a small, hot, orange-red object. I realized that it was a ring. A ring he had had on the flame of the stovetop. I panicked and shouted for my mom. I moved so much that my shirt slid up, exposing the soft flesh of my stomach and back. He couldn't get to my arms or neck like he wanted, so he went with the next best thing, the area between my hip and stomach. Pain tore through me. Burning, searing heat almost made me pass out. I hated that man, hated him with all of me, while I smelled my own burning flesh. My mother found her strength again. She rushed to grab a cast-iron skillet from the counter, then swung as hard as she could and connected with my pop's head.

He stumbled backward. The sounds of sirens blaring had him watching us with restrained fury. It also had him looking at the ring in his gloved hand and back at me. The insanity in his eyes blazed as he smirked. He pointed at me and called me his before he pulled open the back door to the kitchen, then disappeared through it.

I knew without a doubt that while he would forget what had just happened, because he was just that type of drunk and dope user, I would remember it forever.

Which was why I sat in his chair during my short trip to New York City and waited for him to come home. When he got home and noticed me, I gave him a smile that matched the malice he had shown us so many years ago.

I remembered our long conversation. His being shocked that I was there. He told me he was proud that I'd found him, and all the while he downed glass after glass of beer that I had laced. Lacing it hadn't been hard to do, because he kept his product all around him. Drugs, his pills, and even needles. So while I listened to him tell me about people I should meet, *la familia*, I tricked him into using. Dazed, he pointed at that picture I'd checked out, while he mentioned *la familia* and said the old man in the photo would make me a *reina*.

Didn't know what a *reina* was, but I also didn't care. I was on a mission, and pumping him with drugs meant it was about to be accomplished. I watched him die during our long conversation, in which I learned that this *familia* didn't know a thing about me, because he had once thought me so insignificant that my existence wasn't worth talking about.

The stuff I'd thought would be history after I killed him was resurrected when I met Code. I had always thought I looked like my mama, but Code had let me know that it was my smile, the way my eyes turned into pits of blackness when I was killing niggas, and the way I got pleasure from my illegal activities that gave me away. She had said that I had a devil in me, and that this made us *familia*.

Nerves had me shaking now as I clutched my heavy backpack.

Yeah, what I was holding on to was important to me. See, in my backpack was a component for a 3-D printer. Which was why I held my backpack tightly. In addition to the printer component, I had a bundle of cash I had taken from my pop's old savings account. My mom had never closed the account or taken money from it, because she was afraid of it being traced back to us. I didn't know why she was afraid then, but I knew now. Still, since I figured I couldn't be traced and I needed some dough, I emptied the account.

In my backpack was also my small notebook that had the design for a biodegradable gun. I didn't know how to make this shit, just had the idea to create a throwaway gun for when we had to protect ourselves. Since biodegradable bullets also existed—they were made of resin, had a mineral- or petroleum-based center, and were coated in non-biodegradable plastics—I knew Boots would be able to use my notes on that and create something sick with the gun. All of this was important to me, and I wanted no one but Boots to know. Which was why I had texted him and told him that I wanted to go in on a partnership with his crew.

Yeah, so I hadn't been lying to Auto back there in the diner when I said I wasn't talking to Code at that moment. I was talking to her, but I was also talking to Boots too. Auto was on that other type of illegal shit, and I was too. But with how everything was going down, it was time to link up with people who could protect us the right way. I really wasn't trusting anyone. But in this gun game, I knew that by linking up with a man whom everyone wanted to do business with because of his mind and weaponry, I could set us up nicely and protect us from any more attacks. At least I had hoped so until I saw that old man when I was back at the restaurant.

Shit!

The sound of my phone going off had me turning right and finding a spot to hide for the time being. This was good because I could use this time to catch my breath and read my text messages. Code had been blowing me up from a number I didn't know. Only way I knew it was her was that she had told me who she was in the first message. Now she was talking about crap I just wasn't understanding.

I glanced at the words before me, frowning in the process.

Code: Midas touch used to reach into many lands. His fingers would itch when what was touched by his hands disappeared from his hold.

Confusion made my brows crest while I read those words over and over. The hell was she talking about?

What? I texted back.

Blazing car horns had me whipping my head up. My eyes darted back and forth as I watched the cars, which couldn't see me, from the alleyway in which I hid. Checking my surroundings, I saw that this was a huge shopping plaza. People moved around the place with their minds on their own business. Still, I felt exposed in this alleyway and knew I needed to go somewhere where I could blend in. My mental clock started ticking as I decided what to do and where to go so that I would not be noticed.

Glancing around again, I saw that there was a tech school across the way, and a smile appeared on my face. Blending in with the students at the tech school would be easy, and it would get me close to computers. So guess where I headed. Right. To the tech school.

I pulled off my top to expose the white Nike sports top under it, the tats on my arms, and the Egyptian winged tat that peeked slightly out from under my breasts, and then I wrapped the top around my waist. My fingers gathered up my hair, twisted it, and arranged it on top of my head, and then I dropped down to dig in my backpack. I had a pair of geek glasses, so I popped them on. I then quickly headed to the school while looking down at my cell and reading another one of Code's confusing messages, which always took me a while to get.

Code: Midas knowledge is fucking power. It reaches out!

My mind ached as I tried to decipher her message. Guessed this meant that her old man was sniffing around what I had done. I didn't know the method to her madness. Had never understood it, not even back when I met her, before ever meeting Auto and having him bust me out of jail.

See, a couple of days after taking out my father back in NYC, I had been hiding again and had watched the town house my father had been visiting. Blocks were blocks, and even though I had been in the Spanish Harlem barrio, I knew that people would be clocking a new face that wasn't a tourist. So I had had to make myself blend in, which meant I had to look like a tourist or continue to look homeless. I chose the latter. I just wanted to hear the whispers of the streets, and being homeless worked better for this. See, if I could find out who the people were in that town house, then I could know more about my father. Which was what led me to chill in what was a hole-in-the-wall restaurant, at least on the outside, but it also had cool seating for people to eat Cuban food.

Spicy, comforting scents played with my senses, making my stomach flip, dip, and twist, as I was really hungry. My bitch of a stomach got so disrespectful that it shouted out loud, drawing the attention of a girl who looked a smidge older than me. Her height was the same as mine, and she had long legs, like those of a dancer, and a curving, toned body. She had a bounce in the back that I was used to hearing niggas stroke their dicks off too while talking mad disrespect about how they would love to play with her pink slit. Her hair was actually the same length as mine, stopping at the small of her back. Hers had a thickness that revealed the African in her, but it was loose and silky, which showed the Latina in her.

Unlike mine. My hair was thick and coiled up, revealing the African in me, which I was proud of and which came from my mama. But my hair was also slightly wavy, an indication of what I now understood was my Latin and black blood, inherited from my father. This chick and I were almost the same color: I was a light brown sugar to her toffee tone. Our similar copper-brown eyes locked for a moment, which made me nervous. I wasn't trying to draw attention to myself, but I had, anyway. The chick came my way, dropped an ice-cold pop bottle with something yellowish in it in my hand. She disappeared, then came back with a plate with aluminum foil on it. Unsure about taking it, I shifted back in my chair. The girl dropped down low so that I could hear only her while the Cuban music blared.

"Go chill in the alley over there," she said, with a subtle jerk of her chin. "Mi familia don't like ratty dogs and diseased animals near their food or their restaurant, so move out quickly," I heard her add in a calm, light voice.

The edge to her voice took me back for a moment, because it was rude as hell but had a layer of kindness to it. Chatter in the front of the restaurant had me getting up to quickly grab what had been offered. I had to play the role, and I already had this chick's attention, which I didn't want.

"I got money, see . . . ? I'm just a little hungry." I threw down change, pieces of crumpled paper, and a crinkled dollar.

An amused laugh came from the girl. "That's why I gave you more than you can afford." She then mumbled something in Spanish that I understood only a little of and flashed a smile like my father's. "Girl, you're trippin'. Leave before trouble follows."

Her words made me feel some type of way. People walked by, waving at the chick, and others began to come out of the restaurant. This chick had to be related to the people in the town house. She had to be. I just knew it. But because

I did not want to draw too much attention to myself, I had to keep to my game. If I didn't move out now, then, like she'd said, trouble would follow. How she had laughed at me made me feel ashamed, and I quickly left and went to a different alley to eat and watch the restaurant.

The food was mad good. Plantains. Grilled chicken and shrimp. Rice with some onions and peas mixed in, and so much more. Everything was flavored in a way that reminded me of what my father would cook us from time to time when he wasn't being an asshole. Which had me thinking, Who is my father for real? *He wasn't just some vet. Nor was he just some abuser or another black man from the hood.*

Thinking about him, I shook my head. Sometimes it was like he was bipolar. Evil. He would cook for us while ignoring us, and then he would hurt my mom again, and even rape her. I hated it and was glad he was now maggot food. Wiping my mouth with my sleeve, I shifted my position in my hideout and fell asleep. After that meal, I didn't collect much information, if any at all. I just heard snippets about the people on that whole side of the block, including those in the town house, being some type of street kings. The girl from the restau-

rant didn't come my way, but I watched her leave the place and go to that town house.

It wasn't until I was back in ATL that I ended up seeing her again. This time, she approached me as I worked at Morton's. She sat outside the restaurant in a pimped-out speedster. It was black, with silver stripes. On its chassis were lights that flashed from time to time like lightning. At that time, I didn't even know she was the chick from New York. To me, she was just some crazy female who watched me and who then followed me toward the MARTA bus depot.

"Hey, Mami. Come talk to me," she said as she sat in the speedster. She gave a whistle.

A frown spread across my face; then my lip curled upward while I sucked my teeth. "Ew, nah. I'm good." I kept going.

I heard a car door slam, and this was followed by the sound of feet approaching me. I whipped around and stared the girl in the face.

"You need to chill," she said with a laugh.

Hair up in a ponytail bun, she stood with her arms crossed over her fancy-looking white shirt and gold mini jacket, which she wore with white leggings and gold heels. Something about how her eyes seemed to change, like she would eat me out if it weren't for something else, had me feeling mad defensive.

"Yeah? You ain't gay?" I spat out at her, just to see if I could piss her off like she was doing to me. I really didn't care if she was or not. Wasn't something that bothered me.

Old girl stared me down with controlled annoyance; then, in the blink of an eye, the stare was gone, and she gave me a pretty smile and rested a hand on her hip. "Depending on my mood, I am."

Say what? I could not believe she had said it like that. It made me laugh, actually, and had me crossing my arms in the same way she had.

Looked her up and down and shook my head in amusement. "You ain't black. What are you?"

"Oh, for real? You're just going to come at me like this, Mami?" she said with a roll of her eyes. Abruptly shrugging, she gave a dramatic sigh and rolled her eyes again. "Bullshit . . . I am black by race," she added in annoyance.

How she was acting had me laughing to myself. This was what she got. You didn't come at people the way she did and think they would hop on a train with you. I didn't know her and didn't care to.

"A'ight. Well, I'm trying to figure you out, 'cause I don't know who the hell you are and why you in my face like this. I'm not ya friend," I said, then turned away.

"Wait! Malta sea! This is important. My name is Maria Rosa. I remember you from NYC. Been following you for a long time now. I'm your cousin, and you need to watch yourself so you don't get caught by the pack of wolves that is mi familia," *she blurted out, pulling me by my arm to stop me.*

The brand my father had given me with that ring when I was a child—an *O* with a crown in the middle of it—was what had given me away back in NYC. Today I had it nicely tatted over with a tattoo that started at my rib cage and swirled over my hip. It was funny to think back on when I first met Code, because that conversation was what changed everything for us. It was also why we repeated the same words later, when I met her again, for the "first time."

Everything was a show.

I really didn't know she was running with Auto back then, and I didn't know anything about him. So when I ended up meeting his crew, what a surprise it was when I saw my "cousin" chilling among the misfit team. The shock was genuine and true. Now everything was coming full circle.

I left the past behind and focused on what I was doing. Getting into the tech school was easy breezy. When I headed to the computer lab,

all I had to do was say I had forgotten my key
card and hella dudes came my way, offering to
help. I now sat in front of a computer, clicking
away at my keyboard, hacking in to send an
encrypted e-mail message to Boots. What I had
been carrying around was too much to keep with
me. Before coming to the computer lab, I had
hid it in this school, which was the perfect spot.
I let him know that everything was precious
and that the bag I'd put it in had my detailed
instructions in it.

I glanced at my cell, waited on Code to text me
back. I was worried. In so many words, she had
told me that she was being held against her will.
Slowly, I was beginning to understand her lingo,
a secret language she had had years to perfect.

Code where? was all I had texted back, and
I got nothing in return. The waiting made me
nervous.

I hit SEND on my e-mail, and Boots now
had the information on where I had hid my
stuff. I had got a bag from the tech school's gift
shop. And I had put the bag in the ceiling of the
women's bathroom. A buzz on my cell had me
glancing down, and relief hit me.

Code: Can't say. You know why.

She was right; I did. She was determined to
keep me safe.

Code: The wolf is pissed, and the three little pigs won't be enough for his meal. Goldie is safer with the bears. Go to Papa's. Trust me. Do it and don't argue. Lay your head where you can sleep in peace.

I read her message over and over again before wiping it clean. It took me a minute, but I knew the tales *The Three Little Pigs* and *Goldilocks and the Three Bears*. Code was telling me to stay with Auto. After everything that had gone down during my time running with the Eraserheads, he was the only one Code trusted with my life. So I thought on it.

Before she'd gone ghost, she had explained that Auto's home could not be found, for good reason. That even if her old man was watching, and Code knew he was, Auto's home would still never be tracked down. I didn't know why she felt so strongly that Auto's home would never be found, but I trusted her word. I remembered when I had stayed there and how I had been cautious with my leaving. My home was also safe, but the cops had watched me back when I had a case. But now that was cleared up, so I was sure that it was safe there as well.

Every action I took had to be on point at this time.

I had run from Auto. I'd enjoyed the food I ate at the diner and the sly way I watched him, trying to figure him out. Because, for the life of me, I couldn't read him, like he was trying to read me. Now I had to go to him for real safety and bring with me more drama yet again. This wasn't cool.

But Code's life was in danger, and her secret was mine now. I wasn't sure if I would be able to trust Auto like she did, but I knew that he would hate me to my grave if something happened to Code and I didn't open my mouth. Snitching wasn't in me, especially with my DNA, but "loyalty to family" was my motto. Code had protected me, and she was still doing so. And Auto was like a brother to her, so I had no other choice. I guessed this meant that I needed to do the same for her—protect her—because of two things: one, I was her cousin, and two, we both were Eraserheads.

Loyalty over everything.

Chapter 18

Code

Papa had taken me into his custody the night Boots ended Mouse's life. I called it *custody* because he forbade me to leave the house. I'd asked him why. How dare I fix my mouth to question him, as if I had the right? he'd said.

The next day I had gone into the war room, where a meeting was taking place. All around me had sat family members: my mom, aunts, uncles, and cousins alike. They had all sat in chairs in the war room. Shit had reminded me of a dungeon. The middle of the floor was stained concrete. Drawn on the concrete was an oval shape. It was the family's crest, a capital *O* with a king's crown in the middle. There were two step-ups that circled the room as well. The people with the most power in the family sat around that oval shape, while Papa sat front and center at the head, like the king he was.

I'd been so angry when I learned he had been behind everything that I'd rushed right in to confront him, interrupting his meeting with the family council.

"Been hanging around filth so long you've forgotten your place, Maria Rosa?" he snapped at me.

The old man stood and came to stand face-to-face with me. As always, he was dressed the part of a corporate head honcho. In a bloodred dress shirt, wide-legged brown dress pants, and designer red loafers. On his left hand was a ring with the family crest. On his wrist, a black Movado timepiece. His shoulders were squared, and his eyes were unreadable except for the icy glare. The look in his cool eyes had chilled me to the bone. No matter how tough I was, the old man scared me. I'd seen him do shit that I didn't think even the devil would do. The punishment he had inflicted on those who betrayed the family was the worst. Still, I never cowered in his looming presence. To cower only seemed to anger him more.

"Papa, you stole my shit. You put the lives and the livelihood of all my friends in jeopardy. Why would you do that?" I yelled at him.

Family whispered around us. Those who thought the old man showed me way too much favoritism were anxious to see what he would do to me. I was belligerent. Was panicking at the thought of Auto finding out Papa had been behind the thefts all along. Auto and the Eraserheads were the only normal part of my life, and that was saying a lot, being that we stole shit from people and car dealers for a living. Then to have Papa use our shipment of cars to transport his guns and drugs unnerved me. He hadn't taken into account the repercussions, the fallout this would have for me. I couldn't afford to have Auto think I'd betrayed him. Couldn't afford to have the family I'd become a part of look at me as if I was a traitor. They meant that much to me.

"I did not steal anything. I cannot steal that which belongs to me," he countered.

"That didn't belong to you. It belonged to us! We worked for it. Earned the right to have a legitimate business—"

"You lost the last shipment, no?" he asked, cutting me off.

I looked up into his eyes as he closed the gap between us. "*Sí.*"

"Then tell me, How would you have been able to pay me back my investment into your little business?" he asked coolly.

"You took from us before I even borrowed the money, Papa!"

"Still doesn't matter," he spat in his normal arrogant fashion. "You now owe me way more than I took. Therefore, I now own more than half of your business."

"The hell you do."

My reward for my defiance was a backhand that immediately set my right cheek ablaze. I could feel the blood trickling down my face, as he'd smacked me with the same hand that sported his crested ring. Anger bubbled in the pit of my stomach as I slowly brought my face upright and snarled at him. Papa only chuckled, then grunted as my eyes set fire to him. To any other man in my family, that was a signal to run. To Papa, it only hyped his anger.

"Do you want to dance with your old man, Maria Rosa?" he taunted.

To dance with him had nothing to do with actual dancing. I didn't respond to him verbally. I took a deep breath and swallowed my rage for the moment.

"You are already walking on thin ice, no? To tell me no when I asked a favor, and now to defy me for a mutt-ridden family? Fags, cripples, mutes, ex-whores, and a chink are who you go up against me for, little girl?" he yelled at me.

"Your son was an undercover fag, and so was one of his sons—"

Before I could finish the sentence, his open palm struck my left cheek. Then another backhand hit the right one. Papa hated to be reminded that one of his sons used his dick as a weapon on women and men alike. One of Uncle's twin sons had picked up the nasty habit honestly from his father. The old man detested it. Had always cringed at the thought of two men having sex, whether willingly or not. While Uncle had been everything Papa had trained him to be, the one red mark against his legacy with the family was having an affinity for punishing males with his dick.

The old man's slaps made my face sting like I'd been attacked by killer bees. Blood dripped from my nose like a faucet. The fact that he had stepped down to face me showed his respect for me as his favorite grandchild. Anyone else would have had to kneel and look up at him from the floor. The loud and hard smacks on my face was more about showing his dominance than inflicting punishment.

I was so blinded by my rage that I lashed out at him. I swung out at the old man. I could tell that, if for only a few moments, my brazen violence against him stunned him, as it took him a min-

ute to react. My right fist slammed into his jaw.
Then my left one landed full frontal into his nose.
I slapped him, just so my nails could leave their
mark on his face. By the time he realized that his
baby girl was attacking him, I'd done enough to
know there was no turning back. I went to swing
at him again. He caught my left wrist and, with
little to no regard, twisted it hard enough to make
me cry out. I could have sworn in the old man's
eyes there were tears. But I was more than willing
to bet the water I saw was just a natural reaction
from the punches and slaps I'd given him.

He gave me a knee to the stomach that leveled
me. I dropped to my knees in agony. Slobber
swung from my lips as he continued to twist my
wrist. I cried out again. Looked at my mother,
only to see her standing there, looking at me in
utter disgust. Her dark chocolate face showed
that she didn't see the humor in what I had
done. Although it had taken her fourteen hours
to push me from her pussy, she would kill me in
the name of Papa, no questions asked. To show
her displeasure for my actions, she walked to the
middle of the floor and hawked a wad of spit in
my face.

Her show of loyalty to the old man wasn't
anything new for me. She'd given him custody of

me as soon as I'd been weaned from her breast milk. I belonged to him.

"Papa, you're hurting me," I pleaded as I looked back up at him.

If he twisted any harder, he would all but break my wrist. At that moment, he didn't care. The disdainful look on his face showed that he too was now blinded by rage, due to my unmitigated gall to go up against him in such a manner. Papa's hands were bigger than any man's I'd ever seen. So when he balled his fist and introduced it to my face, I blacked out before I fell back and my head hit the floor.

That had been two nights ago.

"I am the night. I cannot be claimed. I am the night. I cannot be tamed. I am the darkness. I cloak the night. In my darkest hour, I can make you question your sanity. While you sleep, I plot your demise. I am the night. I make the wolves cower in silence and make the moon howl with rage. I am the night. The only thing that can make an atheist halfway believe in God . . ."

I repeated those words over and over now as I sat hunched on my knees in the middle of the cold, dark, and damp basement. While many men in my family favored the basement, because it was used as a torture chamber by most of them, it was Papa who'd invented the

method to the madness. The one place no one
wanted to end up was in one of his many base-
ments. Neither friend nor foe. The outcome was
always the same. You were either going to die,
lose your mind, or come out with a new outlook
on life.

Hisses surrounded me. My flesh crawled at
the thought of what had me fenced in. I was
safer in the dark. If I couldn't see the things that
I feared the most, then they wouldn't scare me.

At least that was what I told myself. The hissing got closer. Seemed louder. Sweat poured
down my face as my fists tightened to the point
where I was sure my palms were bleeding. Fear
had always brought me closer to my humanity.
It balanced out the evil that I had been born with.
Fear brought me back down to earth.

My mind went to Smiley. During these two
days that I had been in the basement, Freddie
had brought me food and my phone. The only
way I had been able to text Smiley was because of
Freddie. If Papa knew Freddie had been sneak-
ing me a means of communication, Freddie
would surely be placed somewhere where his
fear of water would consume him. Freddie had
almost drowned when he was three, and as a
result, he was afraid to go anywhere near pools
or bodies of water.

Papa had used that against him too. But now Freddie could hold his breath underwater for five minutes. His specialty was death by water. Still, Papa played on those fears when he saw fit, just as he played on my fears. That was the reason I sat alone now in a basement filled with enough snakes to make my flesh crawl. While none I could see were venomous, the paralyzing fear they caused me was still all too real.

The door to the basement opened, and light shone through. At the top of the stairs stood Papa, Freddie, and Mark.

"Go get her," he ordered them.

Dressed in all black suits, both my cousins descended the concrete stairs. My legs were weak from having kneeled for so long. Stomach still hurt from Papa's knee. It wasn't until hours after he'd kneed me that I realized the blow was harder than I'd thought. Face was sore and swollen from his assault as well. Freddie and Mark practically dragged me up the long flight of stairs. I couldn't stop the tears that were falling down my face. I gazed at my old man through burning tears. As much as I hated him, I loved him. He'd taught me how to ride a bike. Taught me how to shoot a gun. Was affectionate when the time called for it. Had even had no problem talking about things that made most grandfather's cringe, such as when it came to a woman's monthly.

I didn't really have a mother. She was there, but that was all. It was Papa who had nurtured me. Papa who had made many of the wives he had take care of me. It was Papa who had threatened the first little boy who had broken my heart at ten years old. Papa was the first man I'd loved. And for my love, in return, he'd taken my soul. I could never be free of him.

"Why did you make me do this to you, *mi tesoro*?" he asked me affectionately.

I didn't answer him. I let my tears roll down my face, defiance still showing in my eyes, I was sure.

"Take her to her mother so she can be cleaned up," Papa ordered. "Maria Rosa, when you are done, I expect to see you in the war room."

Papa nodded. Freddie and Mark helped me down the long hallway. Once we reached my bedroom, they tossed me face-first onto my king-size bed. I knew if we were alone, Freddie wouldn't have been so careless, but he, too, had to keep up a certain façade.

I grunted loudly as I turned over in the bed. My wrist was screaming in pain. My white down comforter was now covered with specks of my blood. I stared around the room that had been mine for as long as I could remember. It had changed over time: the princess-themed décor had given way to a more mature theme. Pictures of famous female warriors, from both fiction and nonfiction, decorated my walls. All women of color. My room was spotless, as living with Papa demanded this. The maplewood flooring had been polished to perfection.

Upon the gold, cream, and white carpet at the foot of my bed was a trunk filled with guns that I had collected over time. My white armoire was trimmed in twenty-four-karat gold, courtesy of Papa. Closet was filled with everything clothes- and shoes-wise that I could imagine. Yes, the old man had spoiled me. It pained me to know that he had betrayed my trust.

It didn't take my mother long to make her appearance. I'd been trying to rid myself of my soiled clothing for minutes before she strolled in. The bitch always walked like she had a book balanced on her head. For as regal as she walked, she was a deadly pit bull, trained to fight. Her long hair sat plaited against her head. She had on a thin green silk gown that outlined her slim figure.

She didn't say anything as she laid white bath linens on my bed before walking over to help me undress. She was shorter than I was, but her attitude made her seem as if she was a giant. Once I was nude, she looked at the bruises on my stomach and side.

"You deserved it, you know," she told me. "How dare you disrespect my father as such? *Tu me averguenza y eres muy arrogante. Pude haberte matado*!"

She was angry that I'd embarrassed her and acted with arrogance. She was so angry that she told me she could have killed me.

"Is your standing with Papa more important than me, Mama?" I asked.

She stood back and looked at me. "You know the rules in this family, girl. Don't act as if you don't. Father holds you in high regard, and you would so vehemently defy him for the sake of gutter trash! Have you no respect for our bloodline, child? Have you no shame to be associated with such utter filth? People who don't even know where they come from?"

"*Ellos no son basura, mamá*! They are not trash. They are people. They are my friends. They have families. They have survived what you couldn't imagine."

"Trash! I don't care what you say. Choose your battles, Maria Rosa. Do not go up against my father again."

As I held my left wrist in my right hand, I shook my head. "I am your daughter, Mama. You carried me for nine months, sí. What about me? What about what I want?"

The woman who should have had some love in her eyes for me slapped me. With one smooth, fluid sweep of her feet, my back hit the floor hard. She got down on one knee and yanked me up by my hair.

With a darkness richer than the one in my eyes, she told me, "This isn't just about you, *mija*. This is about *familia, la familia Orlando*. And the next time you sully our name, I will have you placed in the dirt, in an unmarked grave next to the rest of the traitors. *Entiendes*?"

She didn't give me time to answer before she got up and stormed from the room. I lay there on the floor, wondering where my life had taken a left turn. What had I gotten my surrogate family into?

It took me over an hour to bathe myself. I wrapped my wrist as best I could. Cleaned the dried blood from my lips, nose, and eyes. Bandaged my ribs so the pain there would ease up, then donned my signature white suit. I forwent the heels and decided to slide my feet into white boots. After pulling my hair back into a neat bun at the nape of my neck, I met the old man in the war room.

"I went to see your friend Auto today," Papa said to me as he and I sat at the dinner table.

The only other people in the room were Mark and Freddie, each flanking the old man. Before me sat a plate with a succulent T-bone steak, asparagus, homemade mashed potatoes, and handmade French bread. Papa had cut into his medium-rare steak and was eating like all was well between us. His white suit jacket hung neatly on the back of his chair. The sleeves of his white dress shirt were rolled midway up his forearms, the tattoos only family knew he had clearly visible.

I simply stared at my plate. No way would I eat anything on that plate. He noticed my hesitation.

"Why aren't you eating, Maria Rosa? I slaved in the kitchen to make your favorite, and you would insult the cook, no?" he inquired.

He had cooked. That was the closest thing to an apology I would get from him. But I was no damn fool. Many men had met their deaths by way of poison at the hands of Papa. He moved his plate to the side, pulled mine in front of him. I watched as he cut into my steak, then took a bite. Next, he ate a spear of the asparagus, then a spoonful of the potatoes. Finally, he took a big chunk of the bread and nodded at me.

"No poison, *mi bella*. I would not poison some-one so important to me over a minor infraction. Give me some credit."

As he talked, he frowned, while pointing his knife at my food. Once he had pushed the plate back over to me, I dug in. I couldn't front like I wasn't hungry. My stomach had started to growl as soon as I saw the spread.

"As I was saying, your friend Auto, I saw him," he continued while he chewed. "We couldn't come to an agreement. I'd like you to help me with that."

I was curious. "An agreement on what?"

"I want to use his business in the auto industry as a means of transport. Think you can help me convince him?"

I knew by the tone of his voice that what he'd asked wasn't really a question. He was testing me. He needed to see how deep my loyalty to family still was. The fact that he had shown his face to Auto alarmed me. Papa showed his face for only two reasons. One, he was confident that he was going to do intricate business with you. Two, he was going to kill you. Neither boded well for Auto.

"I'll talk to him."

"Need you to do more than talk."

"I said I would talk to him, Papa. He isn't one of us. You can't expect him to just hand over a part of the business he's built from the ground up."

Papa cut into his steak again, ate a few bites, then sipped his wine. He took the cloth napkin and wiped his hands before standing.

"Do more than talk, Maria Rosa. Get me results, or things will go from bad to worse," was all he said before he turned his gaze away from me. "Marco, Frederick, come. We have business to discuss."

Once I was sure they were gone, I made a beeline to my car. Was set to pull away, but then Freddie came running out.

"Yo, Code, wait," he called out.

I hit the brakes and then waited for him to get to me.

"You okay?" I asked him.

He nodded once. "I'm good."

"Thought the old man wanted to talk to you."

"He did. I asked to be excused for a moment. You need to watch yourself. After everything that's happened, Papa's letting you leave too easily."

Butterflies settled into my stomach. "You hear something?"

He shook his head. "No, but you know him. Something is off. I don't know. He and Marco have been talking a lot. Talking about war strategies and shit. Supposedly, we've found a new set of *familia* that had been missing." He saw the panic in my eyes. "Not Smiley. Not yet. Football player for the Nightwings. Watch the news when you can. Anyway, just be careful. I love you, a'ight?"

I nodded. "I know. Love you too, cousin. And thank you for always having my back."

"Just like you always have mine. Oh, and I finally got Oya to answer my texts," he said, then grinned wide.

I shook my head, smiling inwardly that he wasn't treading down the same road as other men had in our family when it came to women. I waved at my cousin and sped off.

Chapter 19

Code

I got to Morrow quicker than I ever had. I didn't want the team to see me as beat up as I was. I parked behind the abandoned Sherwin-Williams plant, then eased my way around to the back of the shop. I slowly made my way up the stairs, used my key to open the door, and stepped into the security room.

Auto was already there. I guess he had been as paranoid as I felt. His hair sat on his shoulders. Black, square-toed dress shoes tapped the floor. He was dressed in a gray polo-style shirt and black slacks. His coffee-black eyes took note of the condition of my face. I watched him inhale and exhale hard.

"I would ask where you've been, but judging by the condition of your face, I can guess," he said.

"Where's Smiley?" I asked him.

He told me the story of how she had run off after seeing the old man approaching Colleen's.

"So where is she now?"

He pointed to one of the TV screens. In the computer room was Smiley, doing what she did best.

Auto swiveled his chair back in my direction and looked at me before standing.

"I need to talk to you and the crew, but you first," I said.

He nodded. "Good. Because I was thinking the same thing."

Auto's eyes held apprehension. I could tell by the way he kept his distance that he was questioning his trust in me. That was to be expected. Auto was smart, so it was safe to say that he had figured out that it was the old man who had visited him.

"I want you to know that I love this family, and I would never betray what we've built. Still, there are some things I need to come clean about. First thing is Smiley," I said.

He folded his arms across his sinewy chest as he watched me.

I went on. "She isn't just some random person that pinged our system. She's my cousin. I ran into her months ago at her job. Had met her years before that and had been watching her.

This is hard to explain, and I know right now you're probably wondering why the hell I would lie to you about her being family, right?"

Auto didn't say a word. He kept his face free of any emotion. The only way I could tell his anger was rising was by the way his upper lip twitched in the right-hand corner.

"The dynamics of my family are complicated, Auto. The only way I can explain this to you is like this. I had to keep who she was a secret, lest the old man take her. She, too, is a granddaughter of the old man. And anything with his blood belongs to him and *la familia Orlando*. I didn't want him to do to her what he has done to me. And the only way to do that was to have you spring her from the joint."

"So why didn't you just tell me this from the jump?"

"Because the less you knew, the safer you would be."

"This is bullshit, Code. Bullshit. You used me. You played on the trust we had to further your agenda."

"It wasn't like that, Auto. It's because I trust you that I felt she would be safer here with us."

Auto shook his head. Mumbled something under his breath about every nigga having an agenda. Then he kicked the chair in front of him.

"And she knows who she is to you?" he asked.

"Yes."

"So I'm the only one in the dark about this whole thing?"

I nodded, shamefully so.

"You know I don't work this way. We're family. We never keep secrets like this. I pride myself on being a great leader. I like to ensure everybody on the team knows what's going down beforehand."

"I know, and I'm sorry."

He shook his head, with his lips turned down into a scowl. "What else?" he asked.

This was the part I hated, because I knew that with what I was about to tell him would come the end of my place in the Eraserheads. Still, he needed to know the old man was gunning for him. So I told him everything. From the first shipment being stolen to the last one, which gave us our biggest loss. I told him how the old man had been behind the whole thing. By the time I was done, Auto had flipped his lid, and had it not been for the love he had for me, we would have become mortal enemies. More so on his end than mine.

"I swear on everything, I didn't know. Had I known, I would have prevented it or would have come to you sooner. I didn't know we were going up against the old man," I pleaded.

"I don't want to hear that shit, Code. I really don't. You should have told me as soon as you suspected that shit. I'm left out in the cold, scrambling to cop my losses, hustling for fucking chump change, and you would sit on this info? This is my life!" he yelled, slapping a hand against his chest. "This is *their* lives," he continued as he pointed at the screen on the TV showing the team closing up shop.

It was after eight in the evening. The time when we closed down the shop daily. My phone kept vibrating, but I ignored it. It was more than likely the old man, trying to see if I had made good on my end of the bargain. I ignored him. On the screen, Seymore, Reagan, Lelo, Stitch, Dunkin, and Jackknife were all clowning around as they shut things down for the evening. There were still a few customers in the waiting area, waiting on their cars to be pulled around.

It pained me that I had been part of the reason their lives could possibly be in danger.

"I know, Auto, and I'm sorry."

"*Sorry* ain't fucking good enough, Code."

"I had to be sure it was the old man before I—"

"Before you what? You borrowed money from this motherfucker, and now, because we can't pay him back in the time he deems acceptable, he wants to take what belongs to me? That's not

going down on my watch. And I'll take down
whoever I need to, to ensure it doesn't. Just like
you got people, I have people too. By any means
necessary, I will protect what's mine. If that
means you and I will have to part ways, so be it."

He spoke those last words with such finality
that they stabbed at me, causing greater emotional pain than the physical wounds inflicted
upon me. I watched as Auto snatched the door
open to the security room and stalked out. A
few minutes later I followed in his footsteps, my
heavy burden leading the way. I hoped to find
Auto in his office, but he wasn't there. The door
to his office was open, and I could hear the noise
of the shop.

As always, Auto's office was hotter than the
devil's nuts. The stifling heat was suffocating when
mixed with my deflating emotions. I watched
as Lelo and Stitch argued about whose turn it
was to clean the kitchen once they got home.
They were both wearing the auto shop's uniform
jumper. Each of them had the top part hanging
down around their waist, showing off sleeveless
ribbed-cotton white T-shirts. Sweat made their
skin glisten.

"Nigga, I cleaned that shit last night," Stitch
fussed. "I'm not doing it tonight. I'm going
home, showering, eating, and then chilling with
the kids if they're still awake."

"The hell you say," Lelo quipped in return. "I'm not cleaning the kitchen."

"Ain't nobody about to be living in roaches, either. I know you used to that shit, growing up in the barrio and all, but nah, bruh. You're cleaning that shit right up."

"Ey, fuck you, man. You always got some shit to say about where I grew up. But soon as I make jokes about shit in your childhood, it's a problem."

"Whatever. Clean the kitchen when we get home," Stitch replied.

"Whatever."

Seymore and Reagan were chuckling. Seymore was at the printer. Reagan was at the sink, washing off some part she had in her hand. Jackknife and Dunkin had walked into the waiting area to hand the customers their keys after pulling cars around. Once the customers had driven off, they sat down and flipped the TV to a basketball game. All was well in their world. They had no idea of all the mess we were in. The doors to the garage bays had been pulled down. The workday was done.

I finally pulled my phone out of my pocket. Five missed calls from Freddie and two texts. The first text read, I'm sorry. The next one read, Forgive me. I frowned. To say I was confused was an understatement. *Forgive him for what?*

"Oh shit," I heard Lelo sing in a happy voice. "Code's back."

I jerked my head up, thinking they'd spotted me in the office, only to see Lelo was at one of the garage doors.

"Damn, where she been, anyway?" Reagan wanted to know.

"Probably handling biz for the fam. You know Code. She always working shit out for us," Stitch said, chiming in.

"I don't know, but I'm glad she brought my fucking truck back," Lelo said with a laugh.

Just as he was pulling the garage door up, it hit me. I'd taken Lelo's truck the night we'd all met at Joy Lake. Since Papa had kept me in the basement, I hadn't had a chance to give Lelo his truck back. I rushed from Auto's office just as Auto came rushing down the stairs from the computer room.

"Lelo, don't open the door!" I yelled, but it was too late.

It all happened in slow motion for me. As soon as the garage door came up, there stood my cousin Mark. In his hand was an AK-47 assault rifle. Flanking him were six other men, including Freddie. Lelo never knew what hit him. His body jerked backward as his chest was riddled with bullets. Reagan had to tackle Stitch to the floor.

Seymore took a hit to the chest from a shotgun blast and was sent flying from his wheelchair. Auto jumped over the railing and went for cover. Smiley took a hit to the shoulder as Auto pulled her over with him.

Bullets swept the place as the men marched forward into the shop. I knew Papa had ordered the hit, because none of the bullets came my way and I was standing out in the open. I rushed into Auto's office. Hit the button for the hidden panel on his wall. Grabbed a Desert Eagle and rushed back to the firefight. With perfect aim and precision, I took down two of my male cousins with ease. Two bullets between each one's eyes. I could see Auto flanking Smiley, who was on one knee, still shooting, despite the obvious pain in her shoulder. Auto's aim was just as good as mine. While another cousin had ducked for cover, I sent a bullet to chase him. Reagan and Stitch were in a dire situation. If they moved from their hiding spot, they'd be dead. I turned my gun on Freddie, took his left kneecap out, then his right elbow. His yelps of pain brought tears down my face.

All I saw was Lelo's body hitting the floor. Heard Stitch's yells of no as he watched the man he loved fall to the floor. Smiley came out from under the stairs. Her bullets chased Mark around the room as he ran for cover. Auto dropped his gun. Ran up behind my cousin Rubio, who had set his sights on Reagan and Stitch. Auto looked like something out of a *Rambo* movie when he pulled the hunting knife from the belt of his pants and sliced Rubio's neck from ear to ear. And just to make sure my cousin would die, Auto shoved the knife in Rubio's back, where his kidneys were, four times before he let his body drop to the floor in a heap.

My cousin Jeremy was so thrown off by the fact I was shooting at him that he never saw Smiley sneak up behind him and put a bullet through the back of his head. I looked at Freddie, who was writhing in pain on the floor. I'd shot him only to spare his life, since he had been firing blindly in a direction none of my friends were in. Me shooting him would save his life once the old man found out what I'd done.

Mark rushed out from behind a car to drag his brother to safety. Another shooter, my cousin Tyree, let go a spray of bullets that sent us all ducking for cover.

"You fucking kill your own, Maria Rosa?" Mark called out to me, the panic and alarm in his voice clear. "You're done, *puta*. Finished when Papa finds out. You're done!"

While the gunman kept shooting, I could see Mark dragging Freddie out of the garage to the safety of their getaway car. Auto crept up behind Tyree. Auto's quick slashes with his knife and one stab underneath Tyree's arm stunned him. Two more through Tyree's ribs on either side sent him into a tailspin. Auto moved like lightning, dropped down to one knee, and jabbed the knife into both femoral arteries, pulling the blade out so quickly that blood spewed like a geyser.

Sobs echoed around the garage. My heart started to hurt at the guttural, wrenching sounds coming from Stitch. I turned to see him sitting behind Lelo, his arms wrapped around him, as Lelo fought to breathe. Gargling sounds could be heard coming from his throat.

"Fuck, fuck, fuck, man! Come on, baby. Just relax. Just breathe for me please," Stitch begged.

Lelo was trying to say something, but every time he did, blood pooled in his mouth. He was shaking as he held on to his lover's hand. There was a wild look of panic in his eyes. The same in Stitch's eyes. The shop seemed to spin around me as my vision took in Reagan cradling Seymore in her arms. He was already gone. In the waiting area Jackknife was using sign language to let us know Dunkin was also no longer with us. My hands started to shake as my grip on the handles of the guns got tighter.

"No, no, no, no!" Stitch yelled out. I watched as he rocked back and forward.

Lelo's short spurts of breath started to get slower and slower as the light dimmed in his eyes.

"I'm sorry, man. I'll do the fucking dishes. I'll do whatever you want. Just don't leave me and the kids. Carmen and I can't do this shit alone, man," Stitch pleaded. "We need you. Four kids, baby. We have four. Me and Carmen going to kill each other if you ain't there to stop us. Please don't go . . ."

Bloody tears rolled down Lelo's face. He held on until he couldn't any longer.

"Ahhh! God, why? Why? Why do you take everything from me? Why?" Stitch cried out.

Reagan's muffled sobs crawled up my spine. She had a fistful of Seymore's shirt as she cried into his lifeless shoulder. Smiley was holding her shoulder as she stood back. It was as if the sight of death did something to her. Her body was in the room, but it looked as if her mind had traveled somewhere else. I turned to search for Auto, only to find his gun aimed at me.

"Get out," he ordered me. "Get the fuck out!"

"Au-Auto, what're you doing?" Reagan asked.

"Auto . . . I'm so . . . I'm so sorry," I cried in a whisper.

"Code, get out," he told me as he fought to hold back tears. His lips were set in a tight frown. "Get out before I kill you."

"Auto, stop. She's family," Reagan yelled, defending me in her ignorance at the moment.

I had no words. Had no defense. As I exited the garage, I knew that none of us would ever be the same.

I drove around aimlessly for what seemed like hours. I knew soon enough Papa would come looking for me. Betrayal of family was never left unpunished. I needed help. Needed someone to protect Auto and the team when I no longer could. I was thinking ahead of the game. As I walked in the entrance of the apartment complex, people watched me. They watched the girl dressed in all white with a Desert Eagle in her hand. It was Garden Walk, after all. No one would call the cops. No one would think it was out of the norm for someone to brandish firearms on this side of town. It was the hood, always a war zone. The "no snitching" policy always in effect.

While none of the normal tenants would stop me, Oya, Shango, Alize, and Shredder wouldn't be so quick to look the other way. They all stopped me when I was midway to Boots's apartment, guns aimed, cocked, and ready.

"I need to see Boots," I told them.

"Not carrying heat like that you don't," Shango said.

"What do you need to see him for?" Alize asked.

"This is important. Just get him or get out of my way."

Neither of them moved. If I'd been in another frame of mind, I could have easily taken them out. If I were here to cause harm, I wouldn't have come through the front gate. The loud music ceased. People started to rush inside their apartments. Parents snatched small children by their hands and pulled them inside.

"Nah. Not until you tell us what's so important that you had to come brandishing firearms," Shango replied.

I didn't have time for the games. "Boots!" I yelled loudly.

I knew he could hear me. Knew he could see me. The security cameras on the poles deemed it so.

I called out loudly to him again. "I know you can hear me. We need to talk!"

Just as I thought it would, the door to his apartment building opened. He nodded toward his guards to let me pass. He stood in his signature cowboy boots; these seemed to be made of a skin I couldn't readily identify. Black denims, a white button-down, and a black vest made up his attire. A gun sat nestled against his hip as he studied me.

"Talk," he demanded.

"I know who took your last shipment and replaced it with children and drugs. May be able to help you get your first shipment back, but you have to help me first."

Chapter 20

Boots

"I'm destined to live the dream for all my peeps who never made it, 'cause yeah, we were beginners in the hood as five percenters. But somethin' must've got in us, 'cause all of us turned to sinners . . . ," Nas sang in the background.

In every story, there's always a villain, ran through my mind while I sat behind my screen, staring at the gunplay going down outside a little auto shop hidden in Morrow, Georgia, thanks to PT's correspondence. I had sent him there on the low to watch them and to deliver a message about discussing our negotiating partnership, but that had been cut short by the images being sent to me via PT's cell. It was quite unfortunate that shit had gone down the way it had. It messed with the business I was about to do. More like put it on pause. Nas continued his rhyming in the background. Fingers tented against my lips, I gave a sigh, then turned the monitor off.

"So, son, that's the crew you intended to do business with?" my pops asked out of concern. We were speaking by video chat.

"Yes sir, it is . . ." I paused when I saw a familiar face walking toward my apartment complex on the security monitors. Some shit was coming my way in the form of a lovely devil, and it had me curious about what it was.

"My task was to get close eventually. But thanks to the business with our enemy, he helped me faster than I had intended. Unfortunately, I wasn't able to protect them from this surprise attack. Having my men step in would have exposed my hand and possibly put them at more risk," I explained, hoping he would understand and think along the same lines as me.

"It is unfortunate, but it just shows how he hasn't changed much in how he flexes his power and reveals his pride. If the leader was strong enough to be with my grandson and have his trust, then I hope he is strong and smart enough to see the weakness presented in that attack. Find a way to help them if you truly seek to do business with them."

I gave my father a respectful nod of understanding. It fell on my shoulders to help in my own way. So I would think of something to do that would be as inconspicuous as possible. The enemy of my enemy was now my friend. I could see Code being questioned by my team. After hitting a button on my laptop, I flipped the image so that my father could see what was going on.

He gave a deep chuckle. "The lizard that enters into a scorpion's hole will come back with its rear. That was told to all the young men running with the king. I held it close to my heart, and my first wife snatched your old man's ass due to that principle. Then, later, your mother did the same before she died in her grief, so watch out. She's your type, but I know that the old adage of keeping your friends close and your enemies closer might help in this."

I really didn't know what a lizard's tail had to do with a scorpion's hole or how it pertained to the situation at hand. Still, I listened to my pops. Sometimes the meaning of the things he said came to me later.

"What do you suggest, then, Dad?" I asked out of respect just to gain a little more wisdom here.

"My enemy doesn't have to be your enemy, son. This battle is not your obligation, as I've always told you, and I wish I'd been able to tell your brother and my grandson. But that is

my regret, and not knowing where they were. I
never wanted you to become involved in this
age-old war. I trained you to be the best, to go
beyond me. Gave you additional teachers until
your own mind was sharp enough for even me to
want to follow. Trust in your own plan. Do with
it as you wish. I will be proud always, because
you are my son. This gang family is nothing
compared to that. I lost too much to let it be.
Besides, dipping into an Orlando has happened
with our family of Kings, as you know. It will not
be anything new . . ."

Pride gave me armor while I laughed at his
words. On the monitor, I saw my father reclined
in the backseat of his ride. The interior was
upholstered in houndstooth black-and-cream
leather, and the car's back windows were blacked
out, so he sat in the shadows. I knew he was out of
the country because of our previous conversation.

I glanced at my monitors before answering
him, still laughing at his words. "This fight is
about our justice for my brother and his son, my
nephew. You say I wasn't born into this battle,
but I say I was, Dad. So I'm going to do this even
if I die in the process."

Code stood surrounded by my people, and
the fact that she knew I was watching made me
smile in amusement. "Dad, we'll speak again
soon. Thank you for the details on my new guns.

Make sure to remind the shop to place a smiling face on each one in respect to its creator."

"Of course . . ." A pause came on his end, then the sound of a car door opening and closing.

I glanced over to check on my old man and saw the shape of a second person, a curving leg, then the side profile of a woman I swore was Naomi Campbell. She wore all black with a pop of purple, like my people usually did. In her hand was a machete, which she lovingly tucked into her mink fur coat. Her ruby-red lips parted into a plump curve. That spark of intimacy between the two had me watching her and my father as they reached toward each other in a loving hug before they leaned back and he glanced my way.

Dad had always taught me to remember my surroundings, and this was one of those times where I had to add up the clues quickly. It didn't take me long when I saw the keloid tribal marks that went over her shoulder and down her arm as her hand carefully touched my father's left kneecap. Her hand dropped to feel the false leg there. She was showing her respect, and I liked her for that. The cascading mark she had was something no other woman was allowed to have but her. A woman who was a Supreme Queen, to be exact. A Nigerian Kulu Queen.

Excitement had me hyped at the move my father was making. While I was growing up, I had heard of her tales, how they ruthlessly hunted their enemies and survived their own battle against our common enemy. I had sat at my father's feet, listening to stories about how she and her husband had trained their daughter to be a lethal princess and now the American faction African Queen she was. The ancestors were being resurrected as they tried to protect the next generation.

"I will be off the grid for my meeting, son, and in the air, traveling," I heard my father say. "Continue as we spoke about. I have others to gather. We will speak soon," he added before the monitor went blank, leaving me to my own thoughts and my plan.

After pushing back from my desk, I entered my standard code, then flipped everything back to its typical feed. I grabbed one of my flavored toothpicks, stuck it in my mouth, and adjusted my Glock so that it showed. Then I strolled out to the front of my apartment building to greet my guest. I studied her with a great deal of distrust. She had too many secrets for my taste, but I wouldn't be who I was if I did not desire to know just how deep her game of deceit really went.

So, I shifted in my boots and crossed my arms over my chest. "Talk."

Only seriousness danced behind Code's whiskey-brown eyes. Her lush lips formed a thin line, and the bruises that peppered her face only added to the badass bitch image she gave off. "I know who took your last shipment and replaced it with children and drugs. May be able to help you get your first shipment back, but you have to help me first."

My crew started to put up a loud protest. I grinned at the shorty in front of me for changing this old Shakespearean battle between my family and hers. I knew whatever she was here for would make me shift my chess pieces on the board. So I was very pleased at the maneuver I had to decide to take in the reveal of this new move.

I slid my hands in my pockets, and my tongue moved my toothpick in my mouth back and forth. I had a huge grin on my face while I looked down at her. "Everyone, again, be chill. Before I decide if she's going to eat metal, she and I have to have a conversation. Like any of my guests seeking me out for business, you will show her a little respect. You all know this, right?"

I addressed Code. "Follow me," I said while I moved to the side and held my hand out for her to follow.

Her lovely eyes locked on me, and I saw her uncertainty. My father's words came back to me in full force. *She has too many secrets*, ran in my mind on repeat while I followed her and enjoyed the way her body moved. But she was a bad chick, and I guessed that meant in order to do what I needed to do, getting close to the enemy by making her my friend was the new phase of the plan, for now.

Was this some stupid shit I was doing? Probably, but even so, no matter how interesting pussy was, there was no way that I was about to allow it to control or dictate how I was pursuing my hidden agenda. So for now, I planned to see what she needed, and judging by the looks of things that I had seen on the monitor, and by her appearance, shelter was what it was.

After closing the door to my office behind me, I locked it and saw her turn sharply. "Relax. Tell me what you need, and we can see if we can come to an agreement."

I moved past her, offered her a chair in front of my desk before I went into my pantry, where I kept a med kit. After walking back her way, I waited, then tossed it to her.

"Talk, or we can end it now," I said.

Code flipped the med kit between her fingers, then quietly opened it. "I'm not lying, and I know who has your stuff and why they took it."

"A'ight, and you're suddenly eager to give me all the knowledge of the world for . . . ?"

I poured water into a clear glass with ice, and then I headed to my desk and stood directly in front of her. I handed her the glass of water.

"Protection, and I'm good," she said and shook her head and used her teeth to rip open an ointment packet, then smeared its contents on her arm, then under her shirt. "Look, I just want my crew to be protected. I know what my old man can do and what he will do to them. I just . . . I mean, I know you can give them that."

She was right. I could. However, this request for help had me curious about this whole thing. "I'm tempted to see you strip just to make sure you're not tapped or some shit, but how banged up you are . . . Nah, never mind. When a person is set on playing someone, they can paint a fantasy any way they want just so that they can achieve their agenda. So my thing is this. Mama, what's yours?"

"I'm not here to play games. I need to lay low, and the best place to do that is where I'd never be caught laying my head down at," she explained while carefully rolling her top down.

What she said next had me pulling out my chair and taking a seat. Her pretty brown irises darkened. They used to hold a little light but now held a deep-seated darkness. Something akin to vengeance and grief.

"Say I believe you, then. How is coming here any safer for you or your friends, Mama? You know your friends are being watched. The fact that your old man came after both of our goods and effectively swapped them out shows that he is watching me too. Now, any smart person knows about playing the game of illusion and having a dope-ass sleight of hand. That's what makes any magician a master. So I can guarantee the safety of your friends, but what's your sleight of hand, Mama?"

"Stop asking me that. I don't have one. I just . . . I just need to rest my head here and think . . . ," she said wearily. "Not for long, though, I promise," she added quickly.

The exhaustion in her eyes and body made me sigh. I watched her quietly, then ran a hand over my waves.

"So can you—will you—do it? Help my people?" I heard her ask while I sat in thought.

I said, "I'm thinking."

The loud scraping of her chair as she got up, then the sound of her abruptly slamming it, causing it to fall to the floor, made me look up at her, only to get locked in a stare down. "What do I need to do, huh? It's a simple yes or no. My family isn't known to beg, but this . . . this shit is different. No matter what my old man says and thinks, those people are my family. *Mi familia.* They deserve the best, and not death because of me."

There was so much conviction in her voice that it had me watching her with newfound respect. Clearly, she was in pain from her battle, yet she stood in front of me with a willpower like that of a true queen. No fucks were given with her. Right now it was raw and real, regardless of her secrets, and I had to take that into account in this negotiation.

Cool and collected, I kept my gaze on Code's and never broke it. "So you're loyal to your Eraserheads or to your old man? Which is it? Because you're not at the end of your rope, baby."

"I . . . both," she said with a hint of sadness in her voice.

That was all the answer I needed in this. I stood and moved around the desk. "Then you can't do a damn thing for me until you know where your loyalty lies. I can't help you until then."

"Wait! What? No, see, you can help. Forget me. Help Auto. Help Smiley!" she urged me.

The way her body slightly teetered from exhaustion made even me tired. I stepped forward, then forced her back in the chair, which I had picked up off the floor. I reached out, took her chin, then turned it from side to side, checking for more cuts or head trauma. I saw nothing, so I dropped my hand, then caged her with my arms.

"I'm taking you to your own apartment in here. No snakes, I promise. There you will rest to give yourself time to think. Three days should suffice. If you leave in that period of time, the temporary protection that I give to your people evaporates. Understood?"

Her head bobbed, and she got ready to open her mouth, but I stopped her by raising my hand.

"Two, in those three days, if you do not tell me where your loyalty lies, then again, all security is gone, and they are on their own. Any help they ask of me on their own is between me and them, so don't think about contacting them, because that will then be a breach of contract. Understood?"

A spark of annoyance flashed across her beautiful face. It made me want to laugh, but I wasn't in the mood to, so I stood up to wait for her to acknowledge that she understood me.

"Yeah, fine, whatever. Three days, I can do that, but . . ." she said, looking up at me. "I'm not here to be your bitch. So don't think that I'm going to be free pussy for you or your boys."

That there made me laugh. "Trust me, that's not how we do things. You and your other family might be about that twisted shit, but there are many ways to do business and many ways to torture. Rape is a lazy way to do things. So I'm good. Besides, anything that goes down between us will go down willingly, and my people aren't interested in you in that way. Don't think the power of your pussy is that fly, Mama. It ain't. It's just pussy."

With that, I snatched her up and threw her over my shoulder.

"What the hell is your problem? Put me down, *pendejo*!" Code screamed, then began to thrash my back.

"I'm many things, Mami, and an asshole is one of them, but keep fighting and I'll throw your ass out a window, *entiendes*?" After strolling out of my office, I kept to the back of the apartment. I entered another room, where I ducked down, since she was still over my shoulder, and walked into the closet. I pushed one of the closet walls to the side, revealing a hidden passageway.

"Put me down! Ow!" Code spat.

Sometimes this chick could be a handful, which was why I sighed and shifted my body up so she would bang her head on a hanging rod as I stepped into the passageway. I walked a few feet, then reached out and slid a door open. We stepped into another room, which belonged to another apartment. Light washed over us both when I tapped the light switch. Then I dropped her on the huge bed in front of me.

"Bathroom's behind me. Next to it is the door to the hallway. Take it to the living room and the kitchen. This is Alize's spot. If you decide to leave, my people will grab you in any direction you go, even up or down, understood? Now chill out and rest. If you need me, get Alize or Oya. They'll be your best friends while you stay for a while. Remember our agreement, Mami," I explained, giving her a rundown on how all of this was going to work.

Code pushed herself up on her elbows, then slipped back in exhaustion. She turned on her side, then closed her eyes. "If I need to go, no one will be able to stop me. Know that. Like I said, I just need to lay low. I want to . . . I want to see my people, but I can't. So I know if you can just help them, they'll be good no matter what happens to me. I don't care if I die. Death is my lover, and after today the old man is going to try to give me that kiss by any means necessary."

What she said made sense, and from my having studied her old man, I knew it was the truth. Thinking about what she had just said, I went over to the door that connected this apartment to mine. I closed the door, locked it, and then headed to the doorway of her room. "Check it. Death may be your lover, but only you can turn it around and make it benefit you. Shit, I'd turn into an angel of death if I were you. But you're chicken shit. Copping out in your pain, and about to let your old man make you look weak. He's all about leaders, right? Be one. It's just that simple."

Code stared at me in shock. Her nose crinkled in a cute way; then she gave me a look of annoyance and scowled at me in anger. No lie, I was enjoying pissing her off.

"You know nada! Just look at those ugly-ass boots on your feet. Bet them things stank too," she spat out.

Opening the door that lead to the hallway, I shrugged, then gave her a wink and a nod of my head like a good country boy. "I may not, but I'm not the one playing myself in my grief." Her words had me feeling salty at that moment, and I looked down at my shoes, then back at her. "Don't talk about my shitkickers, Scarface. Anyway, check it again. Whatever you get to thinkin', make sure it's about your loyalty for the sake of your people. We'll speak again."

With that, I walked out, signaled to my people, then went back to my place, with her on my mind.

Betrayal was a dangerous game, and little Miss Spice could use it to her advantage by serving that shit up with shards of glass once she got her head together. It wasn't hard for me to figure out that no matter what, she would always be an Orlando, but without a doubt, I could see her equally being an Eraserhead as well. That was a dangerous combination.

Everyone on both sides had secrets, and everyone was locked in a battle created long ago, before any of us had been born. It was going to be interesting to see where it went, but for now, I had bigger fish to fry, and more customers linked to her grandfather to sell to. A huge smile slid across my face as I thought about what I had learned about a woman named Code, or the person I really knew her as, Maria Rosa; her cousin Smiley; and the rest of the Eraserheads. I then pondered the man I aimed to return the sweet gift of death to, her grandfather, Caltrone Orlando.

As I walked into my office while in my thoughts, I spoke to my right-hand. "Keep her well protected, Shango."

"She will not receive the special treatment reserved for those of her birth. So yes, I will do that, bro," he said in return.

After clicking on my monitor, I watched Code and took in all the ways she moved even in her sleep. She was a piece of work. "How is Oya doing with our friend?"

Shango gave a grunt, then crossed his arms. "She's attempting to get to him without our new friend's people recognizing her or thinking anything about her."

"So, then she'll play a nurse, yes?" I said, not as a question but as a suggestion.

My boy gave a slight sigh, and I knew it was because of his past history of loving Oya. But in every relationship, people had to let go, especially if they couldn't love each other right, like those two.

"Yes, sir. I'll send that her way," he said, then turned my way. "You know Big Boots's informant will be silent for a while since this has gone down."

Rubbing my scruffy beard, I rolled my shoulders and turned away from my monitor. "Of course. But it's all good. If everything goes well, we'll have our own through our new friendship with our guest's cousin, as you suggested."

"Yeah, we might. Oya is feeling him," Shango said quietly.

I walked to my desk, sat down, and kicked my feet up. "And I'm feeling the one on that monitor. Shit happens."

Shango laughed, then strapped up. "Off to hit up that party for the kid you have me watching with Shredder. Dude has a temper. He's cool people in that aspect."

"Right now, but he has the blood of the devil, so be careful and play hard in his world. Make sure you check on the Eraserheads too."

"Will do." Shango gave me dap, then headed out, dressed like a professional sports agent.

Everything wasn't falling as it should, but in the chaos and the battles, there were good pieces of shrapnel I could use to my advantage or not at all. The devil should have never procreated, because in his pursuit to secure his lineage, he had not only sired demons, but he had also created something worse than his wife, Lilith. He had created his own mirror image, a female Satan by the name of Maria Rosa. I definitely was intrigued, and the move was mine.

Hopefully, what I had told Code would make her understand the power she had in herself was bigger than Caltrone himself. Once she recognized that, maybe her true family could help her down the road. With this newcomer on the news, maybe he too would be worth investing in, but I wasn't sure just yet. I was just here to do what

I did best, and that was watch. Until then, all I had to do was wait like the shadow of a guardian angel that I was and gather more pieces. Then I could begin the move in this battle of chess. Checkmate.

Chapter 21

Auto

The front room was heavy with grief. The polished wood flooring was spotless. Pictures of sunflowers decorated the walls, while live ones sat in different areas, in potting soil. Yellow and green sofas sat kitty-corner to one another in the center of the room. On the left side of the room was a fireplace that hadn't been used in so long, it still looked fairly new. The window in the adjoining dining room was open, and the cool country breeze wafted in.

Outside was cloudy and misty. The weather was fitting for the mood in the room.

"No. No. No!" she screamed as her small fist pounded my chest. "When you took my baby away from here, you told me he would be safe. You said you would protect him with your life," she wailed. "You promised me, Devin. You gave me your word."

Seymore's mother's angelic voice washed over me and made me feel even lower to the dirt than I already was. She'd called me by my real name. Something nobody ever did. Most people didn't even know my real name. After I'd gotten Seymore out of jail and brought him home to Augusta, I had told his mother he would be in good hands. Had told her my plans. Had presented myself to her in a way that showed I was about my business.

All she'd asked for in return was my real name and the assurance that her son would leave behind the criminal activity that had paralyzed him in the first place. Out of my arrogance, I'd been so sure that I would be able to live up to that promise. And now, there she stood, with hurt and pain in her eyes because of me. I'd let her down. Her normally pale face had reddened from emotion. Blond hair was still wet from the shower. Her robe was slightly open and revealed the scars from her battle with breast cancer. She'd fought it and won.

Around her front room sat pictures of her other four sons . . . My heart sank to my stomach. She'd lost all four of her other sons to gang violence. Seymore was all she had left, and now I'd taken him away from her too.

"I'm sorry, Mrs. Cleveland—"

Her hard slap across my face stopped my useless apology.

"I ain't got shit left now, Devin. Nothing. I sent him away to save him," she barely got out through gritted teeth. "To-to save him, and you . . ." She was so emotional that she couldn't breathe and talk at the same time.

I nodded. "I swear to God—"

"Get out, Devin. Get the hell outta my house. You ain't nothing but the devil in sheep's clothing. You presented yourself as something you're not. You're no better than the other devils who stole my sons from me. Get out of my house and go to hell, where all of you belong."

Her words stung. They hurt like hell. To be compared to the other menaces to society all but crushed what little sanity I had left. I reached in my pocket and pulled out an envelope.

"Here is some money to take care of his funeral—"

She lashed out at me again. Knocked the envelope from my hand, then shoved me. While she was only five feet three inches tall at the most, she towered over me, and I felt so small.

"Are you hard of hearing? Get out! Leave and never come back here. He was all I had left. He was it. I got nobody and nothing else to live for. Nothing. Nobody. Get the hell outta my house," she yelled with righteous indignation.

I swallowed my shame and resigned myself to the notion that she would forever see me as the devil who took her last and youngest son away from her. I walked out of her house and headed to my truck.

Took me a minute to even push the button to start the engine on the black-on-black Dodge Journey.

"You okay?"

I looked to my right. Smiley had a concerned look on her face, which made me feel worse than I already did. There shouldn't have been any concern for me, only for those who had lost their lives because I had trusted the wrong person. I looked in my rearview mirror. Stitch sat behind Smiley, his face stoic as he stared out the window at nothing. If he was who I knew him to be, his mind was on the scene that had played out between him and Carmen.

Having to tell one lover that another had been killed wasn't easy. Between him and Lelo, they shared four children, all by Carmen. As much of a conundrum as their relationship was, the three had raised their children the way most parents could only dream of. They had had their share of fights among themselves, but the children had always come first. And now they were one parent short. The color had drained from Carmen's dark face when he delivered the news that Lelo wasn't coming home.

She'd screamed at Stitch. Slapped him. Kicked him. Cursed him to hell, same as Seymore's mother had done me. Then she had latched on to the only father her children had left, and had screamed out to God. She, too, wanted to know why He would take Lelo from them. Watching Stitch break down again, same as Carmen, had been too much for me to bear then.

I finally found the strength to crank the car. "I don't know how to answer that," I said.

I pulled out of the dirt driveway, my mind in overdrive, but my body numb. I'd had to deliver this same speech to Dunkin's grandma. And while she hadn't cursed me to hell, the pain in her eyes still haunted me. She'd taken the money, his portion of the insurance policy we all had, and then wished me well. Once she'd closed the door to her home, I swore it felt as if the whole world had closed me out.

"Your face is blank, emotionless, but you haven't shed a tear," Smiley observed. "That's not good. You have to grieve in a way that lets you show emotion."

I heard her, but as I gripped the steering wheel and drove down the long dirt road leading away from Seymore's mother's place, all I kept seeing was the look on the team's faces when I told them about Code's part in all the madness that had befallen us. I'd been kicking myself in the ass for over twenty-four hours. Every nigga had a motherfucking agenda, even those closest to you. How that had slipped my mind would forever eat away at me. It was a motto to live by or one to die to. Either way, I had never seen the shit coming.

"Don't psychoanalyze me right now, a'ight? Don't do that. Let me handle this my own way and we'll be cool," I told Smiley.

The problem with all of that was I didn't know how to handle this tragedy. Four losses in one night. Three physical deaths and the death of a friendship. How the fuck did one deal with shit like that? How?

"You've been handling it your way for the past day and a half, and all you've managed to do is be the deliverer of bad news."

I snapped my head to the right to scowl at her, then looked back at the road. "Yo, fuck you, a'ight? Fuck you. I just lost three fucking friends who were like brothers to me to death. All because a motherfucker wanted what we built from the ground up. You don't know shit about me. You don't know shit about this family. All you know is what Code has told you. You're only here because she didn't feel like you could protect your own ass, so she wanted me to do it for you. So fuck you."

"Hey, you don't get to snap at me because you fucked up, Auto. You did."

I almost swerved the truck as I turned off the dirt road onto a main highway. "What the fuck?"

"I mean, come on. As smart as you are, you didn't think to up the ante on protection around your camp? Someone stole your shit, nigga. Not once, not twice, but three times. Then these big-ass white boys came on your turf, hunted you and your team like animals, and you did nothing."

My hands were gripping the steering wheel so tight, you could see the white of my knuckles. Her words had cut deep. Made me feel like I was less than the man I knew I was inside. There had always been a killer inside of me. One that I'd tried to hide, but he was always lurking just beneath surface. I didn't want to be that person. I had never wanted to be a menace to society, even if it meant I had to survive in an environment that saw me as food.

The saying in the hood about it being a dog-eat-dog world wasn't just for shits and giggles. The few kills I'd made during this whole fiasco hadn't even made me flinch. I had to do what I had to do, right? Still, something innate in me always kept me on the sane side of things. It probably wouldn't make sense right now, but later on it would. I'd like to think that I didn't or wouldn't kill unless I had to.

But Smiley was wrong; I *had* done something.

"I did do something. How do you think we were able to track down Mouse?" I asked her, temper raging at this point.

"And still, it was Boots who ended him. Boots who ended that Chandler dude too. Meanwhile, both those niggas sold you up shit creek too."

"I was going after Chandler. Boots just got to him before I did."

"My point exactly," she said, with such smugness I was tempted to stop the truck and put her ass out on the side of the road.

I would see how far that pretty face and sassy attitude would get her in the middle of Augusta.

I didn't say what I wanted to say to her. Just kept quiet so as not to do something or say some shit I would regret.

But she kept going. "So you can stop putting the blame all on Code now and take your share of the responsibility too. You let your team down just as much as she did. You quote Bruce Lee all the time but didn't take the method to his madness to heart. You took a Martin Luther

King Jr. approach when you should have taken a Malcolm X position. By any means necessary, you protect those you fucking love, Auto. Any fucking means necessary, even if that means having to sit down with the enemy as you plot his fucking demise.

"Fear not the man who has practiced ten thousand kicks, Auto. Fear the man who has practiced one kick ten thousand times. Isn't that what Bruce Lee said? Some shit like that? Notice that the stiffest tree is most easily cracked, while the bamboo or willow survives by bending with the wind. He said some shit like that too. So, see, you may have become like water, but you forgot to bend like the bamboo and the willow. You forgot to fucking bend with the wind, which is why you cracked, easily."

I swerved the truck to the side of the road. Hopped out, then swiftly walked around to the other side of the truck. I saw her reach over and pick up something before I pulled the passenger-side door open, then snatched her out.

"I told you to shut the fuck up!" I barked at her.

"And you mad because I'm telling you the truth," she retorted.

She tried to snatch herself away from me, but I shoved her back against the truck. I expected her to come back swinging, but she simply caught her balance and folded her right arm, which was in a sling, across her chest.

"How about this truth? You can find your own way back to Morrow. How about that hot shit since you know so much?" I shouted.

"I don't give a shit. I can survive anywhere you put me. Toss me to the wolves and watch me come back, leading the pack. So fuck you too, Auto."

I didn't even pay attention to her words as I hopped back in the truck, tossed her backpack out the window to her, and then pulled off.

"You know we can't leave her out there like that. As pissed at Code as we might all be, we don't want her gunning for us about her fam," Stitch told me.

I'd been so heated, I'd forgot he was in the backseat, honestly.

"Yeah, well, let's see how far that fucking mouth gets her now," I snapped.

I looked in my rearview mirror. She was tossing her backpack over her left shoulder. The shorts she had on displayed her toned brown thighs and lush backside, along with the tattoo running down her thigh. The Braves T-shirt covered the bruises on her torso, which I'd noticed while helping her to clean her scrapes and bruises from the jump over the staircase railing when the guns started spraying. Combat boots added definition to her calves.

"Well, shit. We ain't gone make it that far ourselves," Stitch observed.

I glanced at Stitch in the mirror. He still had that sullen, downcast look about him, only now there was a light humor in his eyes.

"Why you say that?"

"Because she got the proximity key to the truck. So as soon as you turn this motherfucker off, we stuck too."

"Ah, shit."

Stitch gave a head nod, then went back to staring out the window. I should have known she had one-upped me just by how calm she had been. The truck had a "push to start" engine, so without the proximity key, I had pretty much fucked myself while trying to fuck her. I sighed, whipped the truck around, and drove back in the direction I'd left her. She was still there waiting, with a look of triumph on her face. Neither of us said a word as she hopped back in the truck and closed the door.

"Can I get my key back?" I asked her.

"Bend with the wind, Auto. I bend with the wind," was all she said.

She didn't give me the key back until we got back to Clayton County, though.

***

Two days later, after Dunkin had been cremated and his ashes carried to the Caribbean by his grandma, after Seymore's mother had all but told us we weren't welcome at his funeral, we laid Lelo to rest. I had never been a fan of funerals. I could never get used to the fascination people had with wanting to see their loved ones' lifeless bodies being put into the ground. All the tears and bereavement unnerved me.

"Code is here," Reagan said.

There was no emotion in her voice. Only the tears in her eyes alerted you to her pain. The weather was bright, and sunshine was dancing across the sky. Birds chirped in the sky as we all gathered at Sherwood Memorial Cemetery to say good-bye to Lelo. It didn't seem like a good day for a funeral, but as Carmen said, that was Lelo's way of telling us not to weep for him.

Afterward, as people left the burial site to head to their cars, Stitch and Carmen stayed seated with their children by Lelo's side. His daughters had been dressed in all white, while his sons had donned all black. Carmen wore white like her daughters; and Stitch, black like his sons. They sat there like they didn't want to let go.

Reagan and I stood close by to lend our support. Reagan pointed suddenly, and I turned in the direction she was indicating and saw Code. She was dressed incognito. Blended in with the rest of the mourners in all black. She saw us looking at her. We all knew there would be no way she wouldn't show up to at least one of the funerals.

No matter what, we had all been family. Still, as Code walked toward us, Reagan walked off in the opposite direction. She wasn't ready to forgive, and no matter what Smiley had thought and said, neither was I. I watched as Code walked over to Carmen and Stitch. Carmen may not have been a part of our operation, but she knew what had gone down, because Stitch had told her after I'd told him. So it didn't surprise me when she damn near slapped spit from Code and then stormed off. The kids trailed after her. Stitch stood up to follow his girl and kids, then stopped short.

He turned to face Code. "You could have told us what we were up against, you know? Even when you merely suspected it and didn't know for sure, you could have said something. You left us open, Code. Showed that in the end, your loyalty lay with your real family, right?"

For as long as I'd known Code, I'd never seen her in as much pain as she was now. As she looked at Stitch, judging by the way she swallowed hard, I could tell she was trying to find the right words.

"I fucked up, Stitch. I know I did, and I know nothing can bring him back, but had I any idea of what was about to go down, I would have warned—"

Stitch shifted his weight from one foot to the other, then shook his head. "But you *did*. You *did* have an idea of what was about to go down. You know your old man better than anybody. Why? Because he's family, right? But what about us? What about my family now? We functioned as a team. Me, Carmen, Lelo, and our children. What were you waiting on?" he said through his tears.

"I had to make sure," Code answer, trying to defend herself.

Stitch seemed to lose patience and yelled, "Why? Why did you have to make sure? You know what this motherfucker is capable of, Code. So, why? Why play Russian roulette with our lives, huh?"

"I didn't know at first, Stitch. I didn't."

"Bullshit. I keep thinking about . . . thinking back to that night out at Joy Lake, when that Mouse motherfucker looked at you and said he couldn't tell who had paid him. The look on your face, in hindsight, said it all. You knew. Had ample time to warn us about the possibilities, but what did you do?"

Code's only answer was her silence.

Stitch shrugged. "Yeah. That's what I thought," was all he said before he turned and walked away.

While Code stood there, drowning in her own demons, I had one last thing to add to all Stitch had said.

"This is where we end our friendship, Code. We can no longer go on as if shit is the same. Your family is the enemy of my family now."

Smiley's words were haunting me. It was as much my fault as it was Code's that my family had been put into harm's way. I couldn't fault her without faulting myself. We had been a team. We had led this team together, and I, too, had let the team members down. Left them open to hell on earth because I didn't want to become what I feared. I didn't want to become that monster I needed to be in order to survive.

With those words, I turned to walk away from a woman I had once seen as my sister. I sent Smiley a text message and told her I was on my way back to my place. I was sure she had been the one to tell Code about the funeral, since Code hadn't been seen or heard from in days. I had to keep in mind that Code and Smiley were family.

Still, I had no doubt where Smiley's loyalties lay. She had no interest in being in cahoots with the old man, but she did care for her cousin Code. That was the only thing I'd have to be careful of.

"Auto, let me help. You can't go against Papa alone. He's not an ordinary opponent. He has too many resources at his disposal, and he will eat you alive. So please, let me help," Code said behind me.

I shook my head. "Nah. See, I got a few resources up my sleeve too. So, the only way you can help me is to stay out of my way. I'd hate to have to kill you in the melee, Code, but that doesn't mean that I won't. The enemy of my enemy is my friend. A friend of mine once left me with sage words, which I will now live by more than ever. Every nigga gotta agenda, Code. And I now know mine."